Praise for Tom LeClair's previous novels

Passing Off

"For all its flashy ball-handling and dead-on outside shot, *Passing Off* is a deeply literary work of art and politics, probing identity, representation, ecology, and, of course, our desperate, down-to-the-buzzer game of words."

--Richard Powers

"One of the most literate and entertaining sports novels of the decade...*Passing Off* is a fascinating book."

--*The Washington Post*

Passing On

"Entertaining, funny, serious, and death-ridden...*Passing On* takes on issues—with humor and irony—not many a serious novelist tackles these days. It's a winner, worth a shot."

--*American Book Review*

Well-Founded Fear

"In the fierce unfinished business of Kurdistan, Tom LeClair has found the documentary edge and human center that makes *Well-Founded Fear* a resourceful and moving work of fiction."

--Don DeLillo

The Liquidators

"The business of America may be business, but too few fine novels prove it. Here's a brilliant exception. To the tiny shelf of classic workplace writing, add this meditation on failure, fiscal and metaphysical....The workingman blues, as if sung by some truck-stop Homer."

--*Kirkus*

Also by Tom LeClair:

In the Loop (criticism)
The Art of Excess (criticism)
Passing Off (fiction)
Well-Founded Fear (fiction)
Passing On (fiction)
The Liquidators (fiction)

Passing Through: A Novel

by

Tom LeClair

Drinian Press/
Huron, Ohio

This book is a work of fiction. As such, names, characters, incidents, and places (real or imagined) are used fictitiously and are products of the author's imagination. Any resemblance to persons, places, or actual events is coincidental.

Copyright © 2008 by Tom LeClair.

Cover photograph © Drinian Press

Drinian Press
P.O. Box 63
Huron, Ohio 44839
Visit our Web site at: www.DrinianPress.com

Library of Congress Control Number: 2008933437

ISBN: 978-0-9785165-9-8

Printed in the United States of America

For Annaliki

PUBLISHER'S NOTE:

Publishers and authors sometimes disagree over the presentation of a book, such as its title. In this case, while author and publisher are in agreement, persons involved with the story have expressed a different point of view. By way of concession, author Tom LeClair has included the following alternate title page as the beginning of the story.

Passing Through: An Athlete Goes to College

By An Academic

Creative Non-Fiction Press
New York

Part I

Chapter 1

Michael Keever was through with the dead and the dying and was happy.

Terminal Tours, the company that got him in all his recent trouble, was now his estranged wife's business. For a year, Michael had escorted the terminally ill on trips they could not manage alone. Then a client that Michael took to Lourdes unexpectedly died there, and the pilgrim's son sued Michael for neglecting due diligence. When Michael lost the suit, he lost his house and wife and daughter, but he felt his daughter, Sara, would come around if he got the job at Queen City College.

He had a one-bedroom apartment and was through with the house that began his problems with his wife. A decade ago Ann agreed to move to Greece for Michael to play in the pro basketball league there because she thought his year-end bonus would get them the house they hadn't been able to afford. When Michael was exposed as lying about his Greek "heritage" and they lost the bonus, Ann wrote *Passing Off*, supposedly Michael's autobiography but actually an eco-terrorist thriller, to make enough money in Greece to buy the house in Cincinnati. It was ten years before Michael replaced Ann's portrait of him as a dumb, deceptive, and money-obsessed athlete, but his actual autobiography, *Passing On*, the account of Terminal Tours, corrected Ann's version of him. Though not a commercial success, *Passing On* also indirectly got him the interview at QCC.

Passing Through

Just because QCC was new, Ann and others in the city thought it was one of those distance-learning profit-turning scams, a school today, a telemarketing operation tomorrow. But the college had a "campus" in a remodeled three-story auto-transmission factory visible and easily accessible from Interstate 71 close to downtown. The college motto—"Shift Your Life"—was on the building to remind Cincinnatians of its former use and to demonstrate QCC's retraining mission. The classrooms all had computer consoles, Internet access, screens for PowerPoint presentations, and ceilings almost high enough for a basketball hoop. The library, mostly CD-ROMs and terminals, occupied a decommissioned Episcopalian church. Sponsored by AOL, the library had the company logo up on the steeple where the cross had been. The dorm, also visible from the Interstate, was a rehabbed residential hotel with an awning in front, a New York touch, and a Holiday Inn billboard on the roof. "After college," the billboard said, "a great room of your own."

By specializing in schools of Information and Dissemination, QCC had plenty of future-oriented young students and a good supply of older students trying to shift into new jobs. The innovative M.C.A. program—Master of Communication Arts—drew from all over the country, from all over the world. According to Ann, some professors at the University of Cincinnati, where she used to work writing grants, said it was because Queen City used its name to cater to gays. U.C. students who had been rejected were cruder and called the school Queer College.

The Communications Department chair and the director of the M.C.A. program who interviewed Michael brought up the school's reputation in the first five minutes. The chair, a short chunky man about forty, who was wearing New Balance sneakers and a tie more expensive than Michael's suit, held up his left hand to show Michael a thick wedding band.

"We don't ask if our students or faculty are straight or gay," he said, "but here's where my heart is."

Michael's right hand moved to his left, to feel the finger where his ring had been for almost twenty years. He missed it, even if he didn't miss Ann.

"Oh, Richard," the director said, folding her long bare fingers in the lap of her burlap dress, "No need to administer one of your little tests. Anyway, Michael, we take students away from U.C. because they're stodgy, not because they're straight. The faculty over there insist on the old fiction and poetry tracks. Creative Non-Fiction is the future for books, and that's why we hope to add you to the staff."

"Forget about books," Richard said, "They'll disappear in ten years. The future is hypertext, the Internet, virtual reality. Objectivity, economy, speed, collaboration. I really love what you're doing with your web site, not just disseminating your own writing but offering a place for others to post their narratives. Like your motto says, the site could go 'on and on and on.' And will in the future."

"Well," Michael said, "I want you to know the truth about that site. My wife began it, and she'll be kind of the co-proprietor in the future. She needs it for Terminal Tours, and I want to keep it because I'll be traveling to terminal places. So we're going to have a dual entry page."

"Now there's a future marriage for you, Richard," June said. "People may throw away their rings and find new consorts, but will keep their URL forever."

"Well they should, well they should," Richard said, "The address stays the same but quick changes, quick changes in content. That's where CNF is going in the future. Books just require too much lag time, to say nothing about reading time. All those labored expositions and thick descriptions to justify charging thirty bucks. We need to close the gap between writing and reading, get closer to real time and real language. You see, Michael, QCC embraces the insult 'quick changes.' I actually prefer 'speed shifts.'"

"You could even use 'automatic transformations,'" Michael offered.

June laughed. Richard chuckled and went on: "June and I are the only full-time faculty in the department. Everyone else is a field service instructor. This way we have web-like flexibility in adjusting to student demands. We continually poll our students for their interests, even when we're recruiting them. We may be the only college that asks students when they're juniors in high school what they would like to take here. When we find demand, we go out and hire someone to teach the course. That's why we have lots of undergrads."

"And why we may be able to offer you a position," June said.

"I'd love to teach here," Michael said, "but I'm not anxious for any more shifts right now. I'd like to settle down a bit. I'm through with *Passing On*."

Neither Richard nor June registered the reference, and afterwards Michael assumed they hadn't had time to read his book, though it wasn't long. Probably just as well, he decided, since he'd confessed there to lying about writing *Passing Off*, Ann's creative fictionalizing of his experience.

"You will keep traveling for *Hell*, won't you?" Richard asked.

"I'll have to. I can make the necessary trips during breaks here."

Passing Through

"If you ever need a new hellhole and guide," June said, "I'll be happy to show you around."

Michael wondered just how serious this ringless young woman was. In her baggy dress and Birkenstocks, she didn't look much like an adventure-travel guide. She also lacked the guide's tan, though she did have squint lines around her eyes, either from gazing into equatorial sunsets or reading too much.

"Where do you have in mind?" he asked.

"Centerville, Ohio, my hometown, a never-changing hotbed of repression in every season."

"You haven't been to the ice of Ludlow, Vermont, my hometown."

"Richard," June said, "We must hire this man. It's so rare that an applicant alludes to anything earlier than Dave Eggers or Paul Theroux."

To Michael, June said, "Which translation do you prefer?"

Michael had no idea what she was talking about. He'd been in the transportation business but that couldn't be it. June assumed the best about his blank look and asked, "Are you really able to read *The Inferno* in Italian?"

Michael remembered about a hundred words of Italian from his two years playing for Lottomatica in Rome, but he knew better than to pretend to know a language June might speak even if her sandy hair, green eyes, and narrow features didn't look Italian.

"I prefer the Greek translation," Michael said. Since he knew fewer than a hundred words of Greek, he strung together the insults that came to mind, "*Malaka pousti aigamisou palio adelphi*" roughly translated as "masturbator faggot, go fuck yourself old queen."

"Beautiful," June said. "Dante in Greek. Imagine that, Richard."

17

"Impressive," Richard said with a grin. "You must have been working on your Greek since Panathinaikos," the team Michael had played for in Athens.

So Richard was a basketball fan, a reader of *Passing Off*. But Michael was used to responding to questions about that book.

"I knew more Greek than I let on. You know, part of the deception."

"Right," Richard said, "cunning."

"*The Inferno* in Greek," June said, still shaking her head as if cultural dissemination traveled only east to west.

Michael wouldn't need to know any literature, ancient or modern, to teach the courses that dominated the QCC curriculum: New Life Writing, Memorable Memoirs, Innovative Journal Keeping, Experimental Blogging, Poetic Advertising, Postmodern Imaging, The Formal List. Though only forty, Michael felt like a graybeard while reading the catalogue descriptions. When he was a General Studies major, U.C. didn't offer any courses like these, not even for scholarship athletes. At his age, Richard was running the show, and June was probably no more than thirty-two or thirty-three. Good, Michael then thought, no graybeard superiors would come to his office and ask him to arrange for a hooker on a Terminal Tour to Las Vegas.

QCC did move quickly. Michael was interviewed in June and would begin teaching in September, two workshop classes: a graduate course called Future Autobiographies and an undergraduate course entitled New Travel Writing. He knew this would be a full-time load at U.C., and he knew half-time at QCC paid a quarter of the salary at the university, but he managed to negotiate tuition remission for Sara and a two-day schedule. He'd have a lot of time in his new home. The old newspaper-insulated and wind-tunnel house with the roots-strangled plumbing had never felt like a home, not like the apartment did. Now that Michael was through with basketball, he wanted home to be like a locker room—small, overheated, great water pressure, his own comfortable seat, big screen for the games, a place to change clothes. Easy to leave, easy to return to, no lawn to have mowed when he was reporting on the famine in Chad or interviewing the stolen-car kings of Albania for *Hell: The Magazine*. If Sara would agree to move in with him, he'd get a two-bedroom in the building.

But right after Sara got her expedited admission, Ann insisted that she live in an expensive dorm, a quarter mile from Michael's apartment, two miles from Ann's new apartment.

"If she has to go to Quick Change College because of your screw-up at Lourdes," Ann told him, "at least she can get the real university experience in a dorm."

Ann believed "the Q," as it advertised itself on AM radio, was a drive-through school that would soon be gone. Sara had been accepted by the University of Michigan, Ohio State, and Miami, but the expense of transporting a dead man from France to Cincinnati meant she had to take the free ride at QCC.

"Think of yourself as an athletic recruit," Michael told her.

"Except that Queen City doesn't have any teams," Sara said.

"Then think of the Q as standing for quality," her father said.

"Quality Country Club?" Sara said.

The week before classes began Michael felt like the day he'd been called up from the C.B.A. for his ten-day contract with the Celtics. Back then Ann used to call him "Cal," for his Vermont homeboy, Calvin Coolidge, man

Passing Through

of few words. Michael worried about what he'd say to Larry Bird and his other heroes, but Larry put him right at ease when he shook Michael's hand: "Don't fuck up," the legend said. That advice wouldn't get Michael through a three-hour session. He'd had a year of American Literature but had never taken a workshop; in fact, he thought workshops were for the dumb kids in high school, the guys who learned how to run a lathe or tune an engine. Michael had never taught anything either, unless one counted blowing the whistle, signaling violations, and assessing fouls when he was a referee. If a player yapped too long or loud, Michael tossed him off the floor. That probably wasn't the best model for education. He had been taught a few things about punctuation and sentences and organization by the woman who edited *Passing On*, but she was in New York and wouldn't be on call. He'd read *The Inferno* (in English) in case he ran into June. Now he knew the bottom of hell was ice, but that didn't mean he'd go to Antarctica or Ludlow, Vermont, any time soon.

Michael spoke to Richard about his anxieties.

"Don't worry," he said. "We don't mind some rough edges. We want authentic practitioners. Originals, Michael, not those literary weaklings fleeing fiction and poetry, desperately trying to power up their careers with CNF."

Put this way, CNF sounded to Michael like one of those illegal dietary supplements sprinters and sluggers used.

Richard also said, "Just be yourself. Tell them stories from your life. Live it, write it. The first couple of sessions use your height. Don't sit down. Intimidate them."

"That sounds like the power-forward school of instruction. I was a point guard."

Passing Through

"I know, but if you stand up throughout the class, you'll look like a hardass to these kids. Then you can ease up later in the semester."

Richard also suggested a couple of books about teaching CNF and gave Michael an article entitled "Nothing But Net," about writing for magazines like *Hell*. Richard's advice in the article was be objective but personal, minimize descriptions, use plenty of dialogue, and keep the language clean.

The undergraduate Travel Writing students had just come from Abercrombie and Fitch, part preppie, part ragged. Most were a couple of years older than Sara, but looked alarmingly young and wonderfully healthy. In the early September heat, they were wearing shorts and tee shirts, displaying their knotted calves and tanned arms muscled by carrying trays at summer jobs. Their hair was blond, not white. They curled into their seats without Michael's assistance. Even from the back row they could hear him and see what he wrote on the whiteboard. No one hobbled with a cane or dragged around an oxygen tank or needed to be pushed in a wheelchair. Yes, Michael thought, these were his people, full of energy like his former teammates the first day of training camp, anxious to be back exercising those young bodies. There was one difference: not one of his fifteen students was black. Michael's questionnaire found that most had gone to Cincinnati private schools—Country Day, Summit, Seven Hills—or suburban high schools in Columbus and Cleveland. Maybe the rich had a way to keep their offspring dewy. Many of the students had traveled to Spring Break destinations, to Hawaii and Mexico, and to Europe. A couple hoped to write for *Let's Go* next summer, but some already had glossies in mind, *Islands*, *Condé Nast*, and other magazines their parents, presumably, read. Travel Writing was one of the courses they'd identified as cool when QCC was recruiting them.

The graduate students in the Autobiography class also seemed young to Michael, more Urban Outfitters than Abercrombie, but still young to be thinking about telling their life stories. He wondered if his year with the dying geriatrics had aged his perceptions. Though in their early twenties, the grads didn't look as healthy as the undergrads—more pallor, more stiffness, and, it seemed to Michael, a post-season feeling of defeat (rather than pre-season enthusiasm). Michael did have one African-American man and a Pakistani woman who could have passed for African-American if she didn't speak with a sing-songy British accent. The students were from colleges all over the country, and had traveled to many of the same places as the undergrads. The grads, though, were fixated on the nuclear family's ground zero, the horrible home, the hated siblings, the detested parents, the gurgling and pawing grandparents, the doofus uncles and cackling aunts. Listening to the students give brief synopses of their projects, Michael vowed to patch things up with Sara before she became a graduate student and signed up for Autobiography.

In both classes, Michael followed Richard's coaching and gave a digest of his travels and occupations—player, assistant coach, referee, surveillance provider, tour guide— just in the last few years. Having told much of the background in *Passing Off* to Ann, Michael believed that writing should stay close to oral storytelling. He got his undergrads to share their best and worst travel anecdotes, which often involved getting wasted in some city not their home. The grads were asked to tell one lengthy episode from their projected work. Michael was shooting for an atmosphere of collaboration, of teamwork, and was enjoying listening. Pre-season coaching required a lot of hard work—screaming at guys out of shape, walking through plays everybody had forgotten, two-a-day practices—but the first weeks of teaching extended summer vacation.

When the work began, when students brought their writing to the workshops, Michael was surprised by the grad students. Work had pulled him around the world and dictated his writing, but the students wanted their work to be their writing. This seemed backwards to Michael, perhaps because he had just started writing. Ann said he had keyhole vision, looking out upon the world from inside the gym, from inside his athlete's body. He didn't expect the undergrad travel writers to have an aperture to shape their perceptions as basketball did his, but he assumed the graduates would have some lens through which they'd view their experience. If the lens wasn't work, then recreation—music, movies, cars, drugs, sex. But their eyes were clear and wide, and they blurted down on paper their conflicts with the people paying for QCC. If the autobiographers couldn't change the ordinary facts of their young lives, Michael thought they might at least imagine a perspective that would make those facts distinctive.

The students' work was "Creative" Non-Fiction, they implied in their first essays and chapters, because they had created it. Michael missed the more demanding athletic meaning of "creative." "Creates in the air," coaches used to say of his ingenious passing. As a point guard, Michael's job was to control the ball, invite the double team, squeeze through tight spaces, mislead the remaining defenders, and, near the hoop, leap into the air, look one way and deliver the other way, send the ball passing through empty spaces only his eyes could see, passages between and among the bodies and extremities clogging the way, passes fans mistakenly called "blind" rather than x-rayed. Most players knew the fundamentals of passing off, but Michael had coached himself in creativity. He analyzed hundreds of hours of himself on videotape—run and re-run and re-run again—to learn how to deceive opponents, surprise teammates, find holes in the moving picket fence of other bodies, fake a shot, make a pass, and get his players easy baskets (if they caught the pass). Ann said his videotape was the only thing he remembered. She was probably right, but tape was his edge, the key to his creative unpredictability that demanded close attention from teammates when he had the ball, made opponents look foolish, elicited special appreciation from hometown fans, and pissed off everyone else. "No game, no gain" was how Michael summarized his approach, the games within the game, deceptions inside deceptions.

When Michael offered passing as a model for writing, no one responded. Students at QCC didn't want to study the "videotape" of other writers' techniques. The students also didn't want to consider their readers as opponents or fans. QCC writers would create and the readers would come. The students felt entitled to their readers. While the writer's point of view was always "I," the prose assumed a "you" like a doting parent or nurturing high school teacher or encouraging roommate. The page was, like the computer screen, a transparent pane of glass: student on one side, reader on the other, real life passing through like a glance, words invisible because predictable, words like the words all the other students used. Any quirks were in behavior, not in the writers' eyes and ears.

After receiving his travel writers' first assignment—"Recall a place you've visited and discuss what more you need to know now"—Michael wanted their next essay to create a different perspective on a new place. He asked them to imagine what he had been doing for the last year: pretend to take a dying person to some local site and describe the place through that person's eyes. The Mr. Abercrombies and Ms. Fitches resisted. Jody Dalton, either a fine-boned WASP or a girl with an eating disorder, was the most vocal, unintimidated by Michael's six feet and three inches. Her comments reminded Michael of Sara's when he started Terminal Tours, but Jody wasn't his daughter, and this assignment wasn't going to embarrass her as Michael had Sara.

"Please don't ask us to do that, Mr. Keever. It will just spoil the place I want to go to."

"Where are you going?"

"The amusement park at Kings Island before it closes for the winter."

"That's perfect. Don't you think a dying person would like to be amused? Imagine how he or she would feel about a scary roller coaster ride or the haunted house."

Michael could see Jody shiver, her blunt-cut blond hair tremble.

"But it won't be fun for me if I have to imagine I'm dying. And if it's not fun for me, how can I describe it as a fun place for others?"

"Maybe travel isn't just about fun."

"Then why bother to do it?"

"To learn something about a place or someone else or yourself. There's a difference between traveling and travel writing."

"We know that, Mr. Keever," Jody said, emboldened by other students' nods and murmurs to speak for the class, "but we don't want to spend our lives walking around with dying people. It's really morbid, and it's not what we came to college for."

"Nice to know I have a reader, Jody," Michael said, hoping to calm her down. "You haven't by any chance just lost someone close to you, have you?"

"No, and I think that's kind of insulting to assume that my opinion is just personal. Ask the other students."

None of them wanted to do the dying person exercise. As a beginning teacher trying to be "sensitive to QCC students' needs and expectations," catalogue copy that may have been written by Richard or June, Michael suggested a grandparent or parent's perspective. This also was deemed too "limiting." How about a younger brother or sister? "Not really." How about someone in a wheelchair? "Oh no." So the students spread out across Cincinnati and reported back just what anyone, experienced teacher or not, would expect from a bunch of nineteen-year-olds who took travel writing to have fun.

Surprised by the undergrads' resistance, Michael asked the graduate students to write a chapter of their self-driven narratives from another family member's point of view. Maybe because QCC was paying some of the graduates to attend (and teach Communication One classes), they were less direct in their response than Jody and her cohorts, whose parents were footing the bill. Gary Gallagher, who had three studs in his tongue and a noose tattooed on his neck, wondered, "Wouldn't that move our texth over into ficthion?" Michael knew the lisp was a product of Gary's studs, rather than some sign of gay affiliation, because Michael had read Gary's page-long description of how his first girlfriend moaned when that metal touched her clitoris. Michael did wonder if that might be fiction and was looking forward to what women in the workshop would say when Gary presented his work. But Michael couldn't bring that up now.

"Don't autobiographies make assumptions and statements about the minds of characters other than the narrator?" Michael asked.

"Yeth, but wouldn't a chapter make that obviouth?"

"Think of it as an exercise. Maybe not something that will be in your finished work but a way to understand others more clearly. Or if you'd rather, write about yourself in the third person."

"That would be difficult, and it juth wouldn't be real, would it?"

"What about that noose around your neck, Gary? That must have been difficult to bear. It's not rope, but it's real—real ink following a real design and implying a real meaning."

Gary fingered his tattoo. "Thith wath a mithtake," he said.

"That's the nice thing about writing on paper, Gary. If you make a mistake, you can revise it." Or replace it or cover it up, Michael thought but didn't say, just as he didn't say "revith" though he felt that the studs were a mistake that Gary should revise even if a non-metallic tongue diminished the pleasure of Gary's sex partners.

Michael looked around the seminar table. All nine students were studying their laps or preparing to say grace. Michael feared he had unwittingly imitated Gary's "lithp" and thought he should probably put a surveillance camera from his old company, Key Security, in the room to keep track of a rookie teacher's faux pas. Used to locker room bantering among healthy equals, Michael worried he had crossed some professor-student line by calling attention to the lines around Gary's neck. Every coach Michael had ever played for would have immediately asked Gary if he planned to wear a turtleneck on court.

"Other questions about this exercise?"

More silence. Then Michael's international student, Rakhshanda from Pakistan, said, "I do not believe fiction or non-fiction is the issue. I am afraid that such a chapter would interrupt the narrative momentum."

Rakhshanda's autobiography had begun with her two sets of impoverished grandparents. She had shown Michael the first fifty pages, and her parents weren't born yet. The narrative was slow in developing but insistently chronological, right down to dates and days of the week for critical events in her ancestors' lives which, now that Michael came to think of it, she must have been fictionalizing.

"Since the narrative is not moving," Michael the athlete-literalist said, "but only the pages, what do you mean by 'momentum?'"

"Reading should be like falling down stairs. Once you start, there is no place to turn off."

"Just tumble and hurt, tumble and hurt. I like it, Rakhshanda," Michael said, thinking of Terminal Tours.

She flapped her hands in front of her face, possibly a Pakistani negation.

"Please allow me to change the metaphor," Rakhshanda said.

"Simile," Michael said, using some of his new knowledge or old knowledge regained from reading the books Richard had recommended. He was against figurative language, but Michael thought it, like Dante, might come up.

"Yes, of course," Rakhshanda said and again flapped her hands, which couldn't be a negation but was a mystery to Michael, just about as opaque as the difference between synecdoche and metonymy, which he'd been trying to remember earlier that afternoon.

Passing Through

"Reading should be like one of those water slides, where all you get is a little splashed at the bottom," Rakhshanda said.

Michael realized he'd been missing something doing Terminal Tours. Amusement parks. Roller coasters and water slides. He believed "no game, no gain," but his students preferred fun and entertainment, the writer's and reader's easy downhill plunge to a harmless end. Then on to another ride. Yes, on and on and on. Michael had believed in or hoped for that once and at an age more advanced than his students, but now that he was responsible for the shape of their minds and narratives he felt the player he'd been speak to him. Sure, the ball passed through thin air and, if well shot, passed through the net with a swish. But the bodies on the court were zigging and zagging, colliding and near-missing, stopping and going, fighting their way through picks and screens for open spaces. The autobiographers, though, weren't training to create this kind of CNF, Competitive Non-Fiction, that would challenge readers' expectations. The students wanted their straight-line narratives of self to fit the commercial sluice they knew was out there, the sluice Ann had sent her craft down when she wrote *Passing Off*.

Going home after the graduate class, Michael thought changes at QCC might be slower and more complicated than he'd initially believed. But no matter how much resistance he met, Michael was happy with and for his students because, given the most recent statistics, even the oldest of the grads, even the Pakistani woman with her impoverished grandparents and their rickets, had fifty more years to live and to learn the modest lessons Michael was trying to teach. He remembered an old phrase—the quick and the dead. Only the dying had to be quick, hustling finally to take the tours they'd put off. In a park Q students frequented, Michael saw some girls and boys throwing a Frisbee, making sure the harmless disk reached the other players, receiving in turn easy throws, ambling to catch the floating disk, enjoying the sweatless play. Watching the Frisbee sail back and forth, Michael thought maybe his students were right. After the pain of Terminal Tours, why not have some fun and give some pleasure? Why not be happy to be through with the dead and the dying?

Chapter 2

"Walk the talk" was the athlete's measure of success. QCC was talk and talk and talk, like post-game interviews, like a coaches clinic, like Dick Vitale on TV. Five conversations:
"Whutup, MK?"
"What's up?"
"You don't remember me, do you?"
"Let me think. Liked to go left, fade away, and shoot the bank, right? Up at the Friars Club during the summer. Back when I was in college."
"You got it. Bobby Jelkes."
"Of course, just like it says on your shirt. How long have you been delivering the mail here?"
"Got the job when they opened. What you doing here?"
"I teach a couple of courses."
"You, teaching? Shoot, man, I thought you were playing ball over there in Europe somewhere. You looking good. You still hooping at the Friars at night? I'll get on up there and run some night with you."
"Nah, Bobby, I'm not balling anywhere. I'm through, finished."
"That can't be, MK. You use to be a legend."

***

"The connection is bad. Where are you?"
"Alaska, on a cruise ship," Ann said.

"Nice," Michael said, though he was happy to have avoided any northern lights or seasickness tours.

"Not so nice. The pilgrim comes out of her room only to eat salmon three times a day."

"Maybe she was an Indian in a former life."

"She's like a totem pole now. She just eats, doesn't speak, and goes back to her berth."

"Be thankful, I'd say. You'll hear plenty of stories before you're through. Maybe she's regressing, you know, going back to her birth."

"Thank you, Michael."

"Is that it? Is that why you called? For sympathy."

The line was silent, and Michael thought the cruise ship might have sailed past an iceberg or something. Then Ann continued: "How do you like the teaching?"

"The teaching is fine. I don't know about the learning."

"How are you on dangling modifiers?"

"We at Queen City College don't attempt to impose our sexual preferences on anyone."

"Do you think it will become a full-time job?"

Michael wondered why she cared.

"Maybe more sections but not full-time. The college likes to keep its options open semester to semester."

"Have you met Bucky?"

"Bucky whom?"

"Bucky who, Michael."

"Is that his real name?"

"That's what Sara calls him."

"Not to me. She just said she'd met a boy down the hall."

"That's Bucky. She brought him over the last time I was home. They seem very fond of each other. He's obviously more than just the boy down the hall."

"How did you like him?"

"He's nice. Seems smart. Very serious and well-mannered."

"Did he seem changed to you?"

"Changed from what?"

"From the way he was before he got to QCC three weeks ago."

"Look, Michael, I want this school to work for Sara, which means I want it to work for you, but I still believe QCC won't be around for her to graduate. Speaking of which, do you have a lawyer yet?"

"What does a lawyer have to do with Sara's graduating?"

"When I get around to it, I'm going to have my lawyer write a clause into the separation agreement about your being responsible for Sara's tuition, wherever she might go to school. You're going to need your own attorney."

"And I thought you were calling for sympathy."

"Today I could use some sympathy, but I can use your responsibility more. Please remember that because you didn't check out Rorque before you took him to Lourdes, we lost everything."

"Did you have an independent medical expert examine your salmon-eater? If she doesn't come out of that berth for the next meal and if you have to break down the hatch or door or whatever they call it on a cruise liner, do you think the captain is going to gather the onboard musicians on deck and let you have a burial at sea? No, Ann, you're going to have to bring her back packed in ice cubes, and when you get to the Seattle airport you'll run into the shit storm that I did in Paris."

Icebergs were floating on both ends now.

"What time is it there anyway?" Ann asked.

"Ten-thirty."

"Okay, time to eat," she said and hung up.

Passing Through

***

Michael tried to avoid June. He wouldn't mind a daytrip with an attractive woman in good health, but he feared further literary quizzing. When he went in one day to pick up his paycheck, though, she was in the departmental office.

"Michael, come in and sit down. I have something to show you."

"A map of Centerville?"

"Your center of the earth," she said and picked up from her desk a copy of *Passing Off*. "After our talk about Dante, Richard loaned it to me. I don't know anything about basketball, but I loved it, even that hellish thermal inversion in Athens. I especially enjoyed the buried text."

"That's *Passing On* with the mausoleums and cemeteries."

Now it was June's turn for the blank look.

"You know, burial grounds," Michael said.

"And you know what I'm talking about. Such a clever Henry Adams technique to make the Keever figure uneducated but sneak in behind his back your own subtextual references to Joyce and Rilke and Pynchon."

Michael smiled and nodded, giving himself credit as well as time to think. He'd sometimes worried, without knowing why, that Ann had put into *Passing Off* evidence that she, and not the dumb athlete, was the author. Now his suspicion was confirmed. No game, no gain. Ann had gained a sense of superiority by keeping him ignorant of the literary game she was playing.

"Those references were kind of a joke," he said, hoping to finesse the issue.

"I don't see them as a joke. They enrich the book. Along with the basketball metaphors, the allusions give the autobiography a more artful texture. Are you using any literary readings in your grad class?"

"Not yet. We spend most of the time workshopping what the students are writing."

"Of course, of course. Their stories. But you should consider using your own book or other texts like it. You know, I'm not as opposed to literature—or books—as Richard is. In fact, I'm one of the 'weaklings' he likes to refer to. My doctoral dissertation at Cornell was about the lattice-like boundary between novels and autobiographies by women."

"I hadn't realized that you were a doctor."

"A doctor and a resident, waiting for a job in an English Department where I can teach Stein, Woolf, Barnes, Allison, people like that. Given all the allusions to male writers in *Passing Off*, I assume you don't read many gay women."

The way June looked when she said those last two words told Michael she wouldn't be showing him around Centerville. He nodded and said, "Not yet. But they're on my list."

"So how do you find your graduate students?" June asked.

"By going to our classroom every Thursday at five."

"Oh, Michael, I like the way you, as a newcomer, make us aware of our speech conventions. I expect you're a breath of literal air for the students. You're not still standing in the seminar room, are you?"

"Now I sit and make the students stand."

"I've heard that you can be tough."

While wondering about the meaning of that, Michael said, "Just on the outside."

"They're young and delicate, those auto-egos, especially the women."

Passing Through

"I think they'll be okay. They outnumber the men seven to two."

"So what do you think about their work?"

Michael knew the chance he was taking but went ahead.

"I guess I wish it was more literary, more creative, maybe more risky." He considered "delicate" but decided against it.

"Exactly! But we're teaching in Communications, so we do what we can, right?"

"Maybe even less than we can," Michael said, thinking of the paycheck he was holding in his hand.

"Precisely," June said and touched Michael's hand in a way that could only be described as "delicately."

***

In late October, Richard dropped by Michael's office during his office hours.

"Just a few more days until the season begins," Richard said.

"Will the students stop writing until June?"

"Maybe school should be in session when the NBA isn't."

They talked some about off-season trades, what rookies would make a difference, how the Pacers were shaping up, and then Richard got to the reason he'd dropped by.

"All the language arts departments, LADs for short, in the area are going to have a league to foster collaboration. U.C., Xavier, Cincinnati State, Northern Kentucky, maybe even Miami will be in. One game a week, beer and pizza afterwards, break down some of the barriers. Since we're relatively new, this should really help us network with other departments."

As Richard went on about the fun and benefits, Michael realized he'd been recruited. To play ball, not to coach writing. He felt like a "bone," a high school prospect, a dumb athlete. So this is why QCC had been so quick to sign him up.

There was no way to finesse his artificial hip, so he waited.

"I sure hope you'll play for us," Richard said, snugging his chairman's silk up on his neck.

"Can't do it, Richard," Michael said and slapped his right hip. "Steel and plastic. I thought you knew this from *Passing On*."

"Jesus, Michael, I'm sorry to hear that. I know I should have read that book, but I was a little put off by the subject, you know. I read 'The Death of Ivan Ilyich' in my first year at college and it scared me right out of literature. What happened to your hip?"

Richard winced as Michael told him about his accident, cartwheeling over a sound boom while refereeing, but Richard's empathy didn't interfere with his quick calculation: "If you can't play, Michael, will you be our coach? We really need help because we're small compared to the other schools. I'm betting you'd make us competitive."

As Richard went on about what Coach Keever could do for the Q, Michael thought about a few of the many reasons he didn't want to coach. Coaches have no pleasure in playing, only pressure to win. They always quarreled with his showboat passing. "Keep it simple" was their mantra. And no matter how hard they tried to be nice guys, coaches always turned out to be assholes in the end. Michael tried to employ his old evasive skills.

"I teach two nights a week, you know."

"We'd arrange practices and games around your schedule."

"I don't know much about X's and O's."

"We'll use A's and B's."

"Would I get a shoe contract and a Lexus lease?"

"If you can get Kobe enrolled in your Autobiography class, yes."

Michael saw no way to avoid Richard's "request": "Okay, I'll help you out."

"Great, Michael. There's one other thing. It's the LADs but also the lassies. The women in the other schools want to be involved, so the teams will have to be coed. I argued against it, but got outvoted."

"Aaiight," Michael said, imitating the black guys he used to play with, "nothing like sharing lockers and showers with the ladies."

Richard didn't catch the fake enthusiasm. He smiled and fingered the thick gold ring on his left hand.

After Richard's visit, Michael realized how much Ann would like to know about his conversations with his bosses, the problems her *Passing Off* was causing him in his new life, the fact that his superiors had not read the book he'd written.

***

"Facts," Michael told both of his classes, "you must adhere to the facts. Look up the words. Adhere, adherent: follower. Facts: from Latin--'something done.' Betray the facts, and you'll be undone. Or overdone, cooked. Forget CNF. What we should be doing is Creative Faction. Fiction is a departure from the facts. The term 'Non-Fiction' suggests fiction is primary, and the facts a departure from it. Leave the facts and you lose 'creative' because anyone can make up stories. Your creativity is finding new facts or putting facts into a new context. You have to treat your material like the facts of life. Your parents may have put individual spins on the facts, but the facts themselves are indisputable."

"Itn't thith juth what I wath thaying?" Gary asked.

"More or less," Michael said, feeling a bit sorry for a sentence that had a lisp in almost every word.

The only black man in the class, a guy about six feet tall whom now literal Coach Keever was thinking about recruiting, asked, "Aren't the facts of life in some question now?"

"What do you mean, Jason?"

"I mean, how many parents tell their kids the actual facts, that not all the birds and bees are straight, that five to ten percent of their kids are and will be gay? Those facts are buried, as if they were facts of death. No wonder gays are successful in the arts, in the counter-factual areas of life. We've learned from early on to distrust the 'facts' in all of their manifestations."

"We?" Jason is gay? Jason is black. In what Michael had read, Jason was a ten-year-old busily plotting the death of his younger brother.

"Jason is absolutely right," a woman named Lauren said. It was the first thing she'd said all semester. Michael had spotted a gap between her two front teeth and wondered if she was self-conscious. She was not. She was hyper-conscious. "But," she went on, "he's avoiding the fact of language. Gay is fey. He's queer, I'm queer. And we queers are going to queer the deal, the contract on facts. We're going to write crooked, not straight. Life is rife. Wife is strife. Fear the queer and praise on the Amazon."

Except for Rakhshanda, the rest of the class was laughing and clapping and shouting encouragement to Lauren: "More you whore."

"Rhyme the time."

Lauren was grinning like a maniac, the tip of her tongue trying to wave between her teeth to her fans. But she had no more rhymes. She stretched out her right arm toward Michael, handing the class back over to him. He'd heard rap drifting out of his teammates' headphones for years, but the only rhyme he knew was "cold beer sold here."

"So," he said, "this is why you all hate your families, but you just haven't gotten around to telling me yet?"

"Lighten up, Mr. K," Jason said, "Lauren's just pretending to be gay. It's okay. Whatever gets the writing done, right?"

"Lauren?" Michael said.

"Ban the man. Pass as lass. Off and on."

Jesus, Michael thought, even the students were reading his books and using them against him.

"Bold queer told here?" he asked Lauren.

The students were laughing and slapping the table.

"Forget the tact and regret the fact," Lauren said, "Michael Keever just wants beaver."

Michael threw up his arms in surrender as the students howled, got up out of their seats, and high-fived Lauren. Michael realized her tongue wasn't waving to fans. It was sticking out at him, the old guy who had gone from the life of passing off to the death of passing on. He took a closer look at the half of her he could see above the seminar table. Short curly hair that was, maybe, authentically red. Blue eyes behind big dopey glasses. A gymnast's neck disappearing into an oversized hooded sweatshirt. Lauren Jones, maybe Irish, maybe a former athlete of some kind. She hadn't turned in any writing yet. Michael hoped it wasn't in some tricky stanzaic pattern like Dante that he'd have to look up.

Rakhshanda was waiting to have her chapter workshopped. The poor skinny grandparents with the names

Michael would never learn to pronounce. These facts Michael didn't want to face right now. Maybe Lauren and the other students didn't either. Possibly the facts of life discussion was a planned digression. Once they took up the Pakistani story, it would be down the stairs for the rest of the class.

"Any of you beavers and studs play basketball?" Michael asked.

The students looked at him as if they were waiting for a second line, something rhyming with "basketball."

"I'm serious. The chair has asked me to coach a team of women and men, graduate students and faculty. We're going to be playing other schools in the area. I think the chair wants to prove we're not a bunch of faggots and lesbos."

"Better yet," Jason said, "as Lauren might put it, we may be gay but we can play."

"Men in the trench, women on the bench?" Lauren asked.

"Nope. The rule is that team A has to match the number of women team B has on the floor."

The students liked the rule. Jason and Gary, the only men in the class, might have to sit while the women defended the honor of QCC.

Rakhshanda had her hand up. She was the only person to observe the formalities now that Keever had been unmasked. Michael had to call on her, even if she was going to ask when the class would be commenting on her manuscript.

"Rakhshanda?"

"I played basketball in Pakistan. In fact," she started and then looked around to see if anyone was going to make fun of her for using "fact." "I was the leading scorer on my high school team."

The other students applauded Rakhshanda and Michael took a closer look at her. Damn the grandparents' rickets. Her wrists were like the spindles in his kitchen chairs. The seminar table caught her mid-breast, which meant she was 5-2 at the most. And she was much too polite to hoop.

"You'll have to come to practice, Rakhshanda. Anybody else play?"

"Not since I was twelve," Jason said, "but maybe I can help out."

"Alllriiight," Michael said.

Michael was disappointed Lauren hadn't responded, but she was so quirky she might show up at the first practice wearing an Alan Iverson jersey and be as uncoachable as he was. Which would be just fine with Michael if she could fill it up the way A.I. did. If not, she could be the court jester and team rhymester, organizing sideline insults that would throw off other players.

Rakhshanda had her hand up again. There was no avoiding it. Now they all had to start at the top of the fact-laden, multistory staircase that she had constructed: "In the village of Prisnavegasta in a remote area of Baobabalab province, itself a remote area in the northeast of what is now Pakistan but was then India, 1927 was a very bad year for crops. That summer, July to be precise and the 15th to be exact, a very hot Friday, an eighteen-year-old woman named Meherunnisa was working in a field next to her second cousin on her oldest maternal aunt's side, a young man named Thul-Jalal wal-Iram. When the time came for his morning prayers...."

Chapter 3

Michael's favorite student was in Mathematics, not Communications, so she wasn't eligible for the team. She was a five-ten blond, sturdy in the legs, lean through the torso, had expensively straightened teeth, his 20-10 vision, and a way of tilting down her chin and looking at you through her eyebrows when she was mocking you. Sara liked her dorm room and roommate but not the food, so she walked over to Michael's apartment for dinner a couple of times a week after putting in her order at midday. The dorm turned out to be a great idea, even if it was Ann's, even if the price per square foot was like Athens or Rome. Sara's roommate, Marcy from Chicago, was also in math. Better yet, though Michael felt guilty thinking this way, Marcy had been molested by her mother—if Marcy was to be believed—when she was twelve. There were worse things than escorting the dying or separating from your wife. Now that Michael was called Mr. Keever at the college, Sara was friendlier than she'd been in a couple of years. Quick change, indeed, Michael thought.

The first visit, all Sara wanted to talk about was Marcy, who was three years older and had left two other colleges before the first semester was over. Although Sara had a large group of friends at Walnut Hills, Cincinnati's college prep high school, the dorm room was like sitting outside a confessional. Michael listened to Sara reveal details that Marcy never envisioned would circulate outside the two-bed container—or details she wanted to circulate for some kind of sick publicity before she became one of Michael's autobiographers. Since Sara was sleeping three feet from Marcy, Michael wondered about her sexual orientation. Michael was not homophobic, but in all the lockers where he'd undressed and dressed he'd never known a gay. He sometimes speculated about his brother, Patrick, who never seemed to leave his police cruiser for female companionship. Michael assumed some of Ann's friends were gay, but Ann and he used to socialize with couples. Now that he had some experience tiptoeing around college students' sensitivities, Michael decided to be subtle and sly with Sara.

"How does Marcy feel about her mother now?" he asked.

"Marcy was in therapy in high school, so she's kind of worked through a lot of her negative feelings. She does have a hard time getting to sleep though."

"I guess that's why you know so much about her personal life."

"No, it's not like that. The only time Marcy can talk about these things is in the shower."

"I thought your skin looked dry. No wonder QCC can't pay me more. Think of the hot water you're using. That therapy never would have worked in our old house."

"I'm not in the shower with her. I have to sit on the floor outside the shower and say 'Yes, Marcy, yes, Marcy' over and over. She'd never let me see her naked, not even in a fire drill."

"That's good."

"Why do you say that?"

"I mean it's good you don't have to be in the shower."

"You're never going to be slick, Dad," Sara said, looking at Michael through her eyebrows. "You or Mom.

At least you agree on this. She asked me practically the same questions. You don't have to worry about me. I met a guy down the hall during orientation. Marcy's jealous, so I'm safe."

"Down the hall?"

"You'd have known the floor was coed if you'd helped me move in."

"Your mother wanted to do that. She's always been in charge of housing."

"Marcy's parents were both there, and they've been divorced for years. You should have been there. Her father was wearing a dress."

"Don't even try to booshit me, girl."

"You better be careful with that brother talk. Marcy is from the south side of Chicago."

"You're rooming with a sister name Marcy? I be damn."

"You're impossible, Dad. If you get fired, you'll have to pay my tuition and work for Mom in Terminal Tours."

"You no foo. You won't report me, will you?"

"I'm telling you, QCC isn't like one of your locker rooms. Other students are paying high fees for high maintenance, high respect."

"Okay, got you. Now what about the boy down the hall? He's not a greaser, is he?"

"You're going to get in trouble here, Dad."

"I'm just playing with you, Sally Pally," Michael's name for Sara before she went to school. He used to believe that the family that plays together stays together, but his jokes and tricks and pranks hadn't kept the Keevers from living in three different places. At least the barbarian pose tonight had started Sara talking about her parents.

Passing Through

On the next visit, Sara handed her father a "Why I Chose My Major" essay she'd written for her math class.

"Didn't you have Susan Stickler for AP English at Walnut?" Michael asked. "I really shouldn't help you with this."

"I don't want you to edit it. I just thought you might be interested in reading it."

Choosing Math

I didn't choose mathematics. It was there and let me in. It didn't choose me but accepted me, at least for now. And not really "me" but some quirk in my neurological makeup that may be, for all I know, as individual as my fingerprints. That quirk can't turn back and study its quirkiness. The quirk will know itself only by the tests it can pass as the discipline imposes its rigor. The quirk has a past but no future, for at any time the quirk may meet the door that doesn't open. My roommate or classmates will go through and enter a larger (or possibly smaller and less populated) room. And I will have to decide if the arithmetic—no longer math—that I know will allow me to stay in the major or find a place outside the major, outside the college.

The quirk allows but isn't just intuition. The quirk or, at least, my quirk isn't operating on some problem while I'm doing Spanish verbs or Renaissance history. The quirk needs isolation, concentration, imagination to apprehend the numbers cavorting chaotically but regularly in their formulas, the planes and curves and imaginary lines passing through each other, the marvelous sex of sets. If I, the habitation of the quirk, am lucky enough to become for an instant some kind of meta-mind, the quirk just as quickly disappears and leaves plain old me scratching my head and wondering how the skull and brain did that trick.

The quirk, so far, produces numbers and letters but not many words, at least not words that are memorable. In fact, writing about the quirk and its processes seems to me dangerous, for what if the quirk has or is consciousness, a consciousness offended by the childish counting games that language seems to be? Although I didn't choose math, I can choose not to say more and endanger its acceptance of me.

"Jesus, Sara, you wrote this?"

"Do you think you can find something like this at Cheatsheet.com?"

"I'm not saying that. It's just that I couldn't have written this in a hundred years."

"You don't have a hundred years, Dad. And if you don't have the quirk, you wouldn't be asked to write 'Why I Chose Mathematics.'"

"What do you think your teacher is going to say? It's pretty short."

"Nobody is sure if the teacher speaks English, so he may not read it or say anything about it."

"You've been going to classes for three weeks, and you're not sure your teacher speaks English?"

"It sounds like English, but it could be a mix of English and some Indian dialect. It's okay. We can follow his stuff on the blackboard."

"People are paying for this?"

"What's synesthesia?" Sara asked, adding "Mikie Mousie," her equivalent of "Sally Pally."

"All those terms are Greek, no problem for me. Did your mother put you up to asking me that?"

"It's okay, Dad. You've got your quirk, just like me. Just like my math teacher. This is Quirk, not Queer, College. I like it. My history professor is two or three hundred years old and whispers. My Spanish instructor is from Portugal. A guy with studs in his tongue teaches us communication skills."

"You have Gary Gallagher?"

"You have Gary Gallagher. He has us. I get this weird feeling that he may be hitting on me."

"Unbelievable. And to top it all off, you live with a black girl named Marcy."

"Marcy isn't really black. I was kidding you about that."

"What about this quirk? Are you just making it up?"

"No, I know my mind doesn't work like anyone I know. It's hard, but it's fair."

That last sentence was one of Ann's favorite sayings, maybe the only one that sounded like an athlete's wisdom. Michael said, "You sound like your Mom. I'm glad she's wrong about 'quick change' college."

"Now you're happy that I sound like Mom? Maybe you're the quick change guy."

"That's better than being the short change guy."

Sara scowled. "You know, Dad, sometimes I wonder how Mom and I lived with you so long."

"You didn't. That's what your Mom never understood. The only way Ann Logan could put up for seventeen years with a barbarian like me was for me to be away much of the time."

"You could have changed. Marcy did. Mom is changing."

"Your Mom is just changing time zones. No, I take that back. She probably should have left that grant-writing job long ago. Maybe come out of the ghostwriter closet and applied for a position over in the English Department."

"That's Mom. What about you?"

"I have an idea about that, something I figured out writing *Passing On*. When your work is play, as basketball was for me, and when that play pervades your whole life—how you perceive and think, how you move, the words you choose—it's hard to change. It's like I was seventeen until the broken hip at thirty-seven, and then I turned sixty-five and hung out with the dying. Now, finally, I feel something like my actual age. But I'm telling you, your Mom doesn't know how hard those Tours will become. The dead and dying were killing me, Sara."

Michael knew from Richard's books that this last sentence was called hyperbole, but he didn't mean it to end the conversation with Sara, who went to the kitchen and started doing the dishes, a task she never did. Although Michael didn't follow up, he believed that sometime and somehow Sara would need to understand why he quit Terminal Tours if she was going to understand why her mother and father were living in separate apartments and why she was going to QCC. An account of Michael's final tour, the figurative killer, was available online, but he doubted Sara had ever been willing to look at his web site.

During the desperate weeks after Rorque's lawsuit, Michael's former physical therapist and friend, who was dying at thirty-two of kidney cancer, asked him to take her on a tour of mausoleums. Alice had read *Passing Off* and wanted to visit countries Michael (actually Ann) had described. He first resisted taking Alice on the tour of terminals, but she had helped him a lot back when he was recovering from his hip surgery. She was like a trainer, the athlete's best friend. Michael also thought she had insurance money. The longer they traveled—from Turkey to Egypt to India—the more Alice seemed to regain her health, and Michael felt he had to keep going on and on for his friend's sake. But when Ann discovered that Alice would probably never pay, Michael tried to shock her into ending her possibly interminable tour. He took Alice to a ships' graveyard in India, a horrible place where ships are run aground and salvaged by hordes of poor men who work with their bare hands in polluted water and poisoned air, the men dying while breaking the dead ships into scrap. Michael ended *Passing On* at that graveyard in Alang. After the book was published, after he got the job at QCC, and after he separated from Ann, Michael continued Alice's story. Sara could read it anytime by going to www.terminaltours.com.

On our way back to Bhavnagar from the ships' graveyard, Alice repeats her one-word response—"Wonderful"—and asks again, "Where will you take me next?" The dead ships and dying men have been neither enough nor too much. Not enough to prove she could face anything. Not too much to face for a terminal patient in remission. I'd believed one of those responses would send us back home. I was overwhelmed by Alang, sickened and scared by all those young athletes soon to be diseased or crippled or dead, melted down by the sun and their torches and the twelve-hour days. But Alang was somehow too little for Alice, and she wanted to keep going on.

"Alang is the worst place on earth," I tell her. "I don't have anything to top that."

"Okay, so what about the best place on earth?"

"You know how I feel about that."

"Athens."

"Right, but that's purely personal, like a player's irrational attachment to his first court."

"And his heroic past?"

"I was the Greek Key," I remind her.

"What do your other clients say is the best?"

"Probably Paris, whether they've been there or not."

"Well?"

"It has a river, just like Cincinnati."

I'm stalling for time, trying to imagine some objection to Paris other than the French people who live there.

"No mausoleums that I can think of," I say.

"You know, Michael, I don't feel I need death as much as I used to," Alice says, as if she were dismissing a silly habit like drinking carrot juice before every meal. She gestures out the back window of our taxi. "That should hold me for a couple of days, so let's go to Paris."

Just like that. That's how the new Alice likes to decide and move, like an athlete, by whims and darts, fits and starts. I'd picked the Alang graveyard. Now Alice is choosing and heading west, which I hope is a good sign.

In the Delhi airport, I look at the departure board and tell Alice flights are going soon to Washington and New York. Arlington National Cemetery, Grant's Tomb. I'd be in the same time zone as Sara and Ann. It wouldn't cost her as much to harangue me about the length and cost of this tour.

"I think it's healthier outside the United States," Alice says, overlooking the dying men at Alang while eating her Sbarro's pizza. It's hard to argue with the results. The remission mission has become Alice's tour for the cure, and now she wants croissants and frogs' legs at the tourist's axis mundi. She buys a Paris guide in the airport bookshop and starts looking for a hotel. That's when I realize that Alice could go to Paris, and I can go to Cincinnati. Physically, she is strong enough to carry her own bag, and I'd given her lots of international airport experience. There must be plenty of unescorted women poking around the antique shops and flea markets of Paris. Yet somehow I still feel my presence is necessary. Alice and I are "in the zone" together, like Stockton and Malone of old, the assister and assistee so close they don't have to—or dare to—speak of the charmed collaboration they are creating. If traveling is saving Alice's life, I need to go on with her a while longer. After watching and smelling and hearing those poor bastards at Alang, I also feel—more than ever before—that metal may go on and on and on, but that I will end or stop or terminate.

In our hotel near the Bastille, Alice is airplane wired and wants to take a walk before unpacking, so with her holding the map we zigzag through Marais to the Seine near where the canal joins the river.

"Yup," she says, imitating a Kentucky farmer to mock my attempt to discourage this trip, "just like that there Cincinnati etcept here it's Paree on both sides."

"Same boats too," I say as a bateau-mouche passes by, looking nothing like the fake paddle wheelers that give tourists a ride in Cincinnati.

"And I guess that building over there must be Paul Brown Stadium, not the Museum of the Arab World."

"You better be thankful about that considering all the Christian-hating Algerians they have in Paris."

"Michael," Alice says as if I've just arrived at her side, "I want to take a swim."

"Sorry, the Seine is just as polluted as the Ohio."

"Not here. On the plane I was reading about the public pools. Tomorrow we buy you a suit and go swimming. That pool at the Best was for kiddies and mosquitoes."

"Are you sure you're up to that kind of exercise? It's a lot more tiring than the walking we've been doing."

I remember my first hydrotherapy session after my hip replacement. I thought I'd drown. It was then I decided I was through with anything athletic.

"I used to swim four times a week. My legs are still in good shape. And I'll drink a bottle of wine for the sugar before we go."

I must look shocked because Alice touches my arm and says, "I'm just kidding about the wine, Michael. Come on, we're in Paris, put away that silly white nurse's cap. We'll get you a beret and maybe a pipe so you can look philosophical if you insist on worrying."

The next morning we take the Metro in from the Bastille to Les Halles, the underground shopping mall where one of Paris's indoor pools is located. I buy a boxer model, and we walk over to the pool. We pay our two euros each and change in the unisex locker room. When Alice comes out of her booth in her Speedo, I can see she has been exercising herself as well as her patients. A bicyclist's legs and swimmer's shoulders. With her short-cut hair under her swim cap, she looks like old photos of Esther Williams, the rounded cheeks of maybe the first bathing beauty. We take a shower and head to the pool. Just as we are walking onto the apron, a young man with a whistle around his neck runs up to me, points at my suit, and says "Non, non, non" along with some other French that I don't understand. I figure this guy must be the French fashion police and that the bright orange I'd chosen is out this season. "English?" I ask. "Non, non, non." I hold out my open palms to show I don't understand. This referee points down at his own suit, a black number about the size of a cocktail napkin—with considerable matching black pubic hair sprouting around the edges. I look at Alice. She shrugs. She is running the point now, but my guide doesn't speak French and is no help with this native. Again I open my palms. The pubic-proud guy points around the pool at other men, all wearing the same cocktail napkin, though in different colors. "American," I tell him and point at the suit. He is clearly not a person who has seen any beach movies or Hawaiian travel shows. "*Non, non,*" he says, "*non-sanitaire.*" "*Sanitaire,*" he repeats. I understand the word but not its relevance. The suit is brand new, we've been in the shower.

Passing Through

Although the lifeguard and "*sanitaire*" protector is clearly upset, he doesn't blow his whistle. Instead, he takes me by the arm, leads me back through the locker room, points out an iconic sign that clearly X-es bathing suits like mine, and then shows me to a vending machine in the lobby where, for six euros, I can buy my own waterproof and sanitary cocktail napkin. By the time I've tucked all of myself into it and congratulated myself on my blond hair, Alice is tooling freestyle up and down a lane, passing the French women and men. They seem afraid to get their hair wet because they are all doing the breaststroke. I realize why the French are called frogs: they are all kicking like bullfrogs and bellefrogs. I lower my almost exposed privates into the water, but I can't do that frog kick, not with the artificial hip. After two laps, the former athlete is exhausted and the former trainer is still churning the water. Yes, I think, Alice is definitely strong enough to do whatever she wants.

I won't bore you with the usual tourist tales, the undiscovered Oberkampf bistros where we can't get a table or the hideaway Beaubourg cafés where we can't get a waiter. Every morning we go to a different pool, and every afternoon we go to a park (if sunny) or a café (if rainy). We don't go to the Montparnasse cemetery near the Luxembourg Gardens when we are there, and we don't go to the catacombs after we have lunch at La Coupole. After four days, I do get a little superstitious and insist we visit Napoleon's tomb at the Hotel des Invalides, an old military hospital. Alice stands up on the walkway above the crypt and laughs while other tourists and French guards look at her. "I thought he was a little fellow," she says, looking down at a casket that could easily have accommodated Shah Jahan and Mumtaz, permanent residents of the Taj Mahal. "Maybe it's one of those Russian-doll caskets," I whisper to her, which makes her laugh louder. I'm respectfully silent, but the coffin is grotesque, grandiose not just in size but in its polished surface and overdone surroundings, the statues and paintings that encircle the old Emperor. The tomb is unlike anything we've seen, more artificial than the Taj, more strange because more recent, the Museum of Death.

"Enough," Alice says as we're leaving. This is the response I was seeking at Alang, but Alice doesn't mean enough travel, just enough mausoleums. I agree. We are no longer on a terminal tour, at least not the one Alice began. Now it's a training trip. Alice doesn't buy any clothes or souvenirs, doesn't ask me to tape her clowning around with mimes pretending to be dead or statues in front of City Hall. She does more and more laps every day while I sit in my bikini bottom and admire French bodies and the architecture of their pools. A couple are like churches, with vaulted ceilings and high stained-glass windows. One reminds me of a Turkish bath or mosque. Pontoise, the "piscine" in the Latin Quarter, is particularly elegant, maybe even elevating and inspiring. It has three floors of changing rooms and walkways surrounding the pool. Everything is in shades of blue, the painted walls, the pool, the blue sky one can see up through the roof of glass.

Alice set out to refuse religion's false hope of immortality, but in Paris she is devoted to the religion of swimming. It's easy to be baptized but difficult to be confirmed, at least for me. I admit I enjoy hanging around pools more than walking through museums, which I don't understand and where nothing moves. I sit on a bench, type my travel notes on the laptop, watch the bathers. The swimmers are athletes, French athletes doing the frog kick, but still athletes, and they aren't dying in their chlorinated water the way the "unclean" men and boys at Alang were dying in their polluted sea. No, the pools are "*sanitaire*," and I take a quirky pleasure in coming to Paris and bypassing the museums and churches and galleries Ann would have been guiding me through. Instead, Alice the athlete is passing through the water, end to end, around and around like a hoopster on court, on and on, passing the frog-kickers, regaining her strength and wind, preparing for me to be through with her.

A call from Ann while Alice is in the room speeds up the process. She can hear "I know," "Not yet," "I can't," "I won't," and "Well, fuck it, then." After Ann hangs up on me, I tell Alice the other half or, actually, other nine-tenths of the conversation.

"I have to go back, Alice. You can keep going on. You don't need me now."

"Rough back in the U. S., huh?"

I still don't want to jinx our zone—composed of travel and tombs, if not the two of us—so I use the secret I've been carrying since Ann called me in Luxor.

"My wife is worried about money. We're being sued. And your father told her you don't have any insurance to pay for this tour."

"That's true," she says, as if it were a well-known fact. "But now I have the rest of my life. Amex may have to wait, but you'll get your money, Michael. Did you think I'd stiff you the per diem?"

"I don't know, Alice. People do strange things when they're desperate."

"I was desperate to get out of Cincinnati but not now."

"It's not just the money. Ann says if I don't return now, she'll change the locks and I'll be living in the security van."

"Do you believe her?"

"That's the trouble with Ann. She doesn't lie."

"So what did you say?"

"'Well, fuck it, then.'"

"Meaning?"

"Meaning I was pissed. I'd like to keep going on with you. You know, on and on and on. But I need to go back. I'm going to get a flight tomorrow."

"Just like that?"

"You must have seen this coming."

"One more trip, Michael."

"No, I'm sorry but this is the terminal for us."

"One more trip, a short one—for you this time."

"Meaning?"

"We go to Athens for a few days, and then we'll fly back to Cincinnati together."

"Very clever."

"Not clever at all. I want to give you this for all you've done for me. I've got room left on my card. And I want to see your best place. After all, it was reading about your life in Athens that gave me the idea for this tour."

"So you want to join the athletes of Athens, do you? The Greeks are different from the frogs, you know. You want hustling and pushing and shoving on the sidewalks, dodging and running and jumping in the crosswalks, the heat and sweat? You believe you're ready for life on the run?"

"There must be pools there."

"Just at hotels we can't afford."

"Doesn't matter. I want us to go there."

"Okay," I say, just like that, just as Alice has been deciding. "I'll show you around. But only if you promise me one thing."

"What is it?"

"You lied to me about having life insurance."

"That's true."

"Now I want you to promise me that we'll go back to Cincinnati together. I want this tour to end how it began."

"Yeah, I'll keep you company going home, Michael. But let's say it will end **where** we began, not how I began."

Chapter 4

A decade ago Athens had felt like home, the home court, to Michael. When he was through as a minor-league point guard in the U.S., his agent got him the contract with Panathinaikos. A tricky dribbler and fancy passer, Michael was a crowd pleaser called, among other names, "White Magic" and "The Greek Key" and Michalis Kyvernos. That last one his agent had made up to get a blue-eyed, blond-haired person of Irish descent into the Greek league. Michael hadn't told Ann about the fancy paperwork, so after he was exposed as an imposter she was constantly suspicious. Even before the exposure, there was conflict in Athens: despite a cold apartment, Michael loved the city, and Ann hated it. Michael felt the city was a gym, always speed in the streets, always competition for tight spaces. And having grown up on a Vermont farm, Michael enjoyed the sun in Greece and the crowds who came to be in it. Years later, he wondered if he had loved the place for itself or for the recognition and adulation he received there from the fans. Ironically, Ann's fiction made Michael a national hero, partly because, she said, Greeks loved cheaters. Or, in her more recent term, "quick changers," people who passed themselves off as other than what they were. "Where else," she used to ask Michael, "is the epic hero lionized for lying?" It was only after Michael read *Huckleberry Finn* along with Sara that he had an answer for Ann, but by then they were living in Spain where, as Michael understood it, the epic hero had read too many lies.

Passing Through

Michael had enjoyed traveling in Greece and elsewhere in Europe with his teammates, and at first he liked being an assist-man again, helping the terminally ill go on their dream vacations. But until Alice came along, the tours were like a team going 0 and 29. Never a happy ending. Everybody died after they returned and reminded Michael that with every trip he was increasing his chances for early termination. When it looked, finally, as if he was going to be 1 and 29, Michael felt compelled to keep going, to have one win, a single success. In fact, he was afraid of coming back home, Alice's home not the Keevers'. So in Paris he agreed to go to Athens, his old home away from home.

On and on and on? Run it backward. No and no and no. Non and non and non.

No, I'm sorry but I can't bear stringing you on, describing the secret spots of Athens, recording Alice's appreciation of those places, observing all the travelogue conventions, the passing scenery, the weather, the odd or irritating locals, the humorous anecdotes, the fucking eternal Parthenon, the little self-discoveries, the happy touchdown on American soil.

Two days after we arrived, Alice started complaining of back pain in the afternoon. I thought it was all the walking we were doing. I got her some aspirin, and she lay in bed until early evening, when we walked the three blocks from our hotel in Exarchia Square to Barba Iannis taverna, sat outside, drank metal carafes of retsina to boost the aspirin, and returned to the hotel. Alice woke me at three.

"I took more aspirin, but the pain is getting worse," she told me.

"Maybe it's from not swimming," I said.

"Maybe so, but it began in Paris, and I thought it was from too much swimming."

Passing Through

I sat with her on the balcony until dawn. The natives here at the center of the world were honking their horns and revving their motorcycles in the square below us. The university students were yelling at each other in the all-night fast food joint, anarchists were talking over their plots in the chained chairs of the closed cafés, addicts were roaming the alleys for a fix. Even in the dead of night, life was going on and on in Athens.

In the morning, I called my Greek translator, the guy who "metamorphosed" *Passing Off* into Greek, and he used his influence and my old name—Kyvernos—to get us in that afternoon to see an English-speaking oncologist he knew. Dr. Sotiris spent a lot of time with Alice, and then called me into the examining room. Alice was rigid in her chair and didn't look at me.

"The cancer has metastasized into her spine. That's why she has so much pain," the doctor said.

"Just like that?" I asked, "so suddenly and so severely?"

"I'm afraid so," he said.

Outside the doctor's office in a second-floor apartment in Kolonaki, life was going on. The buses were squealing and grinding on Patriarchou Ioakim. Cars were braking and accelerating. Shoppers on the sidewalk were walking and talking loud to each other over the traffic noise. A woman was shrieking "taxeee, taxeee, taxeee, taxeee." The natives were going on and on with their lives. But not Alice. She was sitting straight up in her chair, still, her legs pressed tight together, her hands gripping the wooden arms, her jaws clenched, eyes squinted against the back pain. In my chair angled across from her, I tried to catch her eyes, but she wouldn't look at me. I didn't know why. I walked over behind her and put my hands on those swimmer's shoulders. Her muscles seemed to relax, but she didn't move, didn't turn around or look up, didn't say anything.

Hatshetsup. Alice looked like a relief of that stiffly sitting Egyptian we'd seen in Luxor, the queen who planned her whole adult life for her terminal tour.

The doctor was still speaking. I caught, "back to the States immediately." Something like, "prescription for some pain killers."

What happened next? How the hell do I know? I can see and will always see Alice sitting still, I can hear some of the doctor's words, I remember embracing Alice in the hall outside the office. No, no, no. I remember my saying that. Something about that dubious Greek, what does he know, we'll find someone else. "No," Alice said. I remember we were walking hand in hand and weeping on Patriarchou Ioakim. "I'm sorry," Alice said. No, no, not that. Somehow we were sitting in Pero's café in Kolonaki Square. Maybe we were drinking ouzo or beer but what difference does it make, really, what we were drinking, or where we were, or that the Greeks were buzzing away in their chairs, were going on and on about fashion and soccer or about the two foreigners crying into their ouzo or beer or iced tea or a Greek frappe.

No, you're right, I'm not there. I'm recalling these moments from somewhere else, but every time I recall them and try to write them for this serial, this way-too-short serial, I'm there, at least partly. Run the tape backward: café, street, hall, doctor's office. Alice is sitting stiff and gazing into eternity like dead Queen Hatshetsup.

In the café I try again to have her see another doctor. "No." I tell her again that her doctor back in Cincinnati may have a different opinion. "No." I try to lie to her. This whole thing was a fake, a hoax. I had my translator friend set it up. I didn't believe you'd ever go back. I'm sorry. It was a crazy thing to do. I'm really sorry. "No."

Passing Through

"You're making me feel guilty, Michael."

I remember her saying that. Like her parents made her feel guilty for dying? For fucking up this happy ending to our terminal tour?

"No hope, remember?" she said.

I remember that. And trying to lie some more about what her doctor in America might be able to do. Chemo, radiation, spinal replacement, faith healing. Jesus, I don't know what I might have babbled there in Kolonaki Square. If I could remember, I might be able to understand why—here at the keyboard, now—I was taking this death sentence harder than Alice. Or maybe the reason is so transparent that I don't need to explain anything to you readers who were hoping—desperately, right?--as I was for a different ending to this Tour for the Cure.

No cure. Now you can think of it as the tour of courage. And I'll show some spunk the rest of the way.

We walked twenty minutes back to our hotel. I filled the doctor's prescription. Just a few pills, not enough for me. It was too late to go to the airline office. It was much too late to take a nap. We lay on our backs on the single beds in the Hotel Exarchion and replayed the tour, the tours, the five countries, the stone monuments and the Paris pools, the amusing locals and the impoverished men at Alang, little Napoleon, all of it, all of them, day by day, country by country, tomb by tomb, all of that death, the false hope, the collapsed zone I could now tell Alice about. Private stuff, too, that you really don't need to know.

At the end of our recall, here at the end of the outward trip, Alice said, "I can do it now, Michael. I can disappear. You know, like the bodies at Halicarnassus. You gave me that."

"I was just carrying the bags. You did it yourself."

"Do you really think so, Michael? I wish I could trust you, but I know you lie, especially when you're in this country."

We both looked up at the ceiling. Some fool had painted it light blue.

"Tell me something, will you?" she said.

"Anything."

"That's just what I'm afraid of. So tell me the truth: you made up all that saving-the-Parthenon stuff in *Passing Off*, didn't you?"

"Not me, my wife, my ghostwriter."

"And the City-of-the-Dead stuff in Cairo. How about that?"

"I was there, Alice."

"Good. I wouldn't want this whole tour to be based on a damned fiction."

Early the next morning I bought us first-class tickets for the afternoon flight to New York. We had to hustle to the airport. The cabbie was happy to oblige, my last death-defying ride in an Athens taxi. I wanted him to keep driving on and on, weaving through the traffic, faster and faster, in reverse if possible. We waited in the first-class lounge with the executives, dressed to kill, to live forever. I looked out at the brown hills and blue sky. The worst place in the world. I felt like telling the last security agent to keep my passport. I was through with it. My first first-class seat, the new worst place in the world today. Alice had the window, the tourist's seat. The doctor's pills were powerful stuff, so she was in and out of sleep on the way to New York. Like Drinker, I thought, my first pilgrim, dying on the way home from Indianapolis. Unlike Markita, who filled my ears with fears on this same flight when I was just starting out. Other return flights came back to me in this group coffin thirty thousand feet up. The trip home from Turkey at the end of *Passing Off*. The flight from Paris with poor dumb Mr. Rorque down in the deep-freeze. Never before with someone I'd come to love. Westward, deathward, no more flights.

Passing Through

About half way through, Alice jerked in her seat and came wide awake.

"We need to settle some things, Michael," she said, her voice not at all bleary.

"We've got a long way to go yet. New York to Cincinnati, taxi to your parents' in Lebanon. I've got the meter running."

"I don't mean that settling."

"I know you don't."

"Send 'em home laughing?"

"Smiling, if you can."

"Home doesn't look so bad from this seat."

I thought of my own new home in the van.

"Everything looks better in first class."

"I'm serious, Michael, if you get out and around home looks better, something you've chosen. And I did choose, Michael. In Paris, before Athens."

"You did, I know."

"Okay, so that's settled. If you're still keeping notes on your laptop, I want that clear."

"Got it."

"Okay, that's the present. Now, the future."

"Who's to say what's going to happen, Alice?"

"I can say. For example, I knew you were going to say that. Actually, damn it, that's the whole reason to have this conversation. I know what's going to happen, and that's why I'm asking you one last favor, even if I do owe you money."

"Forget the money, Alice, this is the best trip I've ever taken."

"I'm telling you, Michael, none of that bullshit talk like the stuff on your web site."

With effort she turned in her seat.

"There's something we need to get settled."

The dying can say whatever they want, but I wished she would stop using that word "settled." Every time I heard it I couldn't help but remember my parents' graves in Pleasant View Cemetery, Ludlow,

64

Vermont. Both were buried in April when the frost wasn't completely out of the ground. All summer long, no matter how high the caretakers let the grass grow to hide what was happening, the ground was settling, as if the bodies and the coffins were imploding, sucking the sod downward to darkness.

"Michael?"

"Yes, settled."

"I promised you I wouldn't come after you in your hotel room, right?"

"Yes."

"Okay, here's what I'm asking you to do. Will you come to visit me in my hospital room?"

"Of course, you don't need to ask me that."

"Your wife won't like it."

"Doesn't matter."

"You'll be away with other pilgrims."

"No, Alice, no more tours."

"You may change your mind. But I know I'm going to need you to remind me of this no-hope tour. My parents will be working night and day, day and night, with selected clergymen of their choice trying to get me to accept their faith, any faith, in the other side. I'm going to need you there. I don't know if I'll have the strength to resist being saved."

"You could lie to them. That would please them and wouldn't hurt you."

"I knew it. Michael Keever, the Lying Cretan. No, I don't want to lie. I'll be lying for a long time in Spring Grove. I want you in the hospital to remind me of all the people who have disappeared from this earth. Mausolus and Artemisia in Turkey, Hatshetsup and Nefatari, that silly Shah Jahan, all the people from the past and all those pitiful men at Alang. Will you do it?"

"Of course I will."

"No, Michael, not 'of course.' Because it's going to be hard for you, and I don't know if you're strong enough to do it. We're all just passing through like those ships being broken up at Alang. Brief beginning, short middle, quick end. But you want to believe somehow, some way, any way that we go on and on and on. You want to be deceived, so you might start lying to me or my parents or the clergymen. Oh, damn, I don't know."

She turned back away from me and faced ahead. But even in the dim light I could see the tears going down her cheek, the tears she didn't want me to see. I took her hand and squeezed it.

"I'll be there, Alice."

"In the hospital?"

"Yes, I'll be there."

"You were really there in the City of the Dead?"

"Yes, I was there."

"You won't disappear?"

"Not for a few years, I hope."

"And you won't lie?"

"No, I won't lie."

"And you'll be there all the way through, Michael?"

"Yes, Alice."

"Say it, Michael."

"All the way."

"Until the end, goddammit. Because I don't know if I can trust you, Michael."

"I will be there," I said, just the way Drink, my former agent, would have said it.

"I will," I said again.

"Until the end?"

"Yes."

"All the way until the end?"

"Until the end, yes, Alice, all the way until the end."

Michael went back to his old Key Security van for two nights before Ann let him in the house so that he would be available at all hours to argue about spending three unpaid weeks with a woman other than his wife.

"This time is different," Ann said over and over. "Before, you did things behind my back or left things unsaid or lied to other people, but this time you put this trip right in my face."

"You knew exactly where I was, we talked every few days on the phone, I never lied to you about Alice."

"That's exactly what I'm saying, Michael. You'd still be traveling if she hadn't gotten sick. Or still be in Athens, the two of you, the Greek Key and the American keyho'."

"Don't go there, Ann. You know better than that."

"What do I know? Am I supposed to believe you just because this woman is dying now? Did you really believe she was going to live forever?"

"I don't know what I believed. Maybe I hoped. I tried to get her to come back. She agreed to return if we went to Athens. But I just couldn't bring myself to leave her."

"That's a sad story, a sad sack story. You don't even care enough about Sara and me to make up a plausible lie. How will I know if you'll come back the next time you go on a tour?"

"I'm through with Terminal Tours. That's no lie. No more tours, no more lies."

"And what about Rorque's suit? If you stop now, it's like admitting you were guilty taking his father to Lourdes. There's a bunch of emails from people who want to go."

"You take them. No more tours for me."

Over and over again Ann repeated "This time is different."

Michael repeated "No more tours," and no matter how much Sara teamed up with her mother—"Dad, why didn't you think about us?" "Dad, do you want all of us to live in the van?" "Dad, how am I going to college if you don't work?"—Michael refused to transport the dying.

At least Michael could say to Sara what he couldn't to Ann: "You don't understand now. Maybe you will when you get older. I thought I was saving someone's life."

To that, Sara brought the wisdom of the immortal teenager: "That was pretty dumb, Dad."

"Maybe so, Sara, but you may feel differently when your Mom and I are dead."

To that, Sara brought the response of the vulnerable seven-year-old: she stomped off to her room and slammed the door.

Every day Michael drove to the hospital to see Alice, and every day as he headed home it felt worse than the hospital. Confined to her floor and then to her room, Alice was disappearing fast. During her last days, the nurses kept the rails of her bed up. They looked to Michael like bars. He spent some nights in the cell of his van even though he didn't have a surveillance job. His old clients had found companies to replace him, and what new customer would trust a man being sued for not providing the basic security of life itself? Other nights Ann recited the charges against him not covered in Rorque's suit, ranging over their years together. She paced back and forth in front of him, as if imitating his movements while she recalled the tour he'd been on since college: the low-paid years in C.B.A. buses, the recruiting trips for Coach Danny Cater, the flights out of Athens, Rome, and Seville, the years refereeing. Although Ann was a marathoner, the pacing and her anger were enough to work up a sweat in the old house. Her red cheeks looked like a child's too long out in the cold, but she was seething like some kind of mobile volcano that gets to go off only once in seventeen years. "You used to tell me I was the pivot," Ann said, "but you never cared enough about Sara and me to stay with us." There was his failure with Terminal Tours: "Okay, you were back on the road, but I accepted that because it was finally something you'd chosen for yourself. And now you're giving that up." There was the recent background: "Ever since your hip replacement, you seem afraid to come to bed." Partly true. With that steel in his leg, Michael was no sexual athlete. Then there was the deep background: "You never chose me for myself, Michael. If I hadn't been pregnant, we'd never have gotten married." Partly true again. Back then, with the nuns still in the back of Michael's head, he'd chosen life, chosen to save the life that turned into Sara. Michael had never been sorry, but Ann never fully forgave him. Not for the pregnancy. Neither one understood how that sperm had gotten through the defenses. But for not asking The Question before the sperm's athletic feat.

Now Michael didn't want to argue, to compete, and his silence angered Ann even more. "What is this new dumb show?" she screamed. All Michael could think was no, no, no. All he would say was "no more tours." He might have admitted to all the charges if he'd felt like talking. If he'd wanted a talking point of his own, he'd have brought up *Passing Off*, the dumb and selfish athlete charge. Even if it wasn't true, that charge in print would outlast Ann and him and her current indictments. For a person who didn't read much, that book had an odd influence on Michael. It didn't pass through; it stuck in his craw or wherever one was supposed to process food for thought. If Ann didn't forgive him for not popping The Question, he couldn't pardon The Answer she had provided to their financial predicament a decade ago.

Two weeks after Michael returned from Athens, Ann quit her job and was away almost constantly with the backlog of Terminal Tours pilgrims. And still Michael just didn't want to go home. Even after Alice died, the house seemed to be ingesting him. With Ann gone so much, Sara had to call a truce with her father, but that didn't make the old Tudor any more livable. It was like one of those mausoleums Michael had taken Alice to. That was it, the tour of terminals had somehow made his home a place he had to leave. He remembered the Greeks who pronounced "live" and "leave" with the same long "e": "You cannot leeve in this country any longer. You must leeve."

But Michael sucked it up, tried to caulk the windows, bought a space heater for the den, limped along with the occasional surveillance client, and worked on *Passing On*. Three months after Alice's death, Ann came back from Graceland, one of the places Michael was most thankful he never had to visit again, and beat him to the spot, as his coaches used to say about gaining offensive position. Before she took off her coat, Ann told Michael she wanted him to move out. Michael felt he should put up some resistance, offer some defensive questions and comments.

"So this is what a few months with the dying does to you, is it?"

"I like them. They don't scare me like they did you. But I realized when I saw Elvis's grave there in Graceland that you're decomposing here."

"Actually composing."

"You know what I mean."

"You know what I'm going through right now."

"Going through? Wrong phrase, Michael. Ever since we met, you've been just passing through. No matter what I did or where we were, home was the place you got your uniform washed before the next road trip. You're like those polyester uniforms. Nothing adheres to you. Nothing sticks, and you don't stick around. But now that you don't go anywhere, home is like a cemetery. There's really no place you want to be, Michael, and I pity you. At least I won't have to do that anymore."

"You spend a year with the terminal, and you'll be pitying yourself."

"No, Michael. It's a business for me, not a search for something I lost along the way. Maybe if you have your own place and have to support yourself, you'll figure out what's been lost."

Michael wondered if he was being banished for his own good. For all of his differences with Ann, he knew she had always loved him. He also knew he was expected to put up more resistance, but he just didn't feel like it. No, no, no. Instead, he shifted to a question: "What about Sara?"

"You can see her as much as you want, but it seems to me there's really no person you want to be with now that your perpetual-motion companion is dead."

Michael didn't respond to the insult to Alice and didn't argue with Ann. How could he? Both Alice and Ann had used the same phrase, "passing through." What Ann said about him felt right when she said it, and seemed true the more Michael thought about it in the coming days as he moved his few belongings to the new apartment. He didn't know why it was true, but he'd have plenty of time to think about that.

On Michael's last day in the Tudor, his brother called from Vermont, where Patrick the policeman was still living in the Keever homestead, to remind him that divorce was a sin, that he should seek guidance from a priest, and that Patrick had warned Michael about the error of Terminal Tours.

"Patrick," Michael said, "we were never married in a church, remember? We've been living in sin all these years. I don't need a priest. Now I'll be pure as a monk."

"Didn't I tell you about trying to replace spiritual advisers?"

"You did, but let me remind you that the pilgrim who caused me all my present grief was a devout right-hander who deceived me so he could see Lourdes and die."

"You'll regret this move, Mikie."

"Maybe so, Pat, but just for another thirty or forty years."

After Patrick's call, Michael backfilled the manuscript of *Passing On* with a chapter about growing up on a potato farm, the deadly boring winters, his mother dead in a parked car with a hose in the window, his father drowned in an icy river, the fucking stones that came up through the ground every spring, the stone reality of life in Vermont: death. It was a place he left as soon as he could. He'd been passing through places and, according to Ann, lives ever since.

But if that were true, Michael wondered, why did he feel so happy about his new apartment? Why did he stay there and work every day to complete the manuscript he'd started before Alice came to him? Why did the memory of Alice stick with him, stick to him?

Perhaps, Michael thought, the life and death of Alice let him sit still, only his fingers moving on the keyboard, changing a dying friend into a permanent person in his manuscript. When he finished *Passing On*, he sent it, without the Paris and Athens stories, to Other Places Press, a print on demand outfit that got the book out immediately. It first got noticed in Greece, and then started getting reviewed in the United States. "Another staggering work of heartbreaking genius," one critic said.

Passing Through

A reviewer, who didn't know a passer from a shooter, referred to *Passing Off* and called its sequel "Keever Reducks," alluding to Michael's attempted evasions of the dying. Soon after a page-four review in *The New York Times Book Review*, Michael's phone started ringing.

***

"Are you satisfied now?" Ann asked.
"Has Rorque moved in?"
"I'm talking about your book."
"My book doesn't make your book disappear. Anyway, you should be the one satisfied. You're no longer a ghost."
"Now I'm a bitch."
"Isn't that the way you presented yourself in *Off*?"
"That was for the sake of domestic conflict."
"This is for the sake of international conflict."
"You know," Ann said, "I honestly never thought you could write a book, Michael. But you've done it, and that's a great ending at Alang. Great for business."
"Yeah, well I've been continuing Alice's story. I want to post the installments on the Terminal Tours site."
"Since it's my business now, I'd like to see them first."
Michael sent the Paris and Athens installments. For obvious reasons, Ann objected to the second. They compromised on posting the first, emailing the second to anyone who asked Michael for it.

***

"This the skinny-ass white boy use to play fo the Panatholes?"
"This the lawyer use to play a mean muthafuckah to scare the GRs?"
"Michael."

"James."

James Henderson, 6-9 center and power forward who hated the "Slow White League" of Greece, pretended to hate the "GRs," and at midseason abandoned them and Michael for a contract with the Milwaukee Bucks in the NBA. Michael watched him bounce around the box scores—Detroit, Orlando, Los Angeles (the Clippers)--and then saw an ESPN feature about post-hoop successes. James had gone to the University of Michigan Law School and was practicing outside of Detroit. On ESPN, James had not used what he called his steroid scowl or the "GR growl" that Michael immediately recognized on the telephone, but James still liked to shift back and forth from dialect to standard English.

"I read that Times review and figured there can't be another Michael Keever who would get into anything as shifty as this Terminal Tours."

"If I hadn't been shifty on the floor, James, you'd still be eating souvlaki and still be looking for a white girl that would let you squeeze her. And isn't a lawyer calling a helper shifty like the pot and kettle?"

"You too light to be in here ... and be no kettle," James said, hesitating to remind Michael of James's first words to him in Athens. During a scrimmage, Michael had gone into the paint looking for a rebound, James had flattened him, and then noted Michael was both too white and too thin—"too light"—to be in James's "kitchen," even if Michael was the only other American on the team.

"Have you been able to cheat any of those folks out of their inheritance?" James asked, for once setting Michael up—for a lawyer joke. But Michael gave him the facts.

"A dead lawyer and his lawyer son double-teamed me to take my inheritance. You can read about it in the book. Buy a copy. I need the money. While you're at it, buy *Passing Off.* You're in that one."

"You put me in a book?"

"You should read something more than your bank book."

"Never knew you could write, Michael. I never even saw you give an autograph. What you doing now?"

"Looking for work. Doing a few surveillance jobs using my old video camera."

"I might have some work for you."

"I can imagine, James. 'Boy, hand me that file in a good position so I can slam the muthafuckah. Boy, you keep passing to my white associates and I ain giving you no mo rebounds.'"

"I know people with clients all over. They might need some discreet tape from down in Ohio, you know what I'm saying? You used to do a lot of traveling, right? My office is in Dearborn, and I have quite a few Arab clients. If one of them wants to die closer to Mecca, you could hold his hand over the water."

"Thanks, James, but I'm out of the delivery business. Anything else, give me a call. And don't forget to buy those books. You were never as good in the League as you are in *Passing Off.*"

***

"This is a call from *Hell*. We want you working for us."

The editor, Dirk Ryan, enjoyed making cold calls—naturally, he called them "hot calls"—like this, and Michael was, as expected, momentarily taken aback. But the last year in Terminal Tours had him prepared: "I have been working for you. The ones with smiles on their faces are from me."

"Touché, Mr. Keever. We're an online magazine that sends correspondents to hot spots like Alang. We loved your description of the place, even if you did compare it to hell. We never use the word, except in our title. That's one of our rules."

Dirk Ryan made up rules for writers that he consistently broke. That was okay with Michael. He could do without hell. In fact, one advantage of losing almost all of his childhood Catholic faith during Alice's no-hope slide was being through with hell. He loved heat and the whirlpool but could let go of the inferno. Ryan asked if Michael had another worst place in mind. Yes, he thought, but Alice had died and someone else was in her hospital room, someone who might also be dying but Michael didn't have to know that. "No," he told Ryan. He asked if Michael might be interested in Mogadishu. "All depends on what you're paying," Michael said and wished he could consult Marv Drinkman, his former agent. But like just about everybody else Michael knew, Drink was dead. *Hell* was paying more than the pilgrims and was throwing in a million-dollar insurance policy if Michael didn't return from an assignment.

"What if I come back mangled or carrying some fatal parasite?" Michael asked.

"In that case, it's best to fax your copy, disappear, and make your wife a rich woman."

Now there, Michael thought, is the origin of the survival instinct.

"Are all your places obvious pits?"

"Most of them. That way we get not just the place, but the correspondent's danger."

"I do have an idea for a piece. The place is beautiful. But I know it's h-e-l-l," Michael said, spelling out the word, not wanting to break an editorial rule on first contact.

Passing Through

"An interesting angle. Where's the place?"

"I'll write a few paragraphs and you can tell me what you think."

Smell Cincinnati's Mill Creek on a summer day and you know why the Greeks invented a river ride to the underworld for their putrefying dead. The Creek runs by Procter and Gamble and the old pig-rending factories, and carries such a brew of effluents that part of the bed is now a cement-paved trough. On one side of the Creek is I-75 that bisects the city and puts its own toxins into the air from the traffic flow. On the other side of the Creek are railroad tracks and Spring Grove Avenue, four lanes of exhaust-spewing diesels heading toward the interstate from the industrial lowlands of the Queen City.

Between the car lots and equipment rental stores of Winton Place and the car lots and used-tire stores of Northside is Spring Grove Cemetery, the largest private cemetery in the country and one of the city's foremost tourist attractions. Approaching from the north on Winton Road, you can see above the high stonewalls old trees sucking the trucks' carbon dioxide out of the air. Behind those walls, you know, the tractor trailers' roar and the I-75 whine are dulled, perhaps unhearable because the cemetery occupies more than 700 acres of central city land.

From the gates on Spring Grove Avenue, Mill Creek is invisible and, depending on which way the wind is blowing, unsmellable. You pause before driving through the gates because you feel someone must be charging admission or, if not charging, checking to see if you are pure enough to enter these walls. Maybe you know that "paradise" means "walled space." On either side of the gates are imposing stone buildings, one a chapel with a bell tower and arched windows in the Romanesque style. The other building is almost as impressive, and looks as if it might have once been a clerical residence. The cross decorates both buildings. In the bell tower is a clock without hands.

Through the gates, you roll into an area some nineteenth-century landscape designer pictured as heaven: acres of suburban grass and occasional trees, a duck pond, and scattered every fifty or so yards obelisks or statues or little stone houses, some close to the road, some in the scenic distance. Spring Grove looks like a sculpture garden for athletes, people in shape to wander the distances between the gracefully spaced stone works. The little stone houses look more like really sturdy bungalows than tombs, getaway cottages for the affluent. If a person were blindfolded and driven here, nothing would immediately give away the fact that under the grass and trees and sculptures are dead people. Live people are riding their bikes, jogging, picnicking on the grass with their kids.

I've seen people dying by the scores in an Athens heat wave and watched people risking (and losing) their lives in an Indian ships' graveyard, but Spring Grove is worse. It is a permanent—founded in 1845--communication that we don't really die. We just pass from the suburbs of the city to the suburbs of paradise. This is why tourists come here and Cincinnatians bring their children here: for American "death," not the closely packed graves of European cemeteries but the rolling land and occasional marker signifying that in this place Christians are passing on to an even better place where the grass is ever green, the trees always leafed, the ducks forever paddling.

I have come here to visit the grave of a friend who I know to be dead, a person who died with no hope of passing on. The first few acres of the cemetery mock her courage, her final days and hours, her end. Today Spring Grove is the worst place on earth for me, and I believe my feeling is not just personal, not just transitory. The best place in Cincinnati for many natives, Spring Grove disseminates the illusion that in part accounts for the polluted water and poisoned air and grinding sounds just outside the wall. Spring Grove tells us, "Not in Arcadia. It's a happy ending. We're going on to some extraterrestrial Arcadia." At the same time, Spring Grove whispers, "Who gives a shit what shit we leave behind."

Not long after *Hell* published his whole piece on Spring Grove, Michael got the call from Richard at QCC. "We're always looking for new local talent. Will you come and talk to us?" Michael enjoyed being recruited. He hadn't been since he was a high school phenom. His agent had to sell Michael to the Greeks, and on the Terminal Tours web site Michael had to sell his services to the pilgrims—the easy passages, the assured pleasures, the fulfilling returns. But now, less than two months into his new position at QCC, he knew just why he'd been recruited—not to instruct but to play, not to teach but to coach. Long-time deceiver on—and sometimes off—the court, Michael had been deceived. About this, he was not happy. Old Mr. Rorque had an excuse for lying to Michael about his illness: Rorque was dying. Richard was dying to be a local talent, a hoopster, a hoop star. Michael was definitely not happy.

Part II

Chapter 5

"Coach on the floor," sportswriters used to call Michael and every other point guard. "Roach on the floor" was more exact. Hurry-scurry, change direction, say nothing, and keep those antennae alert. Even his coaches called him "coach on the floor," distorting the facts to express their nostalgia for a place they'd never be again. Coaches stand still in their tasseled loafers and move the X's and O's on a slate or magnetic board or sheet of paper. The O's don't slap coach X's wrist, grab his suit, or knock his ass back into his seat. Even "point guard" is a false term. The lead guard is really a rear guard, a behind-the-lines general rather than a point-walking grunt. But that doesn't mean the point won't get ambushed. In fact, he welcomes the double team, being knocked around and then breaking through into open space where he now has the advantage. Though often the smallest man on the court, the point guard has to be toughest if he wants to be the coach on the floor.

Michael was now a coach off the floor and had to think about terms again because the would-be players standing in front of him refused to move without deciding what they'd be called.

"The Communicators," Richard suggested.

"That privileges your department," said a man Michael had never seen. "What about those of us in English and Comparative Literature?"

"You're communicators too, aren't you, Sam?" Richard said.

The English professor laughed, as did about half the others gathered around Michael in the church gym that

Richard had rented for the evening, a gym that might have been built before the Protestants split from the Catholics.

"How retrograde, Richard," professor Sam said. "The referent died decades ago, and you techies haven't heard."

June—who was wearing an improbably pink sweat suit, a pink that no athlete had ever worn even as pajamas in a Vermont winter—suggested "Textists" because "we all study and produce texts, right?"

A woman standing next to Michael's student, Jason, started jumping up and down, pointing her hands at herself, and vigorously shaking her head. Michael wondered if QCC had a mime division. Jason said, "Zed is in web design. She objects to words. If you give her some time, she can come up with an icon for our tee shirts. You know, like the artist formerly known as Prince."

"Let's not split hairs," Richard said.

"Speaking of hares, how about Running Rabbits?" one of the English professor's followers said.

"Too literary," Richard said.

"Too sexist," June said.

"Too fast," Brenda Basso said, joining the group late, panting from the single flight of stairs. Brenda was a tech writer, one of five people who shared an office with Michael. She took up more space than the others because she weighed about 220 and had a voice to match her bulk.

"Cunning Linguists," one of the young strangers offered.

"Yes, that is good," Rakhshanda said. "We are all linguists, even non-native English speakers. This name privileges no cultural group."

Jason whispered in her ear, and Rakhshanda waved those hands in front of her face again.

From the rabbit-minded English grad student, "March Hares."

"The Unnamable," professor Sam offered. His forehead was gouged with deep lines, but, unlike most of the rest, his tee shirt was blank.

For Michael, this was like listening to the Greek and Italian and Spanish players babble in the huddle. He held up his hands in a "T."

"Are you calling a time out or a technical?" the formerly mute web designer asked.

"Let's work on some fundamentals," Michael said.

"I object," Sam said. "'Fundamentals' implies an original real, a first cause. With Derrida, I say there is only a precession of simulacra."

"Jesus, Sam," Brenda said to him, "kick the fucking ball if you doubt the real. Or let me have the fun of kicking you in the fundament."

The "team" broke down into arguing factions, not fact-oriented writing groups but schismatics, English versus Communications, young versus old, men versus women. Michael knew the coach was supposed to say something to quiet the players, start bringing them together. But what words could he use that they wouldn't quarrel with?

He blew his old referee's whistle and with his left hand pointed to the hoop furthest away.

"Run," he yelled. They ran to the baseline. With his right hand he pointed to the other hoop and shouted, "run." They ran to the other baseline. He pointed left and hollered, "run." He pointed right and screamed, "run." They were spread out all over the floor, some coming, some going, Brenda walking. Point and screech. Michael realized this was a new meaning for "point." He felt like a coach already. "Run." He didn't tell the name-crazed "athletes" they were learning to run "the suicides."

After they caught their breath, Michael asked them to jump and touch a wall behind one basket. White people all, even Jason. Watching them dribble and shoot in the lay-up line, he could see through their do-rags, headbands, hair, and skulls, could watch them thinking, using words. "Dribble" and "shoot" clogged their synapses like Alzheimer's plaque. Not even marathon sessions of videotape could cleanse their brains of language, the symbolic lies between perception and action. They ran the figure-eight passing drill. They were playing in the recent past or present, not the future, the next second where passers dwell. He gave them a rebounding drill to check their instincts for the ball. Only Brenda had instincts. And the bulk to shed others when she went for the ball. He made each one defend two others. Only a couple had eye-foot coordination. They played two-on-two rotation. The ball almost never went in the basket, except once in a while when Richard shot from beyond the three-point line, an obvious driveway set shot, or when someone was nice to Rakhshanda and let her push up a two-hander from her belly button. Why, Michael wondered, were these educated people stumbling around as if they were wearing Shaq's sneakers or clown shoes?

Brenda was still sitting on the floor after everyone else had gone to the showers.

"You okay, Professor Basso?" Michael asked.

"Do coaches usually use titles?"

"Just the guys who coached Dr. J. Usually players have nicknames, something short."

"Brenda's not that long."

"No, but it's also not a nickname."

"You're absolutely right about that, Coach. I was called 'Brainda' in high school, 'Bassoon' in college, and I don't know what here. You got something better?"

"BB"

"I like it, small, hard, fast."

"I was thinking basket ball."

"I like that better, Coach."

BB struggled up off the floor.

"Listen, BB, I can tell you used to play, and I like your heart, but I know CNF, not CPR."

"Are you suggesting you're going to cut me from this team of geeks?"

Michael knew better than tell Brenda Basso that he was trying to save her life.

"I'm afraid so."

"That's a piss-ass thing to do after one practice. Did Richard tell you to cut me?"

"He's just the chair. I'm the coach."

"For now."

"Brenda, why would you risk your life to play ball?" Michael asked as they walked, slowly, toward the locker rooms.

"We're about the same age," she said, "so you must remember high school. Well, I grew up in that part of Iowa that still played six girls on a team, three on offense, three on defense. I thought the rules were stupid. I could outrun my brother and most girls my age, and I wanted to run the floor. The coach stuck me on the defensive end."

"So that's where you learned to rebound."

"Rebound and not cross the line. When I got to Iowa State, I didn't have the shooting and passing skills to play. So I went to the library. And didn't come out except to eat and sleep."

"Then you know all about 'the suicides.' I can't let you do it. You'll be wheezing and gagging and dying on the floor before you can ever get in shape. Besides, this team won't last three more practices."

"You better make it happen. That little dick Richard really wants this, Coach."

"I can imagine why. But what about the rest? They have no visible talent."

"Do you really want to know why?"

"Yeah, I've never been around people like this."

"They're bodiless. They want to inhabit themselves. Or they're lonely. They're seeking better grades. They want to lose weight. You'll have to ask them."

Michael knew all the players would have their paragraph-length reasons. Just as a coach was supposed to have extensive verbal analysis of every moment on the court. That was another reason why Michael hated coaching. Speaking to students about writing seemed appropriate, but talking to athletes about playing always seemed to Michael like a fiction, a stick figure simplification of the court's complexity. On his videotape and in his head, Michael had precise moving images of hundreds of opponents and teammates. These images he remembered long after he forgot the players' names and all the other information that came in words no matter what the language. But now he was a coach and had to speak.

Richard was waiting in the locker room: "What do you think, Coach K?"

"Early to say," Michael told him, evading the General Manager like an experienced coach would. "We need to find some talent. Can our mailman, Bobby Jelkes, play for us?"

"Not unless we have him teach the Obsolescent Systems course."

"We need more women. If another team puts five women on the floor, we'll be screwed."

"What about the women we have?"

"I just cut Brenda."

"Good, she's trouble."

"I'm going to cut Rakhshanda"

"Why? She's the only woman who can put the ball in the hole."

"I'm afraid someone will break her in half."

"What about June? Not much of a body, but she's pretty agile."

"Maybe she can learn," Michael said but knew she couldn't. She pranced and hopped, as if the floor was a step aerobic class. Possibly she needed the right music.

"Those people from English are all pretentious assholes."

"That you have just right, Richard."

"Call me Ric, would you Michael? I grew up idolizing Rick Mahorn."

"Mahorn? He was a black 6-10 no-talent banger."

"What can I say? I fell short and had to become a shooter."

"Okay, Ric, but you better become a recruiter."

"If I can find us some women, you should cut Sam. I wouldn't want to take a shower with him, if you know what I mean."

"Yeah, he looks like the kind of guy who might have a serious case of athlete's foot, even if he's not an athlete, even if he'd deny he has feet."

Richard sent an email to all faculty and graduate students, appealing for more volunteers. Michael again encouraged his class to come out for the team. They started giggling, and Jason asked Michael if he was trying to lure more students out of the closet. "Only women whose closet has size ten shoes," Michael said. He'd taken a secret look at Lauren's feet and figured she was big enough to play. After class, he told Rakhshanda that he was putting together a defensive squad of "big, bad motherfuckers" and was cutting her. He figured she would be offended by his language and be happy to leave. But her hands didn't rise to her face.

"You should not cut me," she said, "I came to the practice to help you out."

"Okay," Michael said, "but don't get anywhere near Professor Basso if she shows up."

At the next practice were, from English, Sam (with another blank tee shirt), the Rabbity grad student, and one Rennie Freed: 5-8, good calf definition, some weight in the hips for boxing out, muscles across her blades, visible cords in her wrists, not much hair to get in her eyes, no tattoo, and unattractive. Michael figured tattoos and attractive were trouble. From Communications were Richard, June, Jason, Zed the web designer, a new Chinese woman with volleyball kneepads, and Rakhshanda, who told Michael she had been lifting weights all week and now weighed 87 pounds. From the Keevers there was Sara, whom Michael had invited for the comedy. And from the press was a woman about five feet nine inches tall carrying a still camera and a video camera. Richard introduced her to Michael: "Kara Schmidt is a grad student in our photography and web design track. I thought she might get some photos and tape for the department web site."

"You look like a player to me, the tallest woman I can see," Michael said.

Kara pointed down to her half heels. "I'm not really this big, and the only sport I do is prone."

Michael looked at Richard.

"She probably says that to all the guys," Richard said. "She used to shoot rifles."

Michael hated to be out-witted, out-quicked.

"A shooter, huh? I'm a passer. Every shooter needs a passer."

Kara might have been rehearsing: "Not this one. I'm also a rebounder."

"Me too," Michael said and shook her hand. "I also used to do a lot of taping and need some help with my new web site. Maybe we could talk after practice."

"Sure, I'll try to get some shots of you with the whistle in your mouth."

"Not a coaching web site, a travel site."

"Then I should get some shots of you traveling."

Michael gave up with Kara and put his team through the suicides. Rennie could run. They did some skills drills. She could pass and shoot. But when the drills were through and the players were waiting for Michael's next directive, Rennie said, "The balls are too big."

Sam said, "Are you suggesting there is some absolute and ideal ball which these balls exceed?"

"I'm just saying women play with a smaller ball. These we've been shooting are men's balls."

"You're right," Michael said, "but I don't have any women's balls."

"That doesn't sound quite right, Coach," Zed said, proving that even a web designer secretly thinks about words.

Rennie walked over to her gym bag and brought out a woman's ball. Another argument ensued. Rennie, the only woman who was athletic enough to manage the larger ball, favored the smaller one. Rakhshanda, with the stick arms, argued for the larger. Richard, who probably thought his shooting range would reach four-point distance, went small. Jason, perhaps because he was gay, wanted the man's ball.

Passing Through

"Two balls," Sam said, "is the solution," and the players actually listened to his proposal. "Two balls will be in play at all times. Anyone can dribble, pass, or rebound either ball, but men shoot the larger ball, women shoot the smaller. With this we will simulate the free play of the signifier."

Several players pointed out that the league would never entertain such a proposal. Coach Keever saw its merits. Theoretically, it meant more passing, more shooting, more complexity, more everything at once. A nightmare to referee or coach but an extension of what basketball is, free-form and patterned, random and ruled. Practically, two-ball play would hasten the end of this ridiculous "team" and Keever's coaching career. He'd had too many losses as head of Terminal Tours. Then that final failure with Alice. No, no, no.

"Let's try two-ball," Michael tells the team. Jason points out they have only nine players, so Michael presses Sara into play. She has on deck shoes, but they're adequate for this group. Sara played soccer with boys in Europe. When she came back to the U.S., she gave up sport for the telephone but she could still run. The rabbit-man asks if they'll be going shirts and skins, and Zed tells him only if he meant to say shorts and skins. Michael makes up two teams, throws the balls out, and the players go up and down the floor. With all the turnovers and sudden shifts from offense to defense and back again, Michael has a new awareness of how basketball is all about quick changes—the ball exchanging hands, the players changing directions, the teams changing ends of the court. The players go around and around, women gravitating toward the small ball, men toward the large because they all want to be shooters. Few shots find their way through the hoop, but the players are laughing and scampering as if basketball is play, not a game.

Michael walks over to Kara and says, "Better get as much tape as you can. This could be an historical moment, the invention of a new sport. Biball. Or you might sell the footage to Funniest Human Videos."

"We need two cameras, one to follow each ball."

Michael turns on his internal video cam. This will never be a team. No skills, no will to win. They're having too much fun, just like his undergraduates. Too bad Brenda isn't in shape to teach some aggression. Even Sam is enjoying himself and his creation or decreation. Almost as skilled as Rennie, Richard is in his glory and Michael zooms in on him. Watching closely, Michael notices June is never far from Richard. They're on opposite teams, but Michael sees something in their body language. That something is fuzzy at first, but he senses more than shared administrative duties between them. They aren't just good friends who differ on literature. No, although Richard flaunts his wedding band and June implies she is gay, these two are having sex. Michael doesn't need to tape these bodies and study them later in slow motion, as he used to do to and for himself. He can see through them live, not their tee shirts and shorts, but the way they glance at each other, pass by each other, brush each other. He submits his athlete's intuition to suspicion. He's never watched women and men play together before. Maybe what he's seeing isn't there. He studies other women and men on the floor, how they are with each other, how Richard and June brush by them. Michael tells himself he is seeing what he wants to see, evidence that June is straight. But he knows his eyes don't lie. He wonders if they might both be gay, but senses heterosexual pheromones in their sweat. He can't smell or taste them, but Michael penetrates them with his zoom-lens eyes, his quick-decision quirk. Suddenly he understands how he can end the biball players' fun, prevent their future humiliation, and avoid another no-win job.

After practice, Michael asked Kara if she'd like to get a pizza with him and Sara. She tried to beg off because of her sweaty clothes, but when Kara agreed Michael told Sara he'd drive her to the dorm for a shower and change before meeting Kara at Papa Dino's. In the car, Sara asked why he was so insistent she come along.

"I don't want this to be a date," Michael said.

"I see, Dad. You're asking this almost beautiful woman with crossed eyes and great legs for pizza because you want to discuss web design. You realize, of course, except for those crossed eyes and the Mediterranean nose Kara looks like my mother."

"I hadn't noticed that."

"Maybe it's a good sign."

"What do you mean, that my eyesight is failing?"

"No, that you and Mom might get back together."

"I don't believe that's going to happen, Sara."

"That's what Mom says, too, but it would be nice."

Then Sara could go to another college next year, Michael thought.

"So, Dad, why do you want me along? To get used to having a stepmother?"

"I just don't want to go one-on-one with this woman."

"First Marcy, now you. I'm a college freshman. Why do I have to get involved with others' inadequacies?"

"Use your cell phone and give Bucky a call. You've never introduced him to me."

"'Bucky, how about a double date with my father and some woman that reminds him of my mother and himself?'"

"Myself?"

"The camera, all that videotape of yourself you used to watch."

"I'm the word man now."

"Then you ought to be able to talk to this Kara mia by yourself."

"Kara mia?"

"What a word man. You don't remember any Italian?"

"Ah, 'cara mia.' Nice, Sara. By the way, did you consider I might be interested in her because her name rhymes with yours?"

"You are sick, Dad. I'm bringing Marcy along."

Marcy would have been one too many female students at Papa Dino's. Though Kara was just about twice Sara's age, Kara encouraged the freshman to make fun of her teachers. Michael was briefly happy that he was also a coach, until he remembered how the team would turn out. Sara ridiculed some of the quirkiness she'd tolerated earlier in the semester. Her aged history professor whispered because that was the only way he could keep students listening to him. The Portuguese Spanish teacher spent at least half the class practicing her English, asking her students to correct her idioms. "Remove the lead." "You have a piece of the stone." Gary Gallagher, the noosed narcissist, would not allow his writing students to use "I" or "like" as in "I liked that movie." Kara then joined in, creating an alliance with Sara: Kara's photography instructor refused to look at photos taken after Atget. Her web design teacher was at the other extreme, allowing only streaming video with subtitles, as if the web was a place to make foreign movies. Kara told Sara she could use "I" if she took the Introduction to Journalism class Kara was teaching for her tuition remission. Michael wondered if Kara had gone out with a lot of divorced men with children. Maybe her rapport with Sara came from her professional training.

Kara had graduated from Indiana in journalism, worked on alternative papers in Bloomington and Madison, got a job covering local news for the *Post* in Cincinnati, and five years later decided she'd attended too many council meetings and listened too often to her own voice on the mini-recorder. She was using some savings to shift her life and join the century, even if her photos of the moment had to look like Atget's of Paris.

"Do you know his work?" she asked the Keevers, now both students.

"No," they said, and Kara described the doubled landscapes and enigmatic vanishing points.

"If you want enigma," Michael said, "you should look into the Greek key. It goes on and on forever."

"Da-a-ad," Sara said and explained to Kara that Michael had been called the Greek Key in Athens and that he was also plugging his book and web site with the reference to "on and on."

Maybe, Michael thought, bringing Sara along was not such a good idea after all. But Kara felt a daughter treating her father like just another eccentric professor was amusing. And Sara's reference to the web site conveniently moved the conversation away from making fun of present instructors. They all could laugh at the students and professors on the tape Kara had shot earlier in the evening. Michael asked Kara about her earlier career as a shooter, which led her to talk about growing up on the northern peninsula of Michigan where everyone had a rifle but only a few like Kara refused to shoot at animals. "With eyes like these," Kara said and made her pupils do a wacky dance, "it's best to use only one at a time to squint through a scope at a paper figure."

Passing Through

Michael told stories about deer hunting with his father who liked to give the deer a running chance: "He had an old thirty-thirty without a scope. He always shot behind the deer first, got the buck running, and then tried to hit him. He never got one."

"What about you, Dad?"

"He never tried to shoot at me."

For some reason, Kara found this father-daughter act hilarious.

"Well, what about you?" Kara insisted after laughing.

"I was a passer from the beginning. I never even tried to hit a deer. Maybe my father never tried. Sara's the only Keever who has bagged a buck."

"That's a joke, right?" Kara asked.

"He's talking about my boyfriend, Bucky."

Sara didn't say more about Bucky, and the waitress didn't come around to fill the silence with "More drinks?" Kara wasn't about to intrude on a possibly sensitive subject. Michael veered away from the personal with a question to Kara about web sites, which eventually took them to the dual entry (and dual residences) of Michael and Sara's mother. Sara became downcast until Kara exclaimed about Ann's courage in taking over Terminal Tours by herself. Then Sara inserted a secret, not something about Bucky as Michael had hoped, but about her mother: "She is so busy right now she's asked me if I'd like to take some local people on trips." Kara immediately said she thought that was nice, so Michael didn't blurt out "What the hell?" Sara went on to describe Terminal Tours under her mother's management, and Kara seemed engrossed.

She asked Michael, "Why did you want to get out of that business, anyway?"

"It's a long story," he said. Before Sara could accuse him of another indirect plug, Michael said, "I've written a book about it. I'll put a copy in your mailbox, if you'd like. Maybe you'll have some ideas about how to sell it through the web site."

"Fair enough," Kara said and grabbed the check, an attractive move to someone paid as little as Michael Keever.

Michael didn't want to spoil the evening by asking Sara about working for Ann, so now he had two subjects—Terminal Tours and Bucky—to quiz Sara about. Or maybe Mr. Keever would make it more than a quiz. He might examine her, particularly about this crazy idea of getting involved with the dying.

At the next basketball practice, Michael entertained no verbal or biball foolishness. After pushing the eight who showed up through the suicides, he told them it was time to get serious and split them up into two teams. Richard, Sam, Jason, and Rabbit-man as skins. June, Rennie, Rakhshanda, and Zed as shirts. He also assigned the individual defensive matchups: Richard on June, Sam on the much younger and more skillful Rennie, Jason on Rakhshanda, and Rabbit-man on Zed. They used Rennie's small ball. Michael put on his whistle and called fouls. A point guard, as well as a coach, is supposed to anticipate, see the future. Michael saw these women kicking these men's asses. As he assumed, Richard, though highly competitive, did not smother his lover. June used her bobbing and hopping style to get some offensive rebounds and stick-backs because Richard didn't block her out. Sam had no chance with the also highly competitive Rennie. Jason was too nice to block Rakhshanda's shots, and she was a sticky defender who wrapped her arms around Jason every time he touched the ball. Jason looked at Michael, who yelled "no blood, no foul." Rabbit-man and Zed were a wash, equally lacking in talent and desire. The scrimmage was ugly, full of turnovers and missed shots, but the women were the first to forty. The men had fifteen. While the players were getting a drink, Michael carefully watched Richard. He congratulated the women but walked with the stiff back of the clearly pissed.

"The women wanted this one more than the men," Michael told them all, quoting every coach since grade school. Then he started speaking like his C.B.A. coach, Murray Jacobs, who believed that only loathing and fear motivated players: "Now we'll find out who has the killer instinct you need to play this game. All against all, one person wins. Everyone else runs the suicides." Women were to play one-on-one at one basket, men at the other. Then the champs of these gender playoffs would go head-to-head. Michael knew how this would come out. Rennie easily beat the other women. Richard beat the other men. Rennie wouldn't let Richard get off his three-point shot, and he was too slow to keep her from taking the ball to the basket. The more he bodied her up, the easier she went around him. He wanted to kill her and end this humiliation, but couldn't stay close enough to do damage. Rennie was leading 15-3 when Michael stopped play and sent his players to the showers rather than the suicides.

"Bring him to you, fuck him up." That was Murray Jacobs' motto. While waiting for Richard to approach him, Michael wondered just how much the teachings of Coach Jacobs had affected his post-court life. Competition. It was there with Ann and Sara, with his students, now with Richard. But, Michael thought, Richard isn't going to realize it.

Richard waited for Michael to come out of the shower he didn't really need.

"That was pretty embarrassing up there, wasn't it?" Richard said.

"The women on the team are turning out to be decent," Michael said, avoiding Richard's one-on-one beating.

"But if the other schools put men on the floor...."

"You'll have to hit a lot of threes."

"If one of their men is as quick as that damned Rennie...."

"They will fuck us through the ass, as the Greeks used to put it."

"Sam probably wouldn't mind, but I wanted to show those other colleges we're not a bunch of soft-ass private-school sissies over here."

"If we play our missies, we might be okay."

"If they have one man to play Rennie, June and the other missies will also be fucked."

Michael had not anticipated Richard's concern for June.

"You really can't play, Michael?"

"If everybody agrees to walk, yes. But here's what I can do. Pull a Pat Riley."

"What do you mean?"

"Suddenly quit as the coach. Rakhshanda and Jason will probably go with me. Then you can disband the team." Then Michael added the clincher for Richard: "And nobody will get fucked through the ass."

"I hate to quit," Richard said.

"I realize that, but I don't mind. I'd just as soon avoid any more defeats."

"Let me think about it," Richard said, trying to save face. But Michael knew what the decision would be, so could say, "I'm really sorry about this, Ric."

The next day Michael had an email from Richard, not Ric. He was taking the out and announced in a departmental email Michael's "withdrawal from coaching to devote more time to his writing." The announcement was cordial, but whenever Richard and Michael crossed paths, Richard no longer talked about the NBA, and Michael's sensorium picked up resentment beneath administrative civility. Maybe, Michael thought, Richard missed those chances to rub bodies with June in public, play out their secret on the floor. Or maybe Richard realized that he'd been set up and maneuvered but didn't recognize Michael's altruistic motives.

Chapter 6

"That was a wonderful thing you did for Alice," Kara said immediately after she and Michael sat down with their coffees at Sitwells, a café near QCC.

"You're a quick reader," Michael said, shrugging off the compliment. And then felt he needed to explain: "She died."

"Yes."

"So you've looked at the web site, too?"

"Yes, but I didn't ask for the last installment. I guessed Alice was going to die. I just didn't want to see it. I wanted her in my mind's eye swimming on and on and on."

"Like one of Atget's infinite regresses?"

"So, Michael, we've both done our homework."

"Right, but now you know all about my former home life, and all I know about are the trees and columns of Paris."

"At least you've been there," Kara said, avoiding Michael's implicit question about her "rebound." "I'm almost as landlocked as Alice was. I've traveled north to south, Canada to Mexico, but I don't have a passport."

"Then you'll never have to go to the ship-breakers' yard in Alang."

"I'd go if I could take my camera. You had your video cam. Why didn't you shoot some tape?"

"I was sick to death of tape. I've watched too much tape—game tapes, iso tapes of myself, surveillance tapes, tour tapes. They seem to be the only things I remember."

"Funny you should say that. I'm the same way about most writing, my own included."

Michael laughed, and had to explain again his inappropriate response: "We've just met, and here we are speeding away from each other in different directions." He rapped the table. "This is the court, and we're playing biball, you shooting your photos, me firing up my words."

"Biball looked like fun," Kara said. "And besides, don't we intersect at the web site? You need my images, I need your words."

"I guess we won't be knocking against each other then. The perfect academic relationship," Michael said.

"You think academics are soft?"

"Sometimes, I guess. My students aren't very hard on themselves. I was a self-made athlete, modest body, basic natural talent that I worked hard at improving with the aid of tape and will. I don't want to sound like those embarrassing NBA players who now run up the court beating their chest and thumping their heart, but my students just don't seem to have the heart for self-punishment before self-aggrandizement."

"So I'll bet you believe I'm soft-hearted, don't you? Lacking a killer instinct, evading Alice's death?"

"If it's as cold in northern Michigan as it is in Vermont, I'm sure you're not soft. But maybe inconsistent. You don't want to read about Alice, but you wondered why I got out of Terminal Tours and you encouraged Sara to take people on trips."

"Of course, now I know why you gave up the company and why you'd be against Sara being overwhelmed as you were. But I still envy your ability to get as close as you did to the dying. I was fifteen when my mother wasted away like your agent. My brother was twelve and my sister was eighteen, and they went to visit her in the hospital, but I couldn't, I just couldn't. My legs felt like jelly, my stomach was pudding, my head was a soft-boiled egg. I was soft, too weak to see my mother. So we talked on the phone, and she told me how she was feeling, how she felt about leaving me, and I told her everything. But I couldn't go to see her in the hospital or at the funeral home."

Kara also wouldn't let Michael see her face as she finished this story of bodiless telephone talk. Michael reminded her of his body and her body by reaching across the table and touching her wrist. Then she looked up.

"A parent is different, Kara. I'm glad I don't have a clear image of my mother sitting in her car with the garden hose in the window or my father trapped in a pickup truck cab filled with icy water."

"And Alice?"

"I can stand the image of her in the hospital bed because she held hard and fast against any illusions all the way to the end."

"My mother was just as sure, though more relaxed, even calm, about the opposite belief—that we'd be meeting in the afterlife. I don't really believe that, but I see no reason to rule it out."

"As one of my clients pointed out, I do have reason. Since my mother committed suicide, the only unpardonable sin, we'd be meeting in hell."

"'Unpardonable?' Who judges that, dictates that? Those early Christians who needed to maintain and enlarge the flock. Who's to say what was in your mother's mind?"

Michael was silent, appreciating the amplitude of this woman, maybe hoping she was right.

"Whew," Kara said and pretended to mop her forehead, "that was some heavy-lifting homework. Let's go out and play before dinner."

"It's about twenty degrees out there."

"We're hardened Northerners. You can tell me stories about Miami and Las Vegas and Egypt, and we'll pretend we're there."

"And pretend that we're warm and that we'll never die."

"Fucking right, Keever," Kara said, surprising Michael by throwing the voice of Coach Jacobs in *Passing On*. They walked and talked and walked some more, talking about their small-town high school teachers and their big-city college students, Kara's month in Mexico City, Michael's year in Athens. When they were close to Papa Dino's, Michael suggested pizza for dinner. Kara said she knew from Sara that he cooked, so instead they went to a grocery for his fast spaghetti ingredients.

"I thought you were Irish, and we'd have potatoes and potatoes," Kara said.

"Me, I'm Greek. Wait till you see the salad. I brush my teeth with feta cheese. I rub garlic under my arms for deodorant."

"Don't start with the lying, Michael. Remember, I read your book."

"Ah," Michael said, "Now there you have my soft spot."

***

For the travel writers' last assignment, Michael decided to dictate the place, somewhere none of them had been. He hoped to get more vivid writing that way.

"What subway?" they asked when Michael told them he'd arranged a tour. Not even the Cincinnati students knew that tunnels for a subway had been dug between 1920 and 1925. They were never finished, and no tracks were laid, but the existing tunnels were maintained and Michael knew someone, an engineer with the city of Cincinnati, who could get him and his class into the primary tunnel, which began downtown and ended near QCC.

"Are there Indian graves down there?" asked Jody the amusement park goer.

"The Indians are all out in the serpent mounds," Michael the burial expert told her.

"Then it sounds like fun," she said.

"If we all go to the same place, you know," asked an angelic-looking blond girl named Eden, "where will the creativity be?"

"When you chose your locales, no one went to an original or unusual place. Now you have the chance."

"But my writing will be just like everybody else's," Eden said.

"Not if you really put yourself and some work into the essay."

Michael didn't say so, but work was the reason he wanted them all to write about the same place. Like the grads and faculty playing biball, the undergrads had been having too much fun. The tunnels should stretch and push them, test them and their powers of perception. Teacher-coach Keever then turned up the pressure: "Think of this assignment as a writing contest. You'll submit your essays with code names, so there'll be blind judging. I'll send the best entry to *Cincinnati Magazine*. You might get published; you might make some money."

A boy taller than Michael, a gangly kid named Chad, said, "I don't mind going where everybody else is going, but why should we be competing? If my writing is good, it's good."

Passing Through

"It may be good, Chad, but it may not be the best. Travel writers are competing for space every day. Welcome to the world of professional writing. You all should wear warm clothes and rubber boots. Everyone bring a powerful flashlight and extra batteries. Also, a camera with a flash if you have one."

Chad raised his hand again: "Two questions: will I need to worry about bumping my head and should we bring breadcrumbs?"

Chad's height was wasted on him. Shorter students seemed excited about the underground adventure. Class attendance had been spotty, but the next week everyone showed up at the tunnel entrance at Central Parkway and Hopple Street. Michael introduced them to Joe Baumann, their guide, and told the students to make sure Joe, who was volunteering his time for art, was presented as a heroic figure in their narratives. Like two kindergarten teachers on a field trip, Joe took the point and Michael brought up the rear so as not to lose anyone. Twenty feet into the tunnel, Chad, who was the last student to enter, turned back to Michael and said, "I can't do this. I have claustrophobia or fear of the dark or something."

"Better to realize this now than later, when we'd have to push you up through one of the air vents. Go ahead back."

"What about the essay?"

"See if you can find some photos on the Internet."

Michael caught up with the rest of the students. All their flashlights were doing a good job of illuminating the fifteen-foot wide and thirteen-foot high tunnel. Another parallel tunnel, Joe said, was right next door. Like the walls and ceiling, the concrete floor was smooth, and the curves were mild. For hundreds of yards, the tunnel was just "a hole in the ground," as Michael heard a couple of the students say. At the first station, though, Michael felt the sense of abandonment he'd experienced in Egyptian grave shafts. Platforms had been built for passengers who never waited and trains that never came. Stairways led up from the platforms to cement-block walls. On the platform columns was graffiti by, presumably, people who had somehow snuck into the tunnel. Even the graffiti looked old, not as ancient as Egyptian hieroglyphics, but big clunky black letters rather than contemporary colored swirls.

"The original travel writing," Michael told the students. "Kilroy was here."

"More like killjoy," Jody said while clapping her mittened hands together. Jody's skin and bones made her more of a summer travel writer. Or maybe, like Chad, she was afraid and didn't want to admit it.

"Watch your step," Joe told his charges as he climbed down from the platform to the tunnel. "There's no third rail, but we don't want to drag someone with a broken leg all the way back to the entrance."

Between stations, the group had to squeeze alongside a water main that was put in the ready-made hole in the ground. There was no way to avoid six inches of standing water in some spots, so those who didn't heed Michael's warning to wear rubber boots got their feet wet and, Jody quickly pointed out, cold. The next station was similar in layout to the first. The students were getting bored and chilled. They complained that the empty rooms off the platform had no toilet fixtures, that they couldn't buy coffee, that the walk back would be just the same. What a bunch of sissies, Michael thought.

Joe was good humored about the complaints, maybe because he had a surprise in store. He led them through a narrow passage and took them back in the parallel, outgoing tunnel, part of which had been transformed into a fallout shelter in the 1950s. The metal cots were still demonstrating that rust never sleeps, not even on beds. Most of the students were unimpressed, but Eden said, "Way cool." She lay down on one of the cots and didn't want to leave, perhaps because she had worn rubber boots and a ski parka. She was poking around the cabinets that had once held food when Michael said they had to catch up with the group.

"Go ahead," Eden said, "I'd like to stay here for a while. I can find my way out."

"I can't let you do that, Eden."

Eden turned off her flashlight and said, "You could save me from the dark."

Michael pointed his flashlight at Eden and decided not to play along with whatever fantasy she was enacting: "I want to save myself," he said, "from the lawyers who'd pick my bones clean if anything happened to you down here."

Eden turned her flashlight back on. "Okay," she said, "maybe I can get someone else to bring me down here."

"After you turn in your essay," Michael said.

When Eden and Michael emerged from the tunnel, Joe said, "We're missing one."

Michael knew who was missing, but waited to see how the students responded. They quickly identified Chad, but no one volunteered to go back to look for him. "He probably found a shorter way out."

"Downtown, where he could buy some dope."

"Let's wait for him in the cars."

"Just leave the gate unlocked, and he can come out when he wants." Eden said, "He's probably taking a nap on one of those cots."

"If he is," Jody replied, "they can take his frozen body directly to Spring Grove."

Michael finally told the students that Chad had not been feeling well and had not done the tour.

"That's our Chad," was the general sentiment.

"Hanging Chad," one student said. Chad may not have wanted to compete, but the other students didn't mind competing with him, mocking him, cutting him. Next year, Michael thought, the subway tour would be in the second week. He was learning more about his students from three hours underground than from eight weeks in the classroom.

Although the essays were, contest-style, anonymous, Michael easily identified Eden's. She ignored everything but the fallout shelter. It, she described only minimally. The rest of her eight pages imagined what life would be like after nuclear holocaust. Too few facts, too much creativity. If Eden had been a ballplayer, she'd have been cut, but Michael gave the essay a D. Three essays treated the tunnels as just a hole in the ground that the writers had quickly passed through, and these essays came in a thousand or more words short of the assignment. Jody passed in a two-page paper because she'd caught cold and couldn't write more. These four essays teacher-coach Michael gave an F.

Other essays were better than most of the writing that Michael had been receiving. A couple were excellent. Michael picked the best and asked the winner to identify his or her coded name in the last class meeting: "Who is 'Hole Surfer'?" No one raised a hand. "Don't be modest," Michael said, "someone had to win, and this is a fine essay." Still, no hand. Michael counted heads to make sure no one was absent. "If the winner won't confess, I won't be handing back essays to the losers." The students booed and hissed.

Finally, Chad raised his hand and said, "I'm 'Hole Surfer.'"

"Butthole surfer," a voice said, "you didn't even go in."

"Great faction," another student said.

"A unique perspective," Jody said, "the non-participant, unreliable narrator."

The comments and laughter were directed at Chad but were flying past him and hitting Michael, who said that Chad must have done extensive Internet research, maybe spending more time surfing than others spent in the tunnel.

"And didn't get his feet wet, either," someone said.

"Okay," Michael said, "I'm a bit embarrassed by the result here, but Chad is an excellent writer. Not only does he observe the details others have, he imagines himself into tunnels we didn't visit and into tunnels that might have been drilled, connecting U.S. cities beneath the ground."

Fun-loving Jody was incensed, even before she got her failing paper back: "This just isn't fair, Mr. Keever. If Chad gets an A without going to the subway, that's fine. But all of us who did brave the elements should also receive A's."

Students, including Chad, cheered Jody's proposal, but Michael assumed they weren't serious. When he handed Eden her D, he realized that the person who spent the longest time in the tunnel and was most enthusiastic about it received one of the lowest grades. He assumed Eden wouldn't be sharing that fact with the others.

The autobiographers' last installments, except for one, predictably followed their beginnings. The lives described were changing, but not the writers' perspectives or the water-slide narratives, so Michael felt his coaching had little influence. Gary was tonguing his third lover, whose actual name he'd changed, he dutifully reported in a footnote, to the symbolic "Trish." Rakhshanda got her parents born: Roshanara and Sikander. Jason was now old enough to know he was a gay black boy in an affluent suburb of Cleveland, where his physician parents lived. Michael didn't share Jason's belief that living in the inner city would have been easier. Michael had heard about grade inflation, so he gave these three and five other students B's for the course. There were no A's and one C, which went to Lauren. This grade Michael considered a gift for effort. Lauren's initial first-person installment about her early years on an Arkansas farm was slightly unusual because Lauren hated all the animals, as well as her parents and brother. Her last installment jumped ahead to her freshman year at an unnamed state university and was in the third-person:

"It costs more for the Goatess to buy two pairs of shoes, boots, and sneakers, but walking on all fours during freshman orientation shows her glorious hairy ass to all. When men come on to her, she butts them, not with her ass but with her horns. 'You horny ewe, you,' they cry. 'I am no silly sheep,' she bleats, 'I am the goatess.' She twitches her silken ears in girls' crotches. They rub against her horns before dropping onto hands and knees to make the beast with eight legs in the quadrangle grass. 'Oh nanny, nanny oh,' they whisper, but she corrects them: 'No substitute for your mother, I'm the goatess, the goddess before goatmen and goatboys invented Cancer.'"

The installment goes on from the early days of sexual liberation to describe the difficulties of being a "goatess": taking class notes with hooves, eating while standing in the cafeteria, finding a roommate who will tolerate the goatess' smell, being hazed by sorority girls, finally confining herself to a pen. Michael congratulated Lauren on a "nice try" but said her installment deviated too far from CNF. He also mentioned that he'd never seen a redheaded goat.

Although Michael was disappointed in some of his students' final work, looking at a month's Christmas vacation he was happy with the academic life—the two-day work week, the eight-month work year, the time he'd had in his well-heated home to do his own travel writing and to continue his autobiography. None of his students had died or disappeared. They were, though, disappointed and displeased. That's why Michael was sitting in a meeting with June and Richard on December 8 rather than flying to some destination that was hellish but also close to sparkling beaches.

June and Richard seemed somewhat uncomfortable with the occasion because they fumbled around with who would go first. Finally, June said, "We wanted to speak with you about your grading policies." She hurried on to say, "We often have this kind of chat with first-time instructors, particularly if they haven't been in a graduate program. It's unfortunate, we know, but graduate students now expect an A unless they've been grossly negligent. But you didn't give a single A."

"I read the faculty manual. It said A was excellent, B was good, C was average."

"Yes, that's true in theory, but in practice nearly everyone gets an A. Otherwise, our students won't be able to compete when they apply to Ph.D. programs at other schools or enter the job market. In fact, to counter grade inflation elsewhere we're considering adding the A-plus to our manual."

"Or the double A," Richard put in.

The triple-A would give them roadside assistance, Michael thought but didn't say. "I had no idea," Michael did say. "I'll keep that in mind next semester."

"There's also the matter of Lauren Jones's C," June said, and picked up a sheaf of pages from her lap. "For a grad student, a C is equivalent to failure. Lauren showed me her last installment and your comments. Because she was trying to follow your instructions, and because she showed an unusual degree of literariness, even the kind that marks your *Passing Off*, I couldn't help but wonder if she may have been penalized for her sexual orientation."

"A scapegoat," Richard added.

"I appreciated Lauren's effort," Michael said, "but since I've never seen her walk on four legs these pages are fiction. Too creative and bookish for CNF," Michael said, appealing to Richard.

"But," June said, "she's appropriating and transforming her metaphor from Land's popular memoir, *The Goat*, and she's playing with references to Miller's *Tropic of Cancer* and Barth's *Giles Goat-Boy*."

"In that case," Michael said, brightly he thought, "her pages are derivative, not creative enough. But Lauren has been great in class, so I'll read the pages again and reconsider."

June seemed satisfied. It was Richard's turn to be the coach Michael had quit being.

"The travel writers sent a couple of representatives in to complain about grades, but I'm more concerned about legal liability. The college works hard to attract students. We can't lose any in a hole in the ground. Why didn't you ask for advice before you took the group into a life-threatening situation?"

"Those kids are fictionalizing. Some got their feet wet, but no one was in danger. We had a guide from the city. We all got out alive."

"The parents of QCC students don't pay what they pay to have their kids walking around sewers and get D's and F's for their trouble. I'm sure the president is going to hear about this. One student says she may not be able to return to school next semester."

"That student needs to eat more. The subway is not a sewer. I wanted the kids to have an unusual travel experience, something that would challenge their prose, a test. Some responded, the sissies didn't."

"A local hell?" June asked, sympathetically it seemed to Michael.

"Maybe purgatory. Something to pass through and write about."

"Too creative," Richard said, using Michael's phrase against him, "too risky. And obviously not productive of the grades students expected in a free-elective writing course. If we're going to be competitive with Sam's traditional creative writing teachers, we must make sure students receive appropriate grades. We need to keep up and try to improve our enrollments because, as you may not know, full-time faculty raises are tied to enrollment figures."

He gave Michael a chance to respond, but, double-teamed, he couldn't think of anything more to say.

"In any event," Richard continued, "preliminary enrollment figures for next semester's class are way down. I may have to cancel the section. I'm afraid that would leave you with only the Autobiography class."

In all his years as a basketball player, Michael had never been cut. He had tried out for NBA teams that he didn't make, but he'd never been cut from a team he played for. He couldn't afford to lose half his salary now, even if he had engineered the failure of Ric's team. Trust the body, he must have thought to himself if he thought, trust the quirk of his zoom-lens eyes, the athlete's intuition, the key to every deceptive feint or power move.

"Man," he said, looking down at his feet and shaking his head like a recruit for Richard's benefit, "that would be real bad for me. I've been doing a little surveillance work for an old friend who does divorce cases, but I sure do hate to sit in that van even when it turns up some unexpected tape."

Keep it dumb, he thought, and it doesn't have to be subtle. Talk the athlete's talk. "You can't believe how boring it is waiting to tape some dude zipping up his fly while walking out of his squeeze's crib, you know what I'm saying?"

Richard nodded. Michael wanted to steal a look at June, but kept his gaze on the married man.

"Even with that new tech that lets me listen to all those goatish sounds up inside those bedrooms, I'd rather be teaching, you know what I mean?"

Richard nodded again, and said, "We'll keep our eye on those enrollments. Maybe we can get away with a class under the minimum."

"I'd appreciate it. Like I wrote in *Passing On*, I do hate that van."

That, Michael thought, will teach them to not read an applicant's work. Then he turned to June and said, "You know Jason, the guy who came out for the team?"

"Sure. He's one of our most promising writers."

"Jason said you can't believe everything Lauren says and writes. He says she's only pretending to be gay."

June was not the experienced administrator Richard was. When Michael turned up the heat on her, she blushed or flushed, as if the room had suddenly become an outer precinct of hell.

So, Michael thought while walking back to his apartment, Ann had been right: the Q was passing through its students. But not just passing. The graduates were given A's to impress future employers and other schools like QCC. The undergraduates' parents were paying for A's and B's, not changes—slow or quick—in their kids' experiences or minds. Now all students are like student-athletes, aggressively recruited in high school, entertained and coddled in college, and passed along. But the non-athletes never have to compete, really compete. No matter how many special high-carb meals you ate or how many tutorials you had in the athletes' dorm, you eventually had to perform on the floor or field. High-powered athletic programs cheated in their recruiting to lure impact players. A place like QCC was cheating all its students after they arrived, deceiving them about themselves, their abilities and achievements.

Michael then realized he too had been guilty of coddling students—and faculty—by disbanding the nameless team before they could be humiliated. But that, he told himself, was extracurricular, like the relationship between June and Richard, and was for the non-players' own good. He also thought that Richard might have initiated the team to spend more time with June. Maybe he hoped there would be overnight trips, and not to Centerville either. Michael chuckled at Richard, the would-be baller. Richard wanted to be a legend, not a chair. But Michael amused himself only briefly because if he ever had to go one-on-one against Richard, Michael didn't have tape, not yet anyway. On the positive side, Michael thought, Eden had not accused him of assaulting her on the cot. Maybe he should reconsider her grade as a reward. At the very least, he could email her and encourage her to sign up for next semester's course. Three months of teaching, he thought, and I'm back to recruiting the bones.

Michael called the only colleague he could trust, Brenda.

"You have a problem, but I told you not to cut me," she said. "I could have kept the team going. Richard had his heart set on leading that bunch in scoring. I wouldn't be surprised if he was gay."

"I have reason to believe he's straight. What about this straight-A business June was telling me about?"

"It's true. That's why they won't let me teach graduate courses."

"Is there any way I can recruit students for Travel Writing?"

"Sure. Get some grade change slips from the departmental secretary and change all their grades. Attach a note to the registrar saying that you made a global computational error. They'll believe it, since you're in humanities. Presto, you'll have your students back."

Quick changes, Michael thought.

"Have you done anything like that?"

"Not me, but you might. After all, you cut me to please Richard. I was trying to help his team out, but the two of you didn't believe I'd lose the weight. You guys fucked up. Now you should stock up on noodles, Michael."

Michael was going to explain, but Brenda hung up. So now Michael had no colleagues he could trust. He tried students. Sara wasn't answering, Kara was. He told her about his conversation with the administrators and asked if she had run into problems with her journalism students or with her professors.

"Grades aren't so important to us icon people. We have our samples, our portfolios to show. What possible employer would read your graduate students' autobiographies? But people who need web sites will click around our samples, even if they don't read the texts."

"More and more, I think I'm in the wrong business. I should have become a video consultant for some NBA team."

"Then you'd be back on the road for nine months a year."

"You're right. What about your students?"

"Your problem, Michael, is that you're in the soft-science side of writing. I'm in the hard science: who, what, when, where. It's easier for me to make expectations clear, easier for students to meet them. Plus, as you know, I'm basically easy."

"If you were easy, you'd have stayed and done the dishes the other night instead of leaving me alone to clean up."

"I told you. I had someone waiting for me. He's very demanding. He wants me with him every night by eleven."

"Even the dogs at QCC dictate to the instructors."

"Unless you want to clean up poop in your own house."

Michael thought this was a synecdoche for the grades. Or was it metonymy?

"I'm not changing those shitty grades," he said. "I might consider it with the graduate students, but those fucking travel writers who didn't even go through the motions of satisfying the assignment can suck my dick, excuse the jock language."

"You might find one or two to do that, but isn't it the reverse that you need to propose to them? Just make sure you don't invite them for spaghetti. If one of them can describe the inside of your apartment, his or her 'said' is going to outweigh your 'said.'"

"I assume you know that I'm blushing. Soon I'll start stammering."

"I think it's kind of charming. I could tell from your book you're a closet Catholic. A former Lutheran can deal with that."

Passing Through

"Okay, if sex isn't the answer here, please tell your students about Keever's adventure-travel course."

"Can't do that, Michael. They'll be leaving my next semester's Court Reporting in droves for a field trip to Daytona Beach."

Queen City Court, Michael thought when he got off the phone. The college was like the gym at his final practice, all against all, professors, instructors, and grad assistants all competing for students. Or Quasi College, half-hearted, half-assed. But no matter how disgusted he felt, he remembered that his was a half-time job. No, less than that. Quarter College, and that was too little despite all the time Michael had to write and watch the NBA.

Recalling later his conversation with Kara, Michael realized that she was the one who had invited herself to dinner, and that he had missed the chance to make a joke about court reporting. He also could have told Kara, if she'd been an athlete, that fellatio didn't do much for him. He liked one-on-one, face-to-face, belly-up, toe-to-toe, responding to the other's moves, dictating the other's moves, back and forth, heat and sweat, full-body rebounding, timing that shot, the homunculus Michael Keever passing through the dark and narrow tunnel in search of a soft landing and home.

Chapter 7

During the first week of Christmas vacation, Kara and Michael spent a lot of time together without the distractions of class preparations and students. She invited him to her one-bedroom apartment to meet Frisky and to eat dinner. They ate in Kentucky restaurants where Kara could have an after-dinner cigarette. She got around to telling him about the *Enquirer* investigative reporter she lived with for two years, a man who turned out to be probing the nooks and crannies of other women's bodies when he was on "assignment." "On assignation," Kara said. The reporter still called her at all hours of the day and night.

About this phone stalker, Michael asked every hoopster's first question: "How big a guy is this?"

"Erect or flaccid?" Kara answered. She enjoyed seeing a forty-year-old man blush.

"That was an unpardonable low blow," Michael said, and Kara reminded him that nothing was unpardonable, perhaps the reason why she had caller ID and an answering machine rather than an unlisted number or a restraining order. Michael had Kara and Sara over for an Irish meal of roast beef and potatoes. Again he was surprised at how well the two women got along, particularly when they could make fun of Michael and his apartment, the bench-like sofa, the huge TV, the indoor-outdoor carpeting, the showerhead that could knock over an adolescent.

After Sara left, Kara asked why Michael kept the apartment so warm.

"Reminds me of the locker room and doesn't remind me of the house I used to live in."

Kara got up from the sofa and walked the few steps to the doorway of the bedroom, looking around as if she were thinking about renting the place. "And why do you have a single bed?" she asked from the doorway.

"If the apartment is warm enough, you don't need a double," Michael answered from the sofa.

"You can do better than that, Michael."

"I guess I wasn't thinking when I moved in and bought that one. It's narrow but extra long and firm."

"A priest's bed."

"No, maybe just a pessimist's."

Kara came back to the sofa and sat down.

"Which one are you waiting to pardon you, Michael? Your wife or your daughter?"

Michael was suddenly back in Richard's office with him and June.

"Did you learn this kind of questioning in journalism school?" he asked.

"I learned this in junior high when a boy I wanted to kiss needed permission from his mother."

"Do you mean...? I mean ...."

"Don't press that bumbling charm too far, Keever."

Again, the coach's voice.

Run, Michael thought, run. Not run away but the order Coach Keever screamed at his players doing the suicides. Move, react, shift those legs, move those arms, breathe free, pass through that invisible fence of fear and guilt, the locker's enervating heat.

He moved. It was not easy, after so many years with Ann, and Kara was not easy, for her body had its requirements shaped, no doubt, by the man who called at all hours. But the phone did not ring in Michael's bedroom, where Kara opened a window for the air of Michigan and Vermont to modulate the heat of two persons who had been sleeping alone for months. Like players running the suicides, they moved toward mindlessness, wordlessness, imagelessness in the dark.

When words returned, Michael's first were, "I'm buying a double bed tomorrow."

"Not so fast," Kara said. "You know where I have to be in...." Kara looked at the clock. "Forty minutes."

"You stay here, and I'll walk Frisky. When I get back, you can have the bed and I'll sleep on the sofa."

"You sleep in your bed, Michael. There's no telling what you may have done to your muscles and joints with this prone sport."

After Kara left, Michael wondered if she needed to be home to listen to those calls on her answering machine, maybe her way of pardoning herself for leaving the journalist. Michael thought about taking calls for Terminal Tours and then remembered the "Teleton" offices he saw in Greece, little first-floor lighted rooms where an undertaker's representative sat through the night waiting for his phone to ring, waiting to offer his services to the bereaved and the desperate. Michael also thought that Kara might just prefer her own large bed. Or the brand of cereal she ate for breakfast. Or sleeping with a dog. Or any of a hundred reasons why she wouldn't want to sleep in a locker. Maybe she didn't like the sound of the word, its suggestion of being in prison. Sex must be pulling down the barriers between his synapses. "Lock-her." No, Kara was not a person to be constrained. He hoped she wasn't just passing through, a holiday fling, a flying fuck instead of a vacation flight.

Before Michael could buy that double bed for himself for Christmas, Sara called and asked to come over, "by myself" she pointedly said.

"When are you going to bring Bucky? Your mother knows what he looks like. I want to be able to identify him and give him a good grade if he takes Travel Writing."

"Bucky has gone home to Washington."

"Okay, you're not coming to tell me you flunked something, are you?"

"You must be kidding, Dad. I'd have a 4.0 if your student hadn't given me a B."

"He got one, too. What do you want to eat?"

"Whatever. I'm staying at Mom's place this vacation and doing a lot of cooking for myself."

Waiting for Sara to show up, Michael wondered if she'd just been polite to Kara and now wanted to tell Michael that she disapproved. Michael rehearsed his apologies, his explanations, his version of his marriage, all the while telling himself not to praise Kara or note the differences between her and Ann.

When Sara arrived, Michael asked if he should pull the shades and turn up the TV to cover their voices. "You sounded pretty secretive on the phone," he explained.

"Just the opposite, but I did want to talk to you alone."

"Okay, shoot."

"You'll want to shoot me when you hear this."

"You're expecting triplets."

"Damn it, Dad, be serious."

"Sorry."

"Bucky and I want to get married when he comes back in January. We want to move out of the dorm, get our own apartment."

Wordless a few nights before, Michael was now speechless. This was not one of his undergrads suggesting a goofy travel destination. This was his eighteen-year-old daughter changing her name and address and life, maybe her whole life. If Ann had been in the room, Michael could have blustered, but he'd been a single father long enough and a teacher just long enough to swallow his initial reaction. Or maybe, he thought later, he'd been with Kara just barely long enough not to judge and then regret.

He finally got out, "I beg your pardon."

"I said, Bucky and I want to get married and get our own place."

"If the food is that bad in the dorm, the two of you could eat here every night."

Sara grinned. Instead of being upset now with her jokester father, she seemed relieved that he was willing to play along, at least initially: "But this apartment has only one bedroom, and the sofa doesn't fold out."

"Jesus, Sara, you're only eighteen. You've been in college for a semester. I've never met this kid. You're not even wearing his class ring around your neck."

"High school kids did that in Vermont when you were a boy, Dad."

Michael regretted what occurred to him next—that if Sara married, she would lose her tuition remission. Jesus, Mary, and Joseph, as his father used to say when exclaiming "Jesus" was not enough. Michael was quick enough to say nothing because, he quickly realized, he wanted to treat Sara's desire without economic considerations, if that was possible given the facts, real undeniable facts, that he had lost everything in the suit, had probably lost a course for next quarter, and wanted to buy a double bed.

"I'm sure," he did manage to say, "that even your quirky mathematical mind has thought a lot about this, so please give me your reasons. They don't have to be in writing."

Sara grinned again and said, "Thanks, Dad. First, we love each other." She waited, perhaps assuming that Michael would contest that teenage notion. But he was a youngish father and could remember being eighteen. "Second," Sara went on, "we want to be adults. The dorm is like a stupid summer camp. Both our roommates are crazy."

The word "dorm" gave Michael a powerful urge to call Ann and get her in on this conversation, on the speakerphone if necessary. But he resisted and kept it light: "Have you considered talking Marcy and Bucky's roommate into sharing a room so that you and Bucky could have the other room?"

Sara shook her head, didn't glance up through her eyebrows to reply. So Michael said, "Sorry, Sara. What's number three?"

"Three is a response to your changing rooms suggestion. Bucky and I could just move out and not get married. Some students we know are planning to do that. But the only commitment there is to a lease. Bucky and I want to make this a stronger commitment. Marriage makes the decision harder, more serious. We have been thinking, and we will be thinking, but right now this is what we want to do."

"I respect that, Sara, but it still seems a radical move at eighteen, one with lots of legal consequences you may not be foreseeing."

Confident that he'd have Ann's agreement with this position, Michael asked, "What does your mother say about this?"

"She supports it."

Jesus, Mary, Joseph, and the three fucking wise men. How could this be? The answer was quick and simple: because she doesn't know Sara will lose tuition remission worth 10K a semester. Then another answer, not so simple: because she does know it.

"Your mother supports this?"

"Call her up and ask her when she gets home from Johannesburg."

"Who in hell would want to go to Johannesburg?"

"A dying person, I guess. Mom says it's summer there."

"Crossing the equator may have affected your mother's cognitive processes. Why does she support this?"

"We discussed marriage before she left. She said, 'You choose, Sara. However it turns out, you will have chosen.'"

"Do you know the history behind this?"

"I think so."

"Just so you're sure. When your mother got pregnant, I chose. I chose you, Sara, and your mother. You and Bucky don't ever need to be in the same situation. Your options for safe and sure sex are many and just about foolproof."

"We know that. This isn't about sex. It's about choosing, entering a contract."

Where, Michael wondered, was Sara getting this language? Commitment, contract.

"Are you afraid that you and Bucky won't last if you don't do this?"

This question Sara had not been ready for. Her brain whirred for a couple of seconds.

"Why do you ask that?"

"Some married people choose to have children because they fear splitting up if they don't. I wondered if your wanting to get married was similar."

"I hate to say this, Dad, but I hadn't considered that."

Sara's brain whirred some more.

"I need to think about this and talk to Bucky about it."

Michael silently congratulated himself. Fear of losing. It was not a profound insight, and you didn't have to do Terminal Tours to have it. Any serious athlete knew this fear: of being cut, of being beaten, of being the single damned reason your team was beaten and their season ended before collecting the big bonus. Michael also wondered if Sara's desire to get Bucky under contract had anything to do with her father's absences, the perpetual passing through Ann had identified.

The discussion went on back and forth, but when Sara left, Michael was able to congratulate himself again: he had not mentioned the money. He wouldn't tell Ann either, because then it would filter back to Sara.

But where, he thought in his single bed, was he going to get the money if he lost his course and Sara's tuition remission? Even the income from *Hell* was uncertain. His last column had been about the catacombs of Paris, where thousands of skeletons had been stacked like cordwood. Michael had been there several years before and didn't need to be reminded of the horror when he and Alice were in Paris, so he wrote the essay from memory.

"A good piece," Dirk Ryan had said, "but we'd like you to get out of the boneyards. We want to see live people suffering above ground. Something off the tourist track. You know, a slice of danger. We'd still love a piece on Somalia."

"I did some research. Christmas is not a good time for a white Christian to show up in Somalia. Not even in a red suit."

"Okay, maybe next time. In any event, remember suffering, the human strain."

Michael was planning to make a quick trip to Greece after Christmas, visiting the town of Lavrion down the coast from Athens. Ann and he had read about the town years ago: because the land had been thoroughly polluted and largely depopulated by the lead mines there, refugees from Third World countries were warehoused in Lavrion. Michael thought it was perfect: a hell embedded in the paradise of Greece, a hell partly produced by ancient Greece and partly by the contemporary hells that surrounding countries with human rights violations were becoming. Michael was sure he'd see suffering.

When Michael mentioned Greece to Kara, she immediately asked if she could go along.

"You don't have a passport," Michael reminded her, trying to de-recruit.

"I can get my application expedited. It costs more but is quick."

Michael remembered his quick exit from Athens with Alice.

"I'd love to have you come with me," Michael said, "but Greece in the winter can be pretty damned unpleasant. Bad heating, smoke-filled rooms."

"I'm from Michigan and smoke, remember?"

"Right. But this would be a lightning trip. We should go in the summer when it will be a lot more fun and we can stay longer."

"You'll need photos for your piece. I'll pay my way to have some photo credits in my portfolio."

"Lavrion is a pit, Kara. A literal pit. Lead piled around the harbor, nothing dramatic to photograph."

"Just say so if you don't want me along, Michael."

"I do, but it's an expensive trip, and I'd hate for you to be disappointed your first time in Greece. What if I promise to take you on a tour next summer, the whole holiday hog, black sand beaches on Santorini, flaming sunsets across azure waters, sleeping in caves hollowed out of the cliffs?"

Kara pushed air through her lips, as Michael had seen French waitresses and waiters do when they were irritated.

"Think of this as a Catholic lesson in delayed gratification," he said.

"I'm not good at that," she said.

Anxious to talk Kara out of her irritation, Michael hit upon guilt: "Think of Frisky spending Christmas in a cage. Or your old boyfriend with no one to call during the holidays."

Kara pushed more air through her lips. Guilt didn't work worth a damn with her.

"I'm going to get my passport in case you change your mind," she said.

Since that conversation, Michael had been reconsidering—preparing to offer the Lavrion trip to Kara despite its drawbacks—until Sara sprung her surprise on him. After a couple of days trying to perform magic tricks with figures, including the fare to Greece, Michael decided to follow Chad's example and do the Lavrion piece without going there. He knew the surrounding area. He'd do some library research, grab photos off the Internet, and during his "Greek" time drive to Vermont to talk with Patrick about getting some money out of the property that they had inherited years ago, the land surrounding the house where Patrick was still living.

But Michael was in a professional bind: he couldn't very well tell an instructor of Journalism that he wasn't going to Lavrion. Well, he could tell her and, knowing Kara, she might well pardon such a breach of journalistic ethics, but it was very early in their relationship to confirm any suspicion she might have picked up from *Passing On* that he was a liar. Well, yes he would actually be lying about going to Lavrion, but that was not like telling her he was going to Vermont and then sneaking off to some vacation spot. His intentions were to go to Greece and to take her along. But recent circumstances made that impossible and the deception just about necessary. Unless, of course, another deception was possible. Let Sara and Bucky get married but conceal that fact from QCC, not as easy, given its size, as concealing a trip to Vermont. And if Richard discovered that contract violation, not even tape of Richard shagging Lauren from behind would save Michael's job, which he wanted to keep despite his rookie fuck-ups. He considered telling everybody the truth—Sara that she would lose her tuition, Kara that he couldn't afford to go to Lavrion, Ann that he might not be able to afford the dorm payment next semester, Richard that he didn't have tape but really needed a second course. No, four truths were too many. Those damned Rorques, the dead father and the court-sucking son. Now he had to talk to Ann, get at a truth if not tell one. He thought about inviting her to experience the heat of his apartment but decided against that. He called and set up a meeting at a neutral site, the food court in a mall near her apartment. This would be the first time they'd be face-to-face since he moved out.

"Nice tan," he told her at Skyline Chili.

"I think the client wanted to be darker before she entered eternity."

"How's business?"

"It's back to booming. It must be that well-known syndrome, the dying holding on through the holidays. As for the living…" she hesitated and asked, "How are you doing with Christmas coming up?"

"I may have to take a trip for the magazine I write for."

"You have it made now, get paid to travel but don't have to drag someone down the jet way. Why don't you take Sara with you for Christmas? I may have to be away. A woman will pay double to be in Bethlehem on the 25th."

"This is a solo trip. But I wanted to talk to you about Sara. She tells me that you've offered her some tours. Why would you do that?"

"Why not? She'd be good with the little old ladies who want to be driven somewhere. She could contribute to her dorm expenses."

Michael didn't know if Ann was sticking him or being helpful.

"Sara can play Santa's helper at the mall if she wants to make some money," he said.

"Your parents were both dead before she knew them. My parents will live to get their money's worth from Social Security. We never had a cat or a dog to teach her about death. It would be healthy for her to know someone on the brink."

"She can live without death, at least until she gets married."

Even as he said that, Michael thought: if Sara did a few tours, she might understand why he quit.

"Thanks for that association between death and marriage, Michael."

"I didn't mean that, but marriage is what I really wanted to talk with you about. Why are you encouraging a college freshman to marry?"

"Michael, what's the matter? Can't bear the idea of your little Sally Pally having sex?"

"I told her I'd buy her a decade's worth of birth control pills. Having a sex partner or changing a sex partner is not the issue. I think you're using your support to somehow take revenge on me—for being your sex partner eighteen years ago, for not being your sex partner now."

"Not at all. Sara is living her life, not traveling around or writing her life like your students. She wants to be serious and honest with herself."

"*Gelao*," Michael said, the Greek word that Ann found the most interesting because it meant both "to laugh" and "to deceive." Sara was the opposite—serious and honest—but Michael didn't think Ann was, not completely.

"Sara's getting married is not about you, Michael."

"No, but your support may be. I think she's doing this because she's afraid her relationship with Bucky won't last. I believe you may be encouraging her because our marriage didn't last and you're trying to prove you're not afraid of my opinion."

"Michael, you spend too much time by yourself or with teenagers. You need someone to talk through ideas like this. I'm afraid you're the one who is afraid. Afraid of the dead, afraid of the dying, afraid of your dying. So everyone else seems afraid of everything else to you. Maybe you should get yourself a therapist."

"I had a therapist. She died."

"Or," Ann continued, as if Michael hadn't mentioned Alice, "do some of these holiday tours for me. I have an AIDS patient who wants to revisit the gay scene in Amsterdam. If you did some of these tours, I might reconsider my support of Sara's marriage."

"How about this, Ann? You tell Sara you'll disown her if she gets married, she tells me, and then I tell you I'll do some tours for you."

"*Gelao*," Ann said to this and laughed. "I wouldn't trust you to come back to the Tours without a signed contract."

That word "contract" again. Michael wondered if the lost lawsuit had made Ann and Sara legalistic. Coaches and general managers were the ones obsessed with contracts.

"I stuck around," he said, "until we could sign the marriage contract eighteen years ago."

"But you've been unstuck much of the time since. So tell me, what have you learned being away full-time?"

"That, away from the dying, life is worth living. That I wasn't wrong about choosing to teach once you chose to throw me out."

Ann nodded, as if she were a coach checking a player's progress after graduation, but didn't comment.

"Sara's a smart girl," she said, "and can make her own choice. I know you care about her, but you don't have to be a parent *in loco parentis*."

Michael wasn't exactly sure what Ann meant, but the tone seemed a bit conciliatory. He took the occasion to wish her a happy holiday with the pilgrims who were refusing to pass away. Then he got out of the food court and mall with its healthy Americans spending money Michael didn't have.

Back in his apartment, Michael immediately called James Henderson in Dearborn and, surprisingly, got right through.

"Merry Christmas, James. You sure you're doing okay? I didn't get 'He's in a meeting' or 'He's packing his briefcase with drug dealers' hundred dollar bills.'"

"Gloria said it sounded like a white man to her, so I figured I'd better pick up. Whatup?"

"Just calling to check in, see if you might have any work for me during my break."

Michael then told James an abbreviated version of his course reduction story, including his short coaching career.

"You should have signed a long-term coaching contract. I wish I could throw you some work, Michael, but people tend to sleep in their own beds this time of year. I guess they want to make sure Santy knows where to find them. If I had any surveillance to do, it would be up here."

"I'd drive the van up and buy a good sleeping bag."

"That tough, huh?"

"Very tight, James."

"I really don't have anything right now, but I might have something big in a couple of months. You still white with them Huckleberry Finn freckles?"

"White as the sole of your foot. But those freckles only came out in the Greek sun."

"This might mean a trip to the sun."

"I don't do terminal, James. Didn't you read the book?"

"I did, I did. You haven't ever been to Israel have you?"

"Just to Miami Beach. Why?"

"This might be a case where a Holy Land stamp on your passport wouldn't do, you know what I mean? The details are just coming through in bits and pieces, but I can hear the rustle of auto money behind the white shoe firm that contacted me. A trip could be required."

"This doesn't have anything to do with one-way, no-landing flights does it, James?"

"Nah, nah, Key, nothing like that. Keep checking with me. No telling when the money might come out of hiding for this job. But right now I gotta have my shoes shined by my associate, Ms. Fredonia Whelps, from Yale Law."

Passing Through

It was the "Key" that worried Michael. Henderson addressed him that way only when he was trying to be nice, which was not Henderson's natural style. Or maybe it was just the season or sympathy, and Michael shouldn't sense that he was being recruited—not for a free college ride but for something like a Marine hitch.

Chapter 8

Sixteen hours in the van and an under-heated motel room in Buffalo gave Michael lots of time to think. Ahead to Vermont, back to where he was supposed to be and to Kara. Using her critique of the "unpardonable," he tried to pardon himself for misleading her. And he thought about his mother, whom Patrick had never pardoned. Her suicide seemed to settle Patrick in his faith: damnation was the right punishment for abandoning the three Keever males. Rather than believe that, Michael had sacrificed his faith in, though not desire for, some afterlife. His terminal clients' desperate beliefs hadn't touched him as Kara's story of her dying mother did, perhaps because she didn't try to move, to outrun death. Kara lacked her mother's faith, but staring at all those hours of Interstate going on and on made Michael wonder if the matter was closed. Were we just passing through, as Alice insisted? Disappearing like the ships at Alang? He remembered how animated his mother used to become on the family's annual winter vacations in Florida—and how depressed she would get on the drive back to the potato farm. If the Keever family hadn't been tourists, if they'd relocated somewhere closer to his mother's Virginia home, maybe she and Michael's faith would still be alive, tottering and feeble and cataracted but still breathing.

Of course, if the Keevers had sold off their land thirty years ago, Michael wouldn't be making this drive to see if Patrick could loan him some money against a future sale. Since their father's death when Michael was in college, Patrick had been living in the farmhouse, keeping it up, paying the property taxes, and Michael thought that a fair trade. Nobody was farming the acres, not even growing hay on them. Michael hadn't been back home since his father's funeral, but he figured some trees, as well as brush, now made the meadows more attractive to out-of-staters for their ski chalets.

Given Patrick's persistent concern for the state of Michael's soul, he felt his brother would welcome his return. Michael did not mention to Patrick why he was coming to Vermont, yet Patrick tried to discourage the visit.

"I'd like to see you, but we're real busy this time of year with all the drunk skiers," Patrick said.

"The van doesn't have flashing lights. I've always wanted to ride around in a real police car," Michael said.

"I couldn't let you do that."

"Put me in back, behind the steel mesh. Just like you made me ride in the back of your pickup when you had a girl up front."

"You'd be unhappy up here. It's not the same. I'm afraid I've kind of let the house go."

"I'll do dishes, run the vacuum, and collect your butts while you're getting your quota of speeders."

"Maybe I could get a couple of days off, and we could meet in Boston, see a Celtics game or something."

"You just said the holiday was your busiest season."

"Don't come up here, Mikie. It will just bring back all those bad memories. You've got a new life now. Stay away."

"Maybe I want to talk with you about some religious issues."

"I know that's not true. I'm telling you, don't come up here right now."

Patrick spoke with the voice of certainty, as he always did. But Michael didn't really need an invitation to his own former home. He still knew where the house was, and the inherited land was the only asset he had, so he made the drive and thought about Patrick's resistance, as well as his mother and Kara. She wasn't going to Greece, but at least she didn't have to endure the drive and a resentful host. Although Patrick said Vermont was not the same, Ludlow looked pretty much as it had, maybe more boutiques in the old woolen mill on Main Street, more bistros where hardware and clothing and furniture stores used to be before tourism ruled. The road to the farm was exactly the same, a gravel bobsled run between high banks of snow.

Before the house came into view, Michael knew why Patrick had been adamant. Where their father grew potatoes, vacation A-frames had sprouted up. Six that Michael could see from the road. Patrick had been selling off lots. His brother—Father Patrick, the sanctimonious policeman—had somehow forged Michael's name and transferred titles. And the money? Where did the money go? Patrick never took a vacation, as far as Michael knew. The house had indeed been let go. Originally white, it was gray like most Vermont barns. There was no collection of exotic cars in the tractor shed; in fact, the tractor shed had fallen down and not been removed. Michael found the lockout key where his father had always hidden it. Inside the house there were neither expensive paintings nor a harem of expensive whores, just the same old ratty furniture, water-stained wallpaper, and an odor that suggested Patrick might be storing twenty years of ashtrays in the cellar. In the dining room, Patrick did have a flat screen computer on the round oak table. Maybe he was selling Michael's birthright over the Internet.

Michael picked up the phone, called the police station, and asked for Patrick. "He's on patrol." Could you tell him one of his neighbors believes his house is being broken into? "I'll get him on the radio. He should be there in ten or fifteen minutes."

Michael turned up the thermostat from its fifty-five degrees, turned on all the lights upstairs and down, then went out and waited in the van so that Patrick wouldn't bust in with gun drawn. Twenty minutes later Patrick's cruiser came up the road with its lights off. Michael turned his parking lights on and stepped out of the van. Patrick then put his headlights on. He got out of the cruiser and walked toward Michael, standing in the headlight beams.

"So you're the robber my neighbor reported," Patrick said from six feet away. With the headlights in Michael's eyes, he couldn't see Patrick's face.

"No, Patrick. You're the robber nobody reported. It wasn't too dark for me to see the little village you've founded here."

Patrick came no closer. Michael made no move toward him.

"I told you not to come," the policeman's voice from the lights.

"Did you think I'd just forget all about the beautiful vacationland of Vermont, the property we used to own?"

"Come in the house," Patrick said and stepped out of the headlights. "I've kept records of the sales. I'm going to pay you back."

Michael didn't move. "But how am I going to pay you back, Patrick, for trying to fuck your only brother? Your only sibling. Shit, your only living relative, not counting some raggedy-ass McKeevers probably begging over on the old sod."

Patrick went back to the cruiser and turned off the lights. Then he walked past Michael to the house. Michael felt like getting into the van and driving back to Cincinnati, but the cruiser was blocking the driveway. He waited for a few minutes, trying to calm himself. At least he knew the lots were salable. But remembering the condition of the house, Michael realized he wouldn't see any money from Patrick, not anytime soon.

Where had the money gone? That question and the cruiser took Michael back into the house.

Patrick was in the kitchen, making coffee, smoking a Camel. He still had his coat on, and he looked ridiculous to Michael. Those spindly legs in tight state-trooper boots, the doughnut-police belly, the thick coat further bloating him, the fur hat with flaps, more a hybrid European soldier than a local Vermont policeman. But Patrick couldn't have eaten all the money, not with his taste for canned beef stew and cheap IGA ice cream.

Michael didn't want coffee, didn't want Patrick to take off his coat and hat. Michael just wanted to know about the money.

"Where'd the cash go, Pat?"

Patrick pointed to the computer in the dining room.

"I know Vermont acreage is worth more than that, even if it is a flat screen."

"Gambling, Michael. Internet gambling. First it was an Indian casino over in New Hampshire. Then a bookie in Boston. I still owe him money. I thought you were him, breaking into the house. He's been threatening me. But I've had a couple of good nights on the Internet. I'm hoping to pay him back."

"You're going to pay him and me with your Internet winnings?"

"Start paying him, I hope."

"'Hope'? You're talking to me about hope? If you weren't wearing that gun, I'd kick your miserable ass. I was hoping you could help me out of a temporary squeeze. But hope is shit. My last client told me that. I should have listened to her. Faith, hope, and charity. I suppose you still have the faith."

Patrick was silent but looked smug to Michael.

"Well, Patrick, after a year with the dying I can tell you your faith is just hope, and they're both shit."

Patrick said nothing.

"All those years you were offering me advice on salvation," Michael said, "you were offering lots for sale. How could you do that?"

"I'm sorry, Mikie. I have records. We can sell off the rest, including the house. You'll get your share."

"Not in time. You know as well as I do—no, better than I do—that the flatlanders buy in the summer, when they can see what's underneath the snow and ice."

No reply, and this further pissed off Michael: "I know it's Christmas and all, but what's the county attorney going to say if I ask him to start examining those titles?"

"Your half is still intact. I can prove it to you with my records. But if you talk to the attorney, I'll be finished."

He patted the small pistol on his hip and said, "This and the cruiser are the only things keeping the bookie away."

Michael stared at his fat, sad, begging brother.

"Do you want some coffee?" Patrick asked.

"I'm going to have enough trouble sleeping tonight."

"Look, Mikie, I want to talk with you about all this, but I have to get back on patrol right now. I'll be back at midnight. There's nothing much here to eat. But you can drive into town, and I'll see you later."

"I don't think so."

Patrick was silent. He wasn't trying very hard to persuade Michael to stay. That made him even angrier. He needed and wanted the money Patrick owed him.

Michael said, "You got insurance on the house?"

"The bookie already asked me that. No fire insurance."

"Of course," Michael said. "Who needs insurance when you have your faith and hope?"

Patrick shrugged, finished his coffee, and walked out to his cruiser. After he drove away, Michael walked around the house again, taking a last look, turning off the lights. Then he unplugged Patrick's computer and carried it out to the van. Michael considered this robbery an act of holiday charity. By preventing any further losses, he might even be saving Patrick's life. Michael drove back down the dirt road to Ludlow and then twenty-five miles to Rutland, out of Patrick's jurisdiction. No rooms in any of the motels there. Of course not, this was high season in the high mountains. To find a room, Michael had to drive an hour to the Lake George area, which didn't have skiing. From there, it was just fourteen more hours to Cincinnati.

Michael was too angry to think back to Patrick, how he got started with the gambling, why he got hooked. Wasn't it enough of a thrill to turn on the siren and chase after speeders? Michael wasn't afraid Sara would kneecap him, but he was still desperate. He might be able to pawn Patrick's computer and pay for about two and half hours of her tuition. He might ask *Hell* if they'd like an account of his return "home." He felt like calling Patrick and telling him to get ten grand from a loan shark friend of the Boston bookie. Among these improbabilities, there was one certain thing, which came to Michael on the New York State Thruway outside Syracuse. Passing through

Buffalo, Erie, Cleveland, and Columbus didn't change his mind. We're all just passing through. Alice was right. Pascal's wager was shit. Michael had seen enough of gambling. Patrick was a loser. He'd be surprised when those Camels—or his bookie—finished him. Death was going to be the end for Patrick, as it was for everybody. No second chance, no double or nothing, no long odds long shot, no miraculous change of luck, no last-second rescue like one finds in books and movies. Those rescues were not even hopes. They were wishes, fabricated fantasies of salvation. Patrick would disappear like the ships at Alang, like Alice. Like Michael, eventually. All the more reason to hold onto his new job and life. Michael wished he could take more consolation from his Interstate recognition. It was not a conclusion he could—or would, even if he could—share with Kara. Michael had not visited the cemetery in Ludlow, but he knew where his mother was. He assumed Kara was waiting for him to return from Greece, but her mother wasn't waiting for her. Hard, maybe unfair, but true. Fact of life, fact of death. And to think that he had lied to Kara to make this trip, his first tour since Alice's. When he returned—early—to Cincinnati, he'd have to hide in his own apartment and invent his trip to Lavrion for *Hell*. But no matter how much empty, mind-opening Interstate he drove, Michael could not imagine a way to pay Sara's tuition.

Halftime

Michael parked his van behind his apartment building in case Kara drove by. He took his laptop into the bedroom for the same reason. In his email he found the usual million-dollar offers from Nigeria, an apologetic message from Richard saying that no students had ultimately enrolled in the now cancelled Travel Writing course, a note each day from Kara who was imagining what Michael was doing that day on his Greek trip, and an odd message from a Yahoo account named Sceptic: "If I was planning a tour, I'd check on who was taking me."

Michael forwarded this to Ann and ignored it. The same message came a day later while he was working on his Lavrion piece. Michael replied: "And you'd be right. I'm no longer associated with Terminal Tours, which is now run by Ann Logan. Check her web site for her bio."

A reply came immediately: "She doesn't mention the book she wrote in her bio. Do you think such a person can be trusted?"

This one Michael forwarded to Ann along with his reply: "A person often chooses to leave things unsaid. In the years I lived with Ms. Logan, I always trusted her and I can recommend what she's doing with Terminal Tours."

Again the reply came immediately: "Are you such a person?"

Michael cursed email. Snail mail would need to have a real return address, even if it were a post office box. A telephone voice could be identified. But even a homeless person can walk into a library and set up a free email account. Someone was playing with Michael, someone who'd read *Passing On* and its exposure of Ann as a ghostwriter. If Sceptic was one of his students, Michael felt the teacher who claimed "no game, no gain" should play along.

"Yes. I'm a changed man. In *Passing On* I confessed to all those old Greek deceptions, but now I'm going straight. I write the facts."

He thought "Sceptic's" response to "going straight" and "facts" might reveal the student who was behind the account. But the next email didn't pick up on those phrases.

Sceptic: "So it's an accident that the true happy ending of *Passing On* is just like the fake happy ending of *Passing Off*, implausible if not unbelievable?"

This question let out the undergrads, who would never read two books, no matter how disgruntled they were about their grades. The question could be from someone like Gary, that defender of factual fidelity. It could be from June, possibly more positive than negative. How could Michael ignore a reader of the two books about him? He just hoped they'd been purchased, not checked out of a library for free.

"Alice's remission was implausible, though not unbelievable, to her, to me, to her oncologist. But such changes do happen, and they give us hope."

Before Michael signed out of his email, a reply came in.

Sceptic: "If it's false hope, if Alice was not in remission, why end the book with her recovering her health?"

Sceptic was a real Keever fan, reader of both books and the web site, and must have requested the Alice installment. But Michael didn't have a record of the people to whom he'd emailed Alice's death. And it didn't matter because this could be a new email account. The message could be from Richard, that net-head; maybe he finally got around to *Passing On* and was using it to further humble the no-coach K. The message could be from anybody. Michael re-examined the messages for any trace of dialect, African American or Pakistani. He wondered if Lauren was trying to get his goat.

Keever: "The book ends, but the story keeps going. Everything was eventually revealed about Alice. Following your logic, I'd have to wait until I was dead to write part of my life because only death ends a story."

Sceptic: "Everything was revealed after the book sold whatever copies it did. But no one at Christ Hospital remembers an Alice in the physical therapy department."

This was a shift in Sceptic—from reading books to using the telephone—but easy enough for Michael to parry.

Keever: "Like many Creative Non-Fiction writers, I have changed some names to protect privacy."

The reply was almost as fast as Instant Messenger.

Sceptic: "No one in the therapy department recognizes the picture of Alice on the web site either."

Who the hell was taking the trouble to print a photo off the web site, drive to Christ Hospital, think of some story to tell the therapists there, and show them the photo? Only Ann, that Michael could think of, might be angry enough to do that. But with what purpose? Deflate a book she hadn't written? That seemed unlikely. Brenda was pissed at him, but had no motive to investigate him. Perhaps Richard or June or the two of them were compiling a file to combat the tape Michael implied he had.

Keever: "Alice didn't want her picture used on the web site, so I've used a photo of a friend."

When Michael got no response to his photo reply, he thought the most recent messages might be a bluff he could ignore. Still, he checked his email every couple of hours. Two days later Sceptic was back:

"Lebanon is a small town. I asked around about the tragic early death of a young woman. It was easy to find and talk with 'Alice's' father. He didn't know about your book. When I described it, he said that 'Alice' sounded like his headstrong Clarice. He appreciated all the attention you gave Clarice in the hospital. But, he also said, that Clarice's health never improved on her tour. In fact, he felt that the lengthy tour probably shortened her life."

Michael had written only one book, but he knew about Amazon reviews and book blogs and other places where Sceptic could easily disseminate this information from Lebanon. He'd been exposed once—as a fake Greek—and there seemed no end to the consequences of that fact-finding. Michael didn't want to be Rigoberta Menchu, the Guatemalan woman whose critical success turned into a failed hoax. Or that guy, James Frey, whose popular success turned into a humiliating embarrassment. "Exposure," Michael thought, people died of that in the long winters where he came from. He cursed the Internet, facts and rumors and lies passing through the fiber optics and air at the speed of light.

Keever: "She was getting better until we went to Paris. I can't prove it, but she was. She wouldn't wait. She tried to rush back to normal life with the swimming. What do you want?"

The reply took a day to come in, as if Michael had surprised Sceptic with his direct question. Sceptic's reply was evasive and enigmatic, as if Sceptic had been studying writing with the Delphic oracle: "If someone asks you for something, that someone might be the Sceptic."

Keever to Keever, Michael to himself: time to write the truth. I can't hide behind the third person anymore.

If you're a literary reader like June, you may have seen through my basketball metaphors and guessed that I was the "academic" constructing this "objective" autobiography, this anonymous exposé. Partly as an experiment like the exercise I tried to give my students since I've been writing these pages pretty much as the events happened. Partly as an attempt to satisfy Richard's CNF criteria—quick pace, economy, dialogue, ordinary language, nothing too literary. Facts without fat. Muscular—athletic—prose. Partly because I was sick of the students' "I's" and the "I" of *Passing On*, the former point guard's point of view, the "I" that finally admitted through the web site and earlier in these pages that I could not save Alice's life. And partly because I wanted a new life, a new Michael Keever, one that was solid and reliable, two substantial names, not the skinny "I." But from the day of my job interview, I was out of my league at QCC, recruited to play not to teach, and so I ran through all the old deceptions, lies, and pretenses. After Sceptic did his or her investigation, I felt I'd been outed like someone of the third sex and couldn't continue as a third person.

Sceptic never asked why I constructed the happy ending of *Passing On* and left out of that book the material about Alice I've included here. Maybe my motive was transparent. Alice had no hope and could die that way. I had no hope, couldn't accept it back then, and believed most people were more like me than Alice. So I tried to give them hope, a happy non-ending, the sense that Alice's story, like mine I suppose, went on and on and on. If readers really wanted the truth, they could ask to have it emailed to them. Few did, and yet I've included—imposed, maybe—the end of Alice here.

The truth is what I should have told my students. The most original travel writing would be the blog from some shithole, the posting interrupted in mid-sentence by an assassin's bullet. Or one of those messages in a bottle: "Ate crickets waiting for rescue that never came." Kilroy was here...and died. The autobiographers could aspire to dysfunctions so extreme that their life stories had to be finished by a friend or family member or physician. The great thing about games, I should have told my students, is that everyone always asked for the same thing but someone always lost. The perfect narrative was *The Perfect Storm*. Ocean 1, Humans 0. No return. That's the truth I understood on the way back from Vermont.

I can imagine "Sceptic's" response, your response: "Why should we believe you now?"

Why believe any autobiography or memoir not by a public person whose movements are charted and statements recorded? At least, I've admitted to lying. Most memoirists conceal that fact. Do you really think Frank McCourt could remember all those details in *Angela's Ashes*? Angela's Asses is more like it, all the readers who were taken in. Here, though, you're reading about events that happened just a few months ago, not forty or more years past. These events aren't like other confessions, no flaming addiction, no horrific victimization. No terrifying bad luck like Joan Didion's, who won a National Book Award because her only husband suddenly died when her only child was in intensive care. No, what you'll find in these pages are the attempts of an ordinary man to solve slightly extraordinary financial problems. No gain, no game. Without money, I'd be out of the academic game.

Yes, economics took me to a real hell far from QCC and put my life at risk, but you don't have to believe the personal "me" because much of my remaining narrative is in the public domain. For a time-line of events, you could check my real-time blog, accessible through www.terminaltours.com. If you have questions about facts, you can email me: keeverunlimited@gmail.com. If you, like "Sceptic," find the following account "implausible," you can email the public figures I've already identified and the people I will be identifying. If you, again like "Sceptic," find my ending "unbelievable," you can file a request for public information with the U.S. State Department and check out their travel advisories. The rest of this narrative is frequently about documents and can, therefore, be documented. With hard copies, too, not hundred-dollar-a-year phantom web sites. With published writings available in most libraries. *Passing Through* can also be documented with entry stamps and exit stamps in passports, the hardest copy to finesse or forge.

Here's another reason to trust this "I": after I got the last email from "Sceptic," I began doing my own investigation of everyone, looking for that someone Sceptic could be. Sceptic was clever, forcing me to consider any person who might want something from me. Sceptic could be Sara or Bucky, who were asking for my approval. Shit, Sceptic could be anyone: Henderson priming me to be recruited, Dirk Ryan forcing me to go to Mogadishu, Kara's former lover trying to chase me away, Alice's parents taking revenge, Patrick using some secret police network to get me off his back. Two people were beyond suspicion: Chad, who got the grade he wanted, and Alice, who was dead. Actually, Chad might be upset with my outing him as the absentee writer of the best subway essay. For this investigation, I didn't trust my basketball x-ray vision, not the live, one-time version. To have a record I could examine for clues, I began conducting exchanges with people by email as much as possible. I started secretly recording phone conversations. I put a hidden camera in my office for student conferences. When I couldn't record, I wrote down everything I could remember after speaking with someone. Maybe

Ann had been right about me—that I let everything but basketball pass through me. But no more. I became an obsessive autobiographer, keeping a daily journal, compiling data, scrutinizing others and myself, turning events into words, constructing possible narratives week by week. My quirk was now a self-consciousness that exceeded my graduate students', who could afford to take some liberties with facts as long as they didn't pretend to be a farm animal. This is what someone like June would call the irony of this book: the liar was forced to observe, remember, and stick to the truth…if he was going to prevent another truth from being exposed. No autobiographer functioned under the pressure that I did. Was Angela looking over Frank's shoulder?

When I filled the academic opening at QCC, I thought I was through with passing through. I wanted to settle in, settle down, leave Terminal Tours and Key Security behind. Now I'm Key Insecurity. If one of my students wants a better grade or requests that I suck his dick, I'll have to go along. If Richard asks me to teach Communications One for the fun of it or insists that I coach a co-ed mud wrestling team, I'll need to do it. Ann can make me do the tours to Graceland. Sara can insist on a big church wedding I can't afford. That fucking Dirk at *Hell* could send me to Iraq. "Run," Coach Keever had commanded the biballers. Now anyone could be someone, the coach who needs only to whisper "Jump" to make me move.

Part III

Chapter 9

I wanted to come out of the locker room hard and fast, actually easy and fast, for the second half. Before Sceptic could ask some crazed favor, I'd try to pre-empt, put my opponents back on their heels with the new Michael, solicitous and giving and nurturing, and the old Keever of *Passing Off*, not exactly money-obsessed but, let's say, conscious of certain economic contingencies. And while presenting this speed-shifted Michael Keever—more professor than former player or coach—I'd be scrutinizing others, trying to identify exactly who Sceptic was.

I started my blog, hoping to lure Sceptic out into the open while advertising my new dedication to QCC students and exerting pressure on others who might drop in. The first day of second semester classes, I went in to talk with Richard, who was himself solicitous and apologetic: "I'm really sorry about that Travel Writing class, Michael. I'd have run it below minimum, but nobody, I mean nobody, signed up. There was just nothing that I could do. Maybe you'd like to teach it this summer as a low residency or no residency course via the Internet. But I couldn't run it without a single student."

I wondered if Richard had some way to manipulate the enrollment figures. If he was telling me the truth, my "tape" couldn't have worked. He seemed nervous, too collegial to be sitting on information that would expose *Passing On* as a fake.

"I can scrape by for now," I said, pulling my chair closer to Richard's so my pocket recorder could pick up his part of the conversation. I needed one of those ballpoint cameras to get the surprise—and relief—on Richard's face. I wouldn't be mailing my tape to his wife, not right now anyway.

"At least I'll have more time to write this semester," I said. "I've been working on *Passing Through*, the next stage of my autobiography."

This was just to let Richard know that even if he suspects I don't have tape, I still have words his wife might like to read. And that I'd like to write myself into a better and better-paying school than QCC. But I didn't lean on him. I had come to his office in the student-centric, forward-looking spirit of the Q: "I dropped in to propose a shift in or addition to the curriculum. Unless we can afford to take our students to distant travel destinations, I think the Travel Writing course is always going to be problematic."

This last word I'd often heard floating out of Q classrooms. I liked it because it summed up working there: problems automatic. Richard nodded, and I went on, "Maybe it should be offered only one semester a year. But what I came to suggest is a sequence of courses in Creative Sports Writing, possibly even a graduate program."

"Wow, Michael, I never thought of that."

"CSW," I said, "QCC can be the founder of CSW."

"This I love, Michael. Watch it, write it, read it online that same night, before it loses its immediacy in the morning paper."

"I think we'd attract a lot of students, ones that sometimes go to other schools because of their sports teams. We wouldn't have the expense of building stadiums and equipping teams, but students would be connected to local pro and college sports. And we wouldn't have problems retaining those students, not like the ones in Travel Writing, because there's a constant, year-round supply of games for them to watch, either in the flesh or on cable TV. The way our classrooms are equipped, we could offer mostly night classes and pipe televised games right into the classes."

"Damn, Michael, the possibilities are almost endless. We could have courses on each of the major sports, even courses on extreme sports. You know how students like that shit, the snowboarding and skateboarding. We could find someone out on the wheelchair ramp to teach that. We could bring in players from the Reds and Bengals. This could really prove we've got balls. We'd cover big balls, little balls like golf and ping pong, even no-ball sports like hiking and fishing."

"I know you're not much interested in books, Richard, but there are opportunities there, too. LeBron James published his autobiography when he was eighteen. With all the basketball players jumping from high school to the NBA, publishers are going to need trained ghostwriters creative enough to pad a teenager's life into a book."

"You're right. And think of the teenage girls, the gymnasts and swimmers, the ones with no tits. Who's going to write their lives?"

"We could also start one of those academic journals here, one devoted to CSW. Naturally, it would be online and you'd be the obvious guy to edit it."

"CSW," Richard mused. "You know, I never really liked CNF. There was something negative about it, that 'N' in the middle. Plus if you try to say it, it comes out 'cunf,' which always reminded me of 'cunt', but the 'f' gave it a fairy sound, you know what I mean? But CSW. It slides off the tongue. 'Csaw.' This is brilliant, Michael. I don't know how I overlooked it."

"You have a lot of faculty members to manage. That can't be easy."

"You should have been around last year. A guy who was teaching Animal Communication for us was adjuncting at U.C., Xavier, and Northern Kentucky. His schedule was so tight he bought a pickup, stole a Domino's sign, and put it on his truck so he could speed to his classes. Students called him Professor Pizza until he ran into a bridge abutment on Victory Parkway and killed himself. Tech writers are like six-foot shooting guards. A dime a dozen, but try to find a someone who can teach Animal Communication."

I wanted to ask why he didn't get a real practitioner, maybe a gorilla from the zoo, but sympathized with Richard's plight. I also wanted to move him to another aspect of my proposal.

"It also just occurred to me," I said, "that a CSW graduate program would attract a lot of former college athletes to QCC. Many of them know nothing but sports. Our program would train them to make use of their knowledge to become journalists, publicists, commentators."

Bring him to you. Let him "discover" the closer. Yes, I can see the shooter's eyes get just a little wide.

"And you know what?" he asked.

"What?"

"You'd be the coach of the best fucking co-ed team in the state."

"I hadn't thought of that, Ric, but you could be right, particularly if we make sure we have courses in women's sports, field hockey and dressage, stuff like that."

"Right, right. But don't say a word about this to anyone else. That no-nuts Sam over in English will steal the idea quicker than a Gary Payton pick. They already teach Sports Fiction and Poetry. Sam's same old, same old."

"Well, Ric, I hope you'll keep me in mind for teaching assignments if you start this program."

"Absolutely, Michael, but sometimes the administration delays approval of new programs. Departments can innovate, can put in a few new courses without a lot of supervision, but a program could be two years away."

At which time, I thought, I'll be working for the TSA at minimum wage, a job Patrick once suggested for me. You get your own uniform and send people passing through the scanners, but watching x-rays expose dirty laundry was not what I had in mind for my last thirty years on earth.

Richard talked about the Travel course for the summer. If it was offered as a no residency class, I could be in Greece with Kara, the students could travel wherever they wanted, and the whole thing would be conducted online. Even the A grades could be emailed to the Registrar's office in the old National Bank building. This sounded good but didn't bring in any money now.

My next stop was June's office. Turn on the recorder, turn off the jock lifer. I returned Lauren's pages and said that I'd decided to give her an A for the semester.

"All the way from a C to an A?" June said.

"I read some of the books Lauren was playing with and decided my criteria for CNF were too limiting. I thought her pages were the most interesting I received, but I felt I should be upholding Richard's standards, if you know what I mean."

"Well, Michael, this is quite a change. Next you'll be asking to teach literature."

"Nope," I said, reminding her with my Cal Coolidge negation that I was too simple for that business, "but I do have a suggestion for a course someone might teach: Creative Near-Fiction. It would concentrate on autobiographies—like Lauren's—that play fast and loose with facts. You know, concealing certain things, falsely 're-vealing' others. The books wouldn't necessarily be poetic, like Lauren's, but could still challenge readers' desires."

Competitive Near-Fiction, I thought, but didn't say.

June smiled. "I doubt Richard would approve such a course."

"The nice thing about Creative Near-Fiction is the abbreviation. It could sneak in under the radar."

"That definitely makes it challenging."

I then told June about my Creative Sports Writing proposal. As I assumed, she was less excited, much less excited, than Richard. I kept on fishing, looking for an opportunity to bring up tape. I mentioned that Richard felt our basketball team would improve with new CSW recruits.

"I do hope so," June said, "you could probably tell that I didn't really want to be leaping about in that dirty old gym, but I did it for Richard."

"I thought maybe that was the case after looking at the tape."

"What tape would that be?" she asked.

"From that second practice. Kara shot lots of tape of you all playing biball."

"Oh, that tape." June hesitated and went on, "Maybe Richard should see whatever tape you have. It's so hard to get him to change his mind about something. Maybe watching tape would."

I needed a camera to record the look on my face. Was June implying that she wouldn't mind my non-existent "tape" coming to light? Or was she talking about the biball tape?

"How long have you known Richard?" I asked.

"Two years," she said. "He's very committed to certain things, and that makes him rather stubborn. Slow to shift," she said with a little laugh.

Then she beckoned me a little closer to her and said, "May I ask you something, confidentially, you understand?"

So June knew about "bring him to you, fuck him up." Here it comes, the Sceptic's request, demand, order—to do two impossible things: reveal tape I don't have, sacrifice my job to this woman's desire for Richard, that non-athlete.

"Ask away," I said.

"Do you really read Dante in Greek?"

I felt so relieved that this was the question that I laughed and told the truth: "Of course not. But I've read it in English. Creative Near-Fiction at its best. Dante didn't actually go to hell, but the people are real. Well, some of them are. And everybody gets exactly the punishment they deserve."

Again June smiled, but it was difficult to tell what her expression meant. Did she feel that while dancing around the secret tape of her and Richard we had each revealed a semi-secret—that she has been waiting for Richard to leave his wife, that I didn't know Greek. It hardly seemed an equal exchange.

Listening to the two recordings at home, I felt nothing was proved and my situation not improved, at least not for now. Though improbable, either Richard or June could be Sceptic and biding his or her time. The power of my nonexistent tape seemed to be reduced if June welcomed its release—unless Richard could be somehow made to feel he was being double-teamed. But the fact was Richard wasn't putting any money in my pocket now, when I really needed it, and June had no reason to pressure him to do so.

I also had some creative proposals for the graduate students. First, I apologized for misunderstanding grading policies and promised that I would give them extra credit for their work this semester.

"But great grades alone," I also said, "are not going to distinguish you in your job searches, because other schools are also giving great grades. I've been talking to some writers, and I think the best way to help your careers is to get you published. So I'm thinking about starting an online magazine called *Prodigies*. It would be devoted to the memoirs of writers under thirty or maybe even under twenty-five. I know you're all shooting for book publication of your autobiographies, but getting a couple chapters in a magazine called *Prodigies* would help you get an agent and a publisher. If I can get the support of the department for this, *Prodigies* might even be able to pay for your contributions."

No reason to mention that I assumed I'd be picking up some cash as the faculty advisor and managing editor.

All of the students except Lauren, a surveillance camera would have shown, were enthused. They nodded, grinned, winked at each other. Lauren shook her head, and I thought of horns.

"If *Prodigies* publishes only QCC students," she said, "it will just be a joke."

"Of course," I said, in my best professorial manner, both learned and sympathetic, "the magazine would publish others as well. It's just that it wouldn't have the usual contributors' notes identifying the schools. Our masthead can say that we 'choose work because of its ability to plumb the problems of young people, not because of the writer's academic residence.'"

Rakhshanda now had her hand up: "This is a very good idea, but may I ask how this magazine will help someone whose autobiography cannot easily be excerpted because of its length and connectedness?"

"You may ask, Rakhshanda," I said, and while saying that magic word "ask" came up with an answer I'd not considered before: "I'd also like to start a press with the same name. It would have to be modest, maybe a print-on-demand press like the one that published *Passing On*, but I think that book demonstrated that a POD book can get reviewed. There would be a natural synergy between magazine and press."

Again all the students except Lauren were excited about the possibility of book publication. I wondered how I would fare when "the goatess" got to QCC. I went on to list other "benefits": the students would have to put in some time as interns, they would have to work even harder to make their work worthy of publication, they'd have to accept the judgment of an editorial committee. This last was to prevent Sceptic "asking" me to publish his or her work.

"With these incentives," Jason said, "you should certainly find our work excellent this semester."

"Then we'll all be happy," I said and gave them the rest of this first day off to discuss among themselves how to begin a magazine and press. As dedicated to their own personal experiences as these students were, it would be a long time before I had to act on any of their "committee" recommendations. Then I could see what Richard and June thought of my ideas, yet more new suggestions for the Communications Department by a faculty member who was making himself indispensable.

As part of my public relations program, I emailed Brenda, telling her about CSW and suggesting that she, as a former athlete, should have more courses in the long term. I also went one morning to a college faculty meeting that I didn't have to attend now that I was teaching only one course. Of the thirty or so people there from the School of Dissemination, I knew only June, Richard, Sam from English, and a guy from Art who lived in my apartment building. Maybe because faculty members are not widely known outside their departments, people who spoke identified themselves and their departments. The first agenda item was a course in the films of Merchant and Ivory that English had proposed. The discussion was not something I needed to tape, but I did take some brief notes summarizing various positions:

Sam: "We believe English is the appropriate home for this course because most of the films have been adapted from American and English novels such as *The Golden Bowl* and *Room With a View*."

Richard: "Everyone knows you don't teach those archaic novels anymore. And you don't have anyone on your staff who has studied film as a communications medium with its own special semiotics."

Gerald from Political Science: "As usual, my formalist friends in English and Communications are missing the point, the content of these films. They are about cultural conflicts that Poly Sci is most qualified to explain to our students."

Frances from Women's Studies: "As usual, my esteemed male colleagues in English, Communications, and Political Science have ignored the third member of Merchant-Ivory Productions, Ruth Prawer Jhabvala, who has written most of the screenplays adapting the novels into films. Since Ms. Jhabvala is Indian, she links the issues of the other three departments, and since she is, obviously, a woman, we believe the course should be taught in Women's Studies."

Richard: "Gerald and Frances are both attempting a transparent power grab in the name of politics. The course is about films. These are products of mass communications. They are properly our property."

Sam: "These films are parasites on literary texts, which are our purview. The films can be studied only through the novels, and no one else in the college knows how to read literature."

Wendell from History: "As usual, my short-sighted colleagues ignore the need for historical context that these films demand. Gerald talks about political conflicts, but these must be properly historicized within Third World narratives. The course should be taught in our department."

Svetlana from Anthropology: "Excuse my facial expression, which you native English speakers may call a grin if you like. Wendell prides himself on historicizing. But for him history means rulers, wars, geographical change. Only Anthropology can truly place these films in their cultural contexts, modern and ancient. After all, what were the cave paintings but pre-cinema?"

The inter-departmental wrangling went around and around with each representative attacking whoever seemed to have the upper hand. I thought back to biball and wondered if the argument could be a naming problem. But it was more than that. Although my colleagues wanted to believe the course was a political issue, Merchant and Ivory, as the first name suggested, was really an economic issue—an enrollment issue. But Economics was in the School of Information and unavailable for clarification. Far be it from me to identify the underlying practical issue to my more abstract colleagues. But after forty-five minutes of discussion and with no polite way to escape the room, where I wasn't even required to be, I offered what I thought was the perfect QCC proposal, one I knew the students would love because it would lower their workload.

Michael Keever from Communications: "I'm new here and hesitate to speak, but what if every department offered a course in Merchant-Ivory films? I think they've done twenty or more. Even if there is some overlap, that would be good for students who should hear what different disciplines have to say about the same material. The course might even function as a capstone experience for seniors, a way to bring together our various analyses of dissemination."

June gave me a thumbs up from across the room. Others nodded and murmured assent, just as if mine was a serious proposal. No one argued, and the Dean, known as "The Hostage Taker" for his lengthy meetings, said we should discuss the matter further at our next meeting. He then moved on to the next of twelve agenda items, a proposed course on Al Qaeda videos. That's when I noticed that some of my colleagues had brought brown paper bags and thermoses with them.

I was making possibly long-term friends all over campus, but I was still no closer to solving my short-term financial problem. A possible solution came indirectly from the most unlikely source: an undergraduate. Eden came to my first office hours to talk about her subway essay. Right away she said she knew the paper was "off track" and apologized. I laughed at her pun, accepted her apology, and crossed her off the bottom of the Sceptic list. There seemed no reason to activate the camera I'd installed.

"I don't know what happened," she said, "but I think it was being down there in that fallout shelter alone with you. I started imagining things, you know. I mean, you made me...."

"Excuse me, Eden," I interrupted, "but I'm feeling a bit warm in here and need to adjust the thermostat." I switched on the camera and opened the door, but of course no faculty member would be around, certainly not coming into the office so early in the semester, not when there was money to be made at the real day jobs most had.

I sat back down and enunciated carefully for the camera: "I do know how sometimes emotions can lead writing astray. I'm glad that you realize what happened to your paper, and I hope that in your future courses you will be more rigorous and prevent feelings you might have from interfering with your academic work."

"I don't understand," Eden said. "It wasn't exactly emotion that got me off track. It was this really vivid scene I was imagining while lying on that cot...."

I interrupted Eden again: "Do you see that little thing up on the ceiling that looks like a sprinkler? That's a camera, and we're on videotape."

"So?"

"So our whole conversation has been taped."

"So what if we're on tape. I just wanted to tell you, you know, that I was sorry for all that nuclear holocaust stuff I imagined. You were right, you know, to not let me get away with it."

The camera shows the back of my head, not the blush of embarrassment on my face. I was the one guilty of imagining—first that Eden was attracted to me, second that she might be preparing to somehow blackmail me for a better grade. Although I'm still not sure what Eden's initial intentions were, studying the tape of her led me to a series of questions about another young woman and her motives: What if Sara's intended marriage to Bucky is only a pretense? What if she knows her marriage would cancel the tuition remission and she is faking the marriage? What if she is putting pressure on me to return to Ann, to reform a single household that could afford her dorm and tuition payments? And what if that's the reason Ann is supporting Sara's proposed marriage?

But then I thought, why would Ann want me back? I am a published author, an instructor at Queen City College, and a man who has proved that he can choose his own course, support himself (so far), and live by himself, qualities Ann had always been sceptical about. Ann could be the Sceptic and Sara her partner in crime.

I examined my memory and what I'd already written in Parts I and II for signs that Ann might want me back. Unfortunately, last semester I wasn't taping every human transaction, and the signs were ambiguous. So I examined myself: did I give any evidence to Sara or Ann that I might want to reunite with Ann in a three-bedroom apartment large enough to have a Christmas tree? I didn't think I had. Did I want to? No. Ann had chosen to toss me out, and I had no compelling reason—except for the money, the fucking money—to return. I liked my locker and my new, occasional locker-mate. I didn't feel any guilt about what had happened. Terminal Tours would eventually do to Ann what it did to me, whether or not she met an Alice or Al. And when she came down from all those time-zone crossings, I'd be to blame: for losing the house, for driving her into the Tours, for earning only a marginal wage at QCC.

I needed to meet this Bucky, examine him and Sara together, try to see if their marriage is plausible, and then figure out some way to discourage Ann's interest. If she is Sceptic, "discouragement" won't be strong enough. I'll need disgust.

Chapter 10

"Sara? So you haven't eloped?"

"To the Jamaica branch of QCC?"

"Is Bucky back from Washington?"

"Did classes start two days ago?"

"Aren't students supposed to answer the questions that professors ask?"

"Are you a professor?"

I was now determined that Sara be the first to give up asking questions. Since Sceptic's email, I'd come to dislike questions—from students, family members, even waiters asking me what I wanted.

"Could we get some of these questions answered in person, say you and Bucky Friday night for dinner?"

"Can you do pizza?"

"Would lasagna be close enough?"

"Can you make it meatless?"

"Are you telling me that you're planning to marry a weak-ass vegetarian?"

I could hear Sara trying to cover up a giggle, so she was determined to keep asking.

"How do you think cows and oxen get so big?"

"Why do you think oxen are so dumb?"

"Is it because they're not allowed to think and move by themselves?"

"Do you mean because they're always yoked together like a married couple?"

"Or because they always have someone driving them where the driver wants them to go?"

"If the driver is older and wiser, isn't that his responsibility?"

"What if it's profit, not responsibility, that's driving the driver?"

To that I didn't have a quick rejoinder. I managed, "You realize that every analogy limps, right?"

"If that's true, why try to make the oxen limp?"

"Do you want me to come pick you up with a truck on Friday night?"

"We'll walk over. No meat. No oxen. No jokes about Bucky's name. And remember what Larry Bird said to you."

I hadn't remembered I'd told Sara about Larry's advice. Despite all the questions Sara asked, her orders at the end didn't sound like Sceptic to me. Or maybe ordering is what came after asking. Sara knew some things about surveillance, so I had to be careful rigging the camera in an old CBA trophy. I just had to hope that Bucky's parents in Washington were not in the CIA

On Friday night, fifteen minutes before Sara and Bucky were supposed to arrive, I heard a knock at my door. Through the peephole I saw a distinguished-looking gray-haired man in a suit. Maybe, I thought, it's one of those million-dollar giveaways to settle my financial problems. Or a lawyer representing the estate of Rorque, Esquire, recently deceased in the collapse of a home formerly owned by Ann and Michael Keever.

I opened the door, and the man introduced himself in a gruff voice as "Xavier Romero."

There was something odd about the guy, the voice, the hair.

"What can I do for you, Mr. Romero?" I asked.

"Accept him as your son-in-law," Sara said from behind the door, where she had been hiding from the peephole.

She popped out, tousled Xavier Romero's floured hair, and said, "We thought you might like an older guy."

"And rich," she added, plucking at the suit.

"Pleased to meet you, Bucky. It was being early that fooled me. Sara is never early. Glad to see you have a good influence on her. The 'Xavier' was also misleading. What's the connection to Bucky?"

"My parents said that I used to say 'gimme bucky' when I was a kid trying to understand the value of a dollar. It's easier for people to pronounce than Xavier."

"And has some heroic associations. Do you know Bucky Dent?"

"Of course. Yankees-Red Sox playoff, 1978."

"Bucky Burke?"

"Played for the Trail Blazers a few years ago?"

"Enough sports trivia," Sara said and helped Bucky out of his suit jacket. "My father writes for *Hell Magazine* and likes to keep his apartment overheated."

"Come to the kitchen, Bucky. We'll stand in front of the oven and work up a sweat. By the way, do you play any sports or just collect trivia?"

"Tennis, racquetball, ping pong."

"Sara, you sure this guy isn't Mafia? Sounds like he's in the rackets."

Sara shook her head at me and took Bucky's arm. "It's just one of Dad's tests, Bucky. You're supposed to get the racquet sport joke."

"Romero is Spanish, not Italian," Bucky told me. "Since you played in both countries, I thought you'd have known."

So Bucky had been doing his homework, reading about Michael Keever. Yes, he and Sara were playing me, entering with a joke, feeding me sports trivia, reminding me of my heroic past.

"And what brings a good Spanish Catholic boy to QCC instead of Georgetown or Cincinnati's own Xavier?"

"I'd been to Catholic schools my whole life. I wanted to get out of Washington, and we have an excellent computer science program here. Also, I heard that your daughter was going to be here."

"You knew Sara before coming here?"

Sara started laughing, and Bucky grinned. As far as I could tell, the two of them were up three to zero on me, and the night wasn't fifteen minutes old. Despite being outwitted, I have to say that Bucky was a likable kid, maybe not as polite as Ann had said, but sharp and probably nice. During dinner, Sara and he talked about the silliness and recklessness of people living in the dorm. Bucky's roommate proved his ability to hold his beer by climbing out their fourth-floor window and suspending himself by the sill. After each beer, out he'd go. He said he'd know if he had too many if he couldn't haul himself back in. "Stupidity," Bucky said, "real stupidity."

One too many, I thought, and that kid would have something to write about, if he survived the fall: His three-second travel experience or how he went through life in a wheelchair. Cautionary tales, like the ones Sara and Bucky were telling me. But the dorm stories were still not a reason for eighteen-year-olds to get married, not unless the stories involved bars, chains, beating, bread, and water.

After dinner and on the living-room sofa, where the camera had them in its eye, Sara and Bucky ran through the reasons they wanted to marry, recapitulating what Sara had already told me.

"We're not afraid," Sara said, answering my earlier question. "Well, maybe afraid of someone's stupid prank in the dorm, but not afraid of separating. You know,

Dad, I've had boyfriends before, and Bucky was king of his senior prom."

With future prospects bright for CSW and *Prodigies* at QCC, the new nurturing father could show his willingness to be flexible. Delay was my current strategy.

"The question remains," I said, "why not just get an apartment and get married after six months or so, when you'll know what it's like to use the same bathroom and how the kiwis you were planning to have for breakfast have disappeared into your lover's stomach at 3 AM?"

Bucky cleared his throat. I didn't need the replay to see that he had been practicing on this one.

"Both my parents are pretty conservative Catholics, as you can probably tell by my name. They would withdraw their financial support if we were to live together without being married."

Saved by the Catholics. Hooray for Patrick. Saved also by a long-married couple that could maintain a hard line, preserving principles and principal both. The camera wasn't on me, but I don't think I smiled.

"I hadn't thought of that," I said.

Bucky nodded in appreciation and went on with his rehearsed spiel: "They want us to be married in the Church, but of course that's a huge decision."

Forever, I thought, unless you're a mixed marriage like my parents or Ann and me. Or Sara and Bucky.

"Absolutely," I agreed, "huge."

"But," Bucky said, "they're willing to keep supporting me if we get married in a civil ceremony with the promise to have the vows sacramentalized in six months."

Fucking hypocrites and gutless enablers.

"I can sympathize with their conflict," I told Bucky. "Why not save them the moral compromise which, you must know, will be very painful for them as practicing Catholics?"

"It's just six months, Dad," Sara put in.

The nurturing, pleasing, flexible strategy wasn't working. I had no creative carrot to offer. I decided to lean a little more on Bucky. "I know Cincinnati is not Washington, Bucky. But this can be a rough neighborhood after dark. I'm afraid your parents will go to bed every night worrying that you'll be walking to your apartment some evening, get mugged, heroically fight back, be shot at point blank range square in the forehead, and die instantly without the presence of a priest and in a state—let's face facts here, Bucky—of mortal sin."

Bucky ran his hand through his hair, and more flour fell out. The tape shows an expression that suggests he is not worrying about his parents.

"I don't know," I continued, "if your tennis coaches ever used this term, but why not just 'suck it up' for the next few months in the dorm and have a real marriage—civil and sacred together—in a few months?"

Sara said, "Mom says if we've chosen to get married, we should do it now."

"And not be influenced by the Catholic faith?" I asked. "You know how dismissive she is of Patrick and his dogmas. I doubt she's taking into consideration others' sensibilities."

"I don't really know why," Sara answered. "She seems to want things settled."

"Of the people involved, she and you two agree on that. Bucky's parents and I would like to see you wait just a little, at least until spring break when we'd have time to arrange a reception and celebration. So that's three against three, a tie. Deuce, right Bucky?"

"Dad, this is no time for sports metaphors."

"Okay, say the equation is balanced."

"Or," Bucky said, "the circuits are in equilibrium."

I didn't know if Bucky was showing off his analogy-production or if he might not be quite as anxious as Sara—and Ann—to be married in a civil ceremony and chance eternal damnation because some local thug wanted his racquet-sport sneakers and parent-provided credit card. When Sara and Bucky left, I felt they might have something more to talk about. Hell. Bucky had forgotten hell, a notion Sara's parents had never taught her.

As for Ann, I thought she might be worried that a hot-blooded Spaniard named Xavier, a good Catholic boy with lots of siblings, would be against using birth control. Or, I thought later while staring at Sara's face on the tape, maybe Ann is trying to make me jump. I re-ran and re-ran the tape. Sara really looked puzzled by her mother's rush. Sara had the look of a dupe, an unindictable co-conspirator, but not the person who had traveled to Lebanon to talk with Alice's parents.

As for Bucky, I liked the kid. He and Sara appeared genuinely fond of each other. The romance seemed plausible, not a pretense. I still didn't think it a good idea for eighteen-year-olds to marry, especially if some parents' religious scruples were affected, but I'd have given them my blessings if they'd just been willing to wait until I could cover the tuition expenses by teaching "Basketball Biography" and "CSW: The Feminist Angle," as well as editing *Prodigies*, the magazine and the press.

I considered another face-to-face with Ann but decided I didn't want her scrutinizing my features if I needed to spring on her the confession I had in mind. I'd also have better control of the recording technology if we spoke by phone. And I wanted to catch her off guard, so I sucked up the cost and called her global-access cell phone.

"Is Sara okay?" she said right away.
"Yes, she's fine, except for wanting to marry Xavier."
"Why are you calling me here, then?"
"Where are you?"
"In London, and it's 2:43 AM."
Luck was running my way. Be quick.
"Sara and Bucky just left, and I wanted to talk with you."
"Okay, talk."
"Remember how you used to say lying is the worst offense?"
"What is it, Michael?"
"Have you ever considered asking me back?"
"I sometimes miss you, Michael, but not at moments like this."
"Is that a yes or a no?"
"It's a highly qualified yes, one affected by being in London with an old man who thinks half the time we're in London, Ontario."

Quick, quick, her consciousness is coming back.

"I understand that and appreciate it. But listen, if someone asks you for something, what would you say?"

There was a bit of time lag in the transatlantic connection, but Ann, though only half awake, didn't miss a beat: "I'd probably say yes. Isn't that the lesson of Terminal Tours?"

I hated being questioned, so I tried a surprise, direct attack: "You're the Sceptic, aren't you?"

"About you, Michael, I'm always sceptical."

"And you used to call me evasive."

"Deceptive. There's a difference."

Although the test result was ambiguous, Ann was still the most likely suspect, and the only one who could release the pressure on me.

"You have to promise me you won't tell Sara what I have to say."

"Okay, Okay. Please get on with it."

"Probably Sara has told you about this woman I've been seeing."

"She mentioned goggle eyes."

"Right, anyway. Did she tell you about coming to a basketball practice?"

Silence, not even the 2:44 reminder.

"Well this is a roundabout way of telling you, but these men and women I was coaching at the time wanted to play with two balls. I called it biball."

"You're calling me in the middle of the night to tell me that you named your sacred sport Bible?"

"Not Bible, bi-ball, as in bi-sexual."

"It is QCC after all."

"Right, anyway it was while coaching that team that I realized I was attracted to one of my players, the only black player."

"Are you calling me at 2:45 for permission to have sex with some black girl?"

"The player's name is Jason, and we've become romantically involved."

Exactly three seconds of silence on the replay.

"Michael, I don't believe 'romantically involved' is the right term for what you're doing. But this demonstrates the need for us to be divorced as soon as possible. I do not want to read in *The Enquirer* that the husband of Ann Logan has been arrested by the Vice Squad at the toilet in Burnet Woods for laying his hand on the penis of some undercover cop."

If Ann was Sceptic, she was holding a secret of little use to her now. Say she was so angered by this confession that she was tempted to expose me and cost me my teaching job. She'd know that I could claim that I'd been fired because I was a bisexual, and the publicity would be even more embarrassing to her than Rorque's suit. Once again, there was no money to be made from my pre-emptive strike, but I should be able to delay Sara's marriage if Ann is not pushing it. And that will diminish some financial pressure.

Wrong again. Within the week, Ann's lawyer sent me thirteen pages of a proposed separation agreement that read like garbled CNF. Since we had accumulated during our marriage no assets and considerable debt from the suit, and since I was responsible for the outcome of the suit, and despite my present income (estimated according to standard university salaries), and whereas the heretofore assertions could not be disputed, Ann Logan and her lawyer were insisting that Michael Keever, home address unknown, agree to defray that debt by contractually agreeing to be responsible for all educational and other expenses of his only known child, Sara Keever, etc.

The court was not the college, and the college was not the court. It enforced, as well as dissolved, contracts. No deceiving this court. Not only did I have to pay for the call to London, I would now have to pay an attorney $250 an hour to read and explain to a mere field service instructor of Communications just what these turgid thirteen pages meant. Since this was slow and cumbersome work, which could not even begin until a retainer of $3,000 was received, my "bisexuality" was going to cost me a lot of money I didn't have. And I couldn't be certain that the outrageous demands of the separation agreement didn't issue from a lawyer who had been told Sceptic's secret.

Such is the long arm of the law and the long-term consequences, Patrick would say, of sin. To wit, as Ann's lawyer would put it, the lie that I had written *Passing Off*, a lie in which Ann was complicit and active, came back from a decade ago. Without the published lie of that book's happy ending, Sceptic would never have noted the parallel with *Passing On* and would never have investigated the facts somewhat misleadingly left out of my book. I'd always hated Ann's damned book, and now I had good reason, a great reason. Ann's fucking fiction brought me to the current documentary bind, a non-fiction situation in which no creativity could be brought to bear on the damages, bank accounts, salaries, and other facts of the real life Ann Logan and Michael Keever had together.

Two days after I received the lawyer's documents, I got an email from Ann: "I didn't believe you the next morning, but your call made for a miserable night. Yes, I did hope that we might be able to get back together. I asked you to leave so that you would get yourself together. I thought we might be possible as a family again now that you're successful on your own, but once more you have lied to me and, as you said, that is the 'worst offense.' I don't know what's troubling you or what you're up to, but I hope it doesn't cost you the new life you seem to want or the affection of our daughter. Because we are currently passing through a formal legal process, from now on I must ask you to communicate with me only by email."

I knew better than to respond and to be on record. I just hoped that I wouldn't have to someday produce tape of Jason and me as naked Greek athletes to prove what I'd told Ann in London. That's when I realized I had fucked up with my fictionalizing: I couldn't very well say I'd been fired from the Q for bisexuality if my proof was having sex with a current student. Ann was right, again: lying was the worst offense and the offenses were piling up around me.

Passing Through

One last point here: I could have left Ann's email out of this account, as I left Alice's death out of *Passing On*.

Chapter 11

After Lauren's grade change went through, she wanted to talk after class.

"Can you come during my office hours?" I said. When I'll have the camera and my voice recorder on, I thought. When I'll have had time to think of something more the new Michael Keever can do for you.

"I have another class at that time. Can we just sit here in the hall and talk for a few minutes?"

"Okay," I said, "but no rhyming or bleating." No chance to record, but at least a few students were milling around to hear any raised voices.

"Why did you change that grade?"

"Why didn't you come talk to me about your grade before you went to the Director?"

"Because I wanted to test the two of you."

First Sara asking me questions, now Lauren testing me.

"To see if we'd read the same books you had?" I asked.

"To see if you'd recognize shit when it was under your noses."

"Goat shit?"

"Goatess shit. That earth goddess shit June teaches. It's worse than bullshit, which I assume came from the Minotaur. Invent a fuzzy, feely matriarchal past so you don't have to face what happens to women now, every day, everywhere. All I had to do was make up what a supposedly literary reader wanted, and she went for it. You know, like a fake."

"Did you play basketball in high school?"

"No, but my brother did. You don't have to wear a jock to know what a fake is."

"And submitting the piece to me was a tricky, indirect way to get June to read it?"

"Not just that. I was testing you, too. You saw through it, but then changed the grade. Jason told me about biball. That change of grade seems like no balls to me. I thought you really wanted to challenge us, make us work harder, take risks. But a little pressure comes and...."

I said nothing, but I was thinking "no game, no gain," one convert.

Given the pause, Lauren shifted: "Now it's this *Prodigies* crap. Not prodigies, Queen City Children. Why are you going along with this place anyway? You're a published author. Does that mean if I publish a book, I'll end up teaching at Queen City Community?"

"You're not tape-recording this conversation, are you?" I asked.

Lauren laughed. "Should I be?"

"For posterity. The first interview with Michael Keever."

"But you haven't said anything."

"I'm afraid to. This is my first year teaching. I don't understand the politics here. I used to be a referee: bang, bang, call 'em like you see 'em. No reversals. Take off the striped shirt and go home. But I do want to keep this job, and I'd like to have more classes next year."

"So what happens at QCC is 'no blood, no foul'? Don't you see that students' blood is being drained away by the low expectations and false praise?"

"It's up to you to keep your blood up, Lauren."

"Why are you whispering?"

"Because this is a secret," I said. And because no tape recorder a student could afford would catch this old-man whisper Sara's history instructor had perfected.

"I wrote *Passing On* without a workshop, without teachers, without a single reader. If the 'goatess' is shit, think up a better persona. Shift your orientation. Take a real risk. Don't blame people who don't ask enough of you. You're someone who can ask something of yourself."

I didn't really think Lauren was Sceptic, but I threw that awkward phrasing in to see how she'd respond.

"I know that," she said.

"So this little conference was another test?"

"You passed, Mr. Keever. Maybe I'll throw away all that farm girl stuff. I grew up in San Francisco. The only thing I know about farms is what I saw in Paris Hilton's series, but who cares about the life of a spoiled Sausalito kid who had sailing lessons at six?"

"I grew up with farmers. I believed all of it, until you got down on all fours."

"I guess I'm glad. But still, so what? If I'm going to invent stuff, there might as well be some excitement, some stakes, maybe even some weight."

"That's probably true," I said.

"Passed again, Mr. Keever. I fail as a writer, you pass as a professor."

"How old are you, Lauren?"

"Isn't that kind of personal?"

"I'm not asking your sexual orientation. Your birth date is on my grade list."

"Twenty-one."

"So the truth is you are a prodigy, a graduate student at twenty-one. You're almost exactly half my age."

"So I need to wait twenty years for something to happen to me."

"Make something happen for you."

"Yeah, I could quit school and move to Afghanistan."

"Don't do that. I need all the students I can get. Which is why I probably shouldn't say this, but have you thought of transferring over to the Creative Writing program?"

"What, and write some silly water slide novel with a 'Wow, we just got damp' ending?"

If you were on the edge of bankruptcy, I thought, it wouldn't be silly. It might even be a creative solution.

"You'd have to choose," I said and realized I sounded like Ann speaking to me, me speaking about Sara. So, what the hell, I also said, "It's hard but fair."

Lauren said "Yeah" and got up. "Thanks," she also said and walked away. When she was out of sight, I took out my notebook and scribbled down what we'd just said, though I won't claim I have absolutely everything exact. I wished I had a tape so I could demonstrate to someone—anyone—that at least one graduate student appreciated Coach Keever's demands.

"Two graduate students," Kara said when I told her about my conversation with Lauren. "I like your sexual demands."

"They're caused by the single bed."

"Well, maybe you shouldn't get the double then. Whatever happened to that purchase, anyway?"

"I'm waiting for a two-for-one sale."

"You don't like my bed?"

"I may need to buy one for Sara. She and Bucky are talking about getting married."

"Don't you want a double before they graduate?"

"They want to do it during spring break."

"Frookin frackin," Kara said, some upper Michigan exclamation that she translated as "holy shit."

"Wouldn't it be a better idea to send them to Cancun?" she asked.

I almost never mentioned Ann to Kara, but I told her that Sara and Bucky were insisting and that Ann was supporting them. Kara wanted to know why, so I had to tell her what I thought and speculated, the whole, but compacted, history of Ann and me from just before she—or "we," as Ann used to say—got pregnant.

"Frook frack," Kara said, "so you're waiting for three, not two, women to pardon you."

"Three?"

"Alice, Sara, Ann."

"Four. I really didn't want to lay all this on you."

"You're forgiven. See how easy it is? Really, I wondered what was bothering you lately."

"Not enough demands?"

"Just the opposite. You seem to be trying to please everybody. Except, of course, when you travel alone to Greece."

"You'll forgive me for not taking you when we're lying on the black sand in Santorini. As for everybody else, I'm investing in my academic career."

"Maybe the best investment would be taking classes elsewhere instead of teaching them here."

"I don't have your savings. Losing the travel course could be the least of it. *Hell* wasn't pleased with the Lavrion piece. They basically said they wanted to see me sweat in Somalia next time or else. But that's also small potatoes, as my spud-farming father used to say. If Sara and Bucky get married, she'll lose her tuition remission."

"Sara knows this fact and is still asking to get married now?"

"I don't know if she knows."

"You didn't tell her?"

"No."

"Because...wait a second...wait a second...I've got it. Because you don't want money to interfere with a decision like this?"

Ann knew all my faults. I liked getting some credit.

"Ann and I got married because we had to. I don't believe we ever got over that fact. I don't want Sara to say in her autobiography that she stayed single or lost Bucky because she 'had' to."

"So you're afraid, the nearly single father's fear of not responding to his only child's request."

"I guess you could put it in those terms," I said and thought of the goofy things I'd done the last couple of weeks because of my free-floating fear of Sceptic. Like players who come out too pumped up for the second half, I'd been over-reacting, over-exerting, trying to make up a deficit all at once.

"That reminds me," I said, "does your former guy know about me, know my name?"

"Not that I know of, but I suppose he could. Why?"

"I got some weird emails. I thought it might be him trying to chase me off."

"Threatening emails?"

"Not physically. Just the kind of thing that, as you said, encourages me to please everybody."

"Including not telling Sara about the tuition?"

"Maybe."

Kara looked at me as if she was expecting more, but I definitely didn't want to get into the content of the emails. So Kara continued, "And by not telling Sara, you also prove Ann wrong in *Passing Off* about your money obsession, right?"

"When did you read that?"

"When you were in Lavrion. If I couldn't go there, I'd armchair it to Athens."

Kara looked around my bare living room. "I thought you traveled light, Michael, but that book...."

"I don't really understand it myself. No hope, no afterlife, Alice said. But my life in that damned book will be out there passing through readers' hands until Richard has his way and books are used to build telecommunications relay stations."

"'Keep it simple, Keever.' Which coach told you that?"

"Murray Jacobs, the Master of Loathing. He also said, 'Bring 'em to you, fuck 'em up.'"

"Just tell Sara the truth, tell her what you've told me."

I didn't say so, but this sounded like advice Ann would give.

"I'll think about it," I said.

"No you won't. You won't change your mind about this. You didn't change any of those undergraduate grades, did you?"

"No."

"That's the man I love."

"Frackin frookin, sweet Jesus, 'love'?"

"Just this moment. Never before, maybe never again."

"I know, I know. Passing through."

"What?"

"Something someone told me," I said and then led Kara away from Ann's meaning with an abbreviation: "PT. It's the hoopster's primary target: playing time."

"And after years of that, physical therapy."

"Right," I said and thought again of my physical therapist and her meaning of passing through..

Kara immediately sensed the association with Alice and said, "What if we rearranged the words. Physical time, playing therapy?"

"Or add letters: PTOD."

"Isn't 'tod' German for death?"

"I meant PT on demand."

"Frookin frackin," Kara said.

And then she said, "Maybe there's something we could do together...."

"Something other than sex?"

"You're taping everything else. We could collaborate on a home movie for sale on the Internet."

"Procreative Non-Fiction?"

"Keep it simple, Keever."

Without knowing it, the two graduate students had made it difficult to keep it simple. Even if Sara delayed, I was looking down the barrel or preparing to wear one. My rent was overdue. *Hell* was holding up payment, "encouraging" me to go to Somalia even if facts were difficult to check there. Ann's lawyer was pressing me. There wasn't a single welfare or insurance cheat to be taped in Cincinnati. Patrick had to sleep with his boots on in case a collector from Boston burned down the house. After Kara went home to Frisky, I lay awake and let wacky ideas speed through my head: maybe I could somehow use my blog to set up the opponents I sensed all around me, perhaps I could blackmail the graduate students by threatening to mail their autobiographies to their parents, blackmail Richard for an advance on future courses, sell June the film rights to the book she liked, tell Bucky's parents I was bisexual and HIV positive, write a waterslide novel. I could confess to Ann, beg her pardon, beg her to let me come back to her and Terminal Tours. I wondered if there were still debtors' prisons, if they had hot water like my "locker." I was boxed in. I definitely needed to change my orientation, shift my strategy. Make something happen for myself, as I'd told Lauren. I thought again about "passing through," my sneaking out of tight spots on the court, my quick trips through airports around the world. I remembered Henderson talking at Christmas about a tour and auto money. Maybe Henderson could be my creative solution.

"How much do you charge an hour for divorce work?" I asked Henderson on the phone the next morning.

"Nobody has enough money to get me to do domestic relations. I'll do international relations for half. Are you and Ann splitting up?"

"Yeah, she asked me to move out six months ago. Now that there's no chance of reconciliation, her lawyer has hit me with a meat-grinding separation agreement."

"Sorry to hear that, Key, but anyone who read *Passing On* wouldn't be surprised. That was a tough business you were in. But there could be an upside to this separation."

"Damn right. Her name is Kara."

"Another white girl, I expect."

"It's too late for me to try for an NBA point guard like Jason Kidd."

"That boy have a jumper if he darker."

"But would he give up the rock?"

"Yeah, you right. If I'd been playing with him, I might not have had to go to law school. But I'm glad you called. You saved me a dime. I was going to call you."

"One of the Pistons sowing his seed down here in Ohio?"

"No, it's the case I mentioned before Christmas. I know a lot more now. Your passport still good?"

"Yes, but I'd rather not get back into the terminal business."

I'd refused to escort the dying for Ann, but if the money were right I'd do it once for Henderson.

"The person in question is young, and she's in good health."

"Where does she want to go?"

"There's a place she needs to leave."

"This isn't someone in the witness protection program, is it?"

Henderson laughed.

"Civilians don't transport those people."

"Okay, good, so where is this someone asking to leave?" I said, realizing as I was saying the words that I was using Sceptic's language.

"This is a place that her American representative is willing to pay someone a lot of money to help her get out of."

This didn't sound like a job for a professor. I beat James to the trash talk: "This is a place so fucking dangerous that you won't even mention its name, right? In which case, James, why don't you take your big black ass to this shithole and bully yo way out?"

"I told you, Key, this is a job for a white boy. My black face wouldn't work. I won't say it's dangerous. A bit risky. But big money."

Henderson sounded like rhyming Lauren: bit risky, big money.

"I want you to come up here and talk with the American representative. See what you think. I believe that, with your tour experience, you're the man for this job. That's why I was fixing to call you. But it's your choice. I'm not jumping you anywhere."

Henderson was using our former agent's terms: Drinkman moved players in the U.S., jumped them overseas.

"It's Libya, isn't it? You want me to bring out one of Khadaffi's daughters, the one we didn't kill in that air strike years ago."

Henderson laughed again. "A whole lot easier than that, my man."

"But not so easy you'll tell me the country."

"Will you come up here and talk to the money man?"

I remembered my futile four-day trip to Vermont.

"Will he pay me a per diem, one day up, one day back in the surveillance van?"

"This white man will pay for you to fly up here and send a car to the airport to pick you up."

"Okay, I'll come up. Where is this place?"

"My office?"

"No, James. The country."

"Algeria."

"Fucking Christ. I know about Algeria. A would-be client asked me to take him there because he said that we'd have a good chance of seeing someone killed in the streets. I did a lot of research and ended up refusing him, the only person I ever refused."

"Conditions have changed. They have a new government. I'll email you some information and send some tourist brochures. And I'll arrange the ticket up here. What days do you teach?"

I told Henderson Wednesday and Thursday. I didn't want him to think I was desperate, even if I was, especially if I was. I wanted him to think that I, like high school kids going on recruiting trips, had a lot of options, a lot of suitors offering deals worth thousands of dollars in tuition, room and board, incidental expenses, travel allowances. But no one else was saying those two most beautiful words in the English language: "big money."

Passing Through

I knew what Henderson's information and brochures would say: "Welcome to beautiful Algeria, the undiscovered Mediterranean destination with charming local customs and European sophistication, sparkling beaches and mysterious desert, the best of North African and French cuisine, etc."

I checked the State Department's site on Algeria, which gave some recent history and current conditions, the facts. When Islamic candidates were going to win elections and create an Iranian-style state, the military stepped in. For a decade, Islamic terror groups killed Westerners, murdered Algerian intellectuals, and slaughtered men, women, and children. The government clamped down on the media, started "disappearing" suspected Islamists, and may have disappeared some dissident journalists while blaming the Islamists. After a recent election, security conditions improved around Algiers, but the State Department still advised not traveling to the country. A private web site was more specific: "Have someone you know pick you up at the airport, stay in your international hotel, and conduct your business there. If you go to the Kasbah, you will be dead within fifteen minutes."

Algeria was dangerous, unlike what Henderson said, but if done quickly and carefully a trip might be merely risky. A terminal tour in reverse. I decided to take the free ride to Detroit.

Henderson's eighth floor office was in the tallest building I saw in Dearborn. The doorplate, like his letterhead, said "Henderson and Henderson." The receptionist looked like she'd been imported from Denmark to do the job. Henderson came out to greet me: the Afro clasp, the half-hug, then two arms on my shoulders to remind me I was a skinny-ass point guard retired, while Henderson was huge, maybe 400 pounds on his 6-9 frame. He had on half-lenses that he looked over, and there was a lot of gray in his short Afro. His suit looked expensive, even if it was made by a tentmaker. Always vain about his feet, Henderson had on shoes I knew must have pinched the toes that had to support that much weight. He never showed me any love in scrimmages, knocking me around as if I'd come from South Africa instead of Central Vermont, but all I'd have to do now is stump around for five minutes in a game of one-on-one to put Henderson in an oversized casket. The only thing I could think to say was "living large, James."

He laughed and said, "Let me introduce you to the beautiful Henderson."

He took me through a door behind the receptionist and into an office where a woman sat with her back to her door, typing on a laptop. Her hair was black and looked ironed, and I thought it odd that a race man like Henderson would have a wife who conked her hair. But when she turned around, I realized she could have been Rakhshanda's older sister or a dark cousin from Sri Lanka or maybe from Algeria. She was beautiful: high cheekbones, a mouth fuller than Rakhshanda's, and a very long neck.

"Sahar, meet Michael Keever, the man who got me to the NBA."

"Pleased to meet you, Sahar, particularly pleased because this is the first time James has ever acknowledged my assistance in his leaving Athens. And, I might say, abandoning his teammates to an early playoff loss."

"He's talked a lot about you lately," Sahar said, "and believes he has a job for you that will make up for whatever you lost in drachmas."

"Drachmas," James said, shaking his big head. "In those days you weren't supposed to leave the country with more than a 150 dollars' worth of Greek money.

When I walked through passport control, I looked almost as big as I am now." He tapped his midsection where the drachmas had been.

"No more drachmas," I told Henderson. "All Euros now, and no more currency restrictions. No need for money smuggling."

Sahar and James were both silent for a moment. These are lawyers, I realized, paid to talk at five or more dollars a minute. I should have used some professorial euphemism for "smuggling."

James looked at his watch and said we should get to his office for the appointment with Will Franklin of Saintsbury and Herndon. James's office was exactly the size of Sahar's, so it was hard to tell which Henderson was first on the letterhead.

"James, do you mind if I tape this conversation?"

"I doubt Franklin would agree."

"What about bringing in one of your secretaries to take shorthand?"

"Those secretaries are long dead, Key, and besides I doubt that Franklin will want anyone else in the room."

"Someone has to be smuggled out of Algeria, is that it, James?"

"Not exactly smuggled. Let's say liberated. But I'd rather let Franklin tell you himself, because he may have some new ideas since I talked with him last."

Franklin did not look like any lawyer I'd ever seen—in person or on TV. In fact, he looked like my image of Ann's attorney. Franklin was a smaller, junior version of that former wrestler who was governor of Minnesota. Either Franklin had shaved his head this morning, or he had been bald at birth. James could have gone to Franklin's body builder and put that fat into the steel beneath Franklin's blue suit, blue shirt, and blue tie. His eyes were brown.

"Nice to meet an author," he said. "James gave me your basketball book. He's a bit bigger now, isn't he?"

"But just as ugly," I said, to see how close this Franklin guy and James were. Not very, because Franklin was a bit taken aback by a white guy calling a black guy ugly, maybe because Franklin was on the ugly side himself. This was no time to be the new QCC nice guy. The negotiations would get rough, and the lawyers had the weight and ugliness advantage.

Franklin looked at his watch. Lawyers were like players, very aware of the twenty-four-second clock. $2.50, $2.50, $2.50.

Franklin began, as if reading from some script projected on the wall behind me, "Our firm represents an entity that has a serious interest in seeing another entity transferred from the country of current residence."

James interrupted and explained to me that "entity" could mean a person or a group or a corporation. Someone asking something.

"James has given me some details," I told Franklin. "It sounds to me like there's some risk involved here, so please speak as plainly as possible."

"Ah yes," Franklin said, "James said you'd want our proposal direct. All right then, my client wants a woman out of Algeria. I assume you know about the situation there. This woman started a feminist group when she was at the university. The organization became more and more radical in their opposition to something called the Family Code and offended the repressive government. When the state outlawed her organization and brought serious charges against her, she went into hiding. After the fundamentalists issued a fatwa on her life, she was wounded in an assassination attempt, possibly staged by the government. If she is arrested, she would serve a lengthy sentence, but being in jail might not protect her from the fatwa. So she moves between three or four safe houses in Algiers. But this situation cannot go on forever. One day someone will inform on her or she will be apprehended as she tries to pass through the streets."

Franklin paused and looked at me.

"Okay," I said, "that sounds about right from the research I did on Algeria. Where do I come in and, more importantly, where do I get out?"

"There is someone who can supply a fake American passport to this person."

"No need to be circumspect, Will," said James. "That's me. Being in immigration and criminal law, I know some people who know some unsavory characters."

Like Patrick, I thought, with his forged titles.

"And you want me to go all the way to Algeria to deliver this passport?"

"That's one thing we want," Franklin said.

"How many things are there?"

"Two."

"The second?"

"We want you to go to the airport with this woman. We want you to pretend to be her husband. Her passport would have your last name and your home address in it."

"Wait a minute. Why doesn't she just use the fake passport and leave the country?"

"Because it's very unusual for any woman to come into or leave the country alone. She would be scrutinized very carefully and would probably be identified."

"I don't want to talk myself out of a job here, but why can't she leave with some Algerian woman or man?"

"A woman with an American passport? No, the only way she can escape is if she pretends to be a tourist married to another tourist. Her people there are sure of this."

"Someone who is white and looks innocent," James put in, "like you, Key."

Someone who is white and dumb and deceptive and money-obsessed like me, like Ann's construction of me in her book.

"What does this woman look like?" I asked.

James spoke to Franklin: "He means what color is she."

"Quite light-skinned from the photo I've seen," Franklin said.

"Does she speak English?"

"Yes, but her second language is French, so we don't really know how good her English is."

"Maybe we could both learn sign language."

Both Franklin and James were puzzled.

"I don't speak French. Algerians do. The people at passport control will also speak a little English. If there are any questions, you don't want your woman speaking English with an Algerian accent. You don't want her talking to anyone. You want her dumb as she can be."

Franklin said, "We didn't think through the language issues."

I was feeling confident and said, "This is the kind of touring expertise I get paid for."

I wanted to see if Franklin would shrink from a word like "paid." He asked, "If you agreed to go, when could you do it?"

"I assume I have to be in Algeria for a few days if I'm posing as a tourist. I also know it can take a while to get a tourist visa for Algeria. You need some time with the passport. Have the woman dye her hair blond in the photo you're going to use. Slather on the lipstick. I'd want to walk out with a bimbo. It would have to be during my spring break, which comes up in a month."

"The timing should work," Franklin said. "There is one other thing."

This is the time a former athlete still needs his agent, the late Marv Drinkman, the lawyer who steered me around Europe and then, damn his good-hearted soul, steered me into Terminal Tours.

"You said 'two things.'"

Franklin smiled for the first time. It wasn't pretty on that pink hairless head. He said, "Think of this next thing as ancillary to the second thing. You need to take a woman with you, a person of your choice, preferably not someone to whom you're married."

"So I leave Algeria with a wife and a mistress. Christ, James, what are you getting me into?"

"Low, Key," James said.

Franklin continued, "You and your 'wife' will enter the country together, but she will leave a day after you. Because she's an American traveling on an authentic American passport, is not married to you, and has no legal connection to you, she should have no problems traveling alone."

"So I'm supposed to put another person in jeopardy? No, I can't go along with that."

"Let's think about this," James said. "Maybe there's a solution."

"Do you want to send Sahar with me," I asked him, "and have her wait in Algiers for a day to see if the guy she came with has been shot at the airport for trying to smuggle contraband? Which reminds me, how do I know I'm not escorting one of bin Laden's many daughters?"

Franklin was quick to answer the second question: "We can give you a lot of information about her and even some of her essays translated from the French. Her name is Lalla Kahina, and she's an anti-terrorist, which puts her life at risk in a state accused of using terror to fight a terrorist Islamist movement."

"Okay," I said, "I think I remember reading about her when I was looking into a tour to Algeria." Then I turned to James, "Now do you think Sahar would like to spend spring break in Algiers?"

Henderson was not pleased with this question.

"At her billing rate," he said, "Will's client might not be able to afford you both. But how about this: the 'wife' leaves a day early? There's no possible danger to her. Maybe some hassle at the airport, but she's an authentic American and has no reason to be detained."

"That's better," I said, "unless the Algerians are keeping track of tourists' wives."

"Tourists are monitored," Franklin said, "if they leave Algiers, but this isn't like the old Communist countries. You wouldn't have a minder. Journalists, though, need a special visa and are accompanied wherever they go. The government wants tourists back and will do just about anything to control media reports of any continuing violence."

"Continuing violence" slowed down the conversation. The lawyers looked at me. I looked at them. Then I said, "I can't even begin to think about this without knowing what kind of stakes are involved here."

Franklin said, "We would buy three round-trip tickets...."

"Three?" I said.

"The outgoing half of Ms. Kahina's wouldn't be used."

"Of course, sorry."

"We'd put you up three nights in the best hotel in Algiers, pay you a per diem of $300 each, handle all your transfers...."

I started laughing. "This sounds like a tour package. Next you'll be telling me about the special native rug shop your guide will take me to. What about the fee?"

Franklin didn't laugh. "What would you require?" he asked.

I asked James, "How much does Sahar bill at?"

"It varies with clients, but nothing below $300 an hour."

"Okay, let me see: three nights and four days in Algiers is about a hundred hours. At $300 an hour, that's a thirty-thousand dollar fee."

"That's kind of high, Key," James said.

"Call in Sahar and see if she'll go for that."

Henderson and Franklin looked at each other.

Franklin said, "I'll have to talk to my client. Have you considered the good you would be doing, Mr. Keever?"

"I have," I said, "and that's why I'm asking only thirty to risk my life."

"We wouldn't ask you or anyone to do this if we thought you were risking your life."

"Maybe not literally. I don't really worry about a shootout at the airport. But if something goes wrong with this plot of yours, I could be in Algeria for more than spring vacation. I have a job I like, a daughter getting married, a new significant other. In short, a life."

"I understand, but Ms. Kahina is literally risking her life with an escape attempt. You'd be saving her life. James tells me you used to be great when the pressure was on, but we wouldn't want to engage you if you felt you couldn't handle the job."

I did wonder just what James's role was. He'd obviously coached Franklin: "pressure on," handle the job like "handle the rock," give the old point guard a challenge. James was billing this meeting and might be getting a percentage of my fee. But he might also be trying to help out an old broken-down teammate in a time of need. Or even this woman in Algeria.

"There's a lot to think about," I said, "for all of us."

That was it. We all told each other how valuable our discussion had been, and Franklin left.

"What about this guy?" I asked Henderson.

"He and his firm are straight up. You'd get your money, for sure. But it would come through me because Saintsbury and Herndon don't want to be in the paper if something goes wrong."

"Who's the client?"

"I don't know. At first, I thought it was Ford money, but now I think it's some feminist organization that wants Kahina out of Algeria. Apparently, her writings are quite well known, at least by those who read French."

"How old is she?"

"Looks about twenty-five in the photo I saw."

Between Sara and Kara in years and a death sentence on her head. Twenty-five and confined to three safe houses, worse than my security van and the old House of Usher. Franklin was right. There was some good I could do—if I was willing to risk my life for thirty thousand dollars, which would cover Sara's tuition, apartment expenses, small wedding, and my own double bed.

"I can understand why me, James. But why you?"

"I represent a lot of Arabic-speaking clients here in Dearborn."

"Where's Sahar from?"

"Her parents were from Zanzibar."

"James, tell me you don't wear one of those Farrakhan bow ties when you're meeting with black folks."

"You're not as dumb as you can look. No bow tie, but I converted when I married Sahar."

Be damned, I thought, big James got himself an Ann, someone to dance him around.

"So, James, basically I can't trust you. I mean the information you give me. You're invested here."

"Sahar is, yes, as a woman. But Kahina is not a practicing Muslim. She's a little like you, a nonbeliever in a real tight spot. Read her stuff. See if you think she's worth saving. This is your kind of job, Key. Clock be winding down for Lalla, buzzer could blow on her any minute. Her time may be short as Alice's."

So James did get around to reading *Passing On*. He was speaking me to as a brother and as a player, but I couldn't let that shit get through to me. I had to think hard about this. Algeria, fucking Algeria, without a doubt one of the worst places on earth. A trip there would be no Merchant-Ivory soft-focus production, no ride-the-slide tour. That asshole at *Hell* would love it. I was surprised he hadn't thought of it. "Greece off-season," Ryan said about the Lavrion piece, "doesn't sound that dangerous, as long as you take mittens and a hat. If you want to keep writing for us, we need you to suffer. Nobody really gives a damn about foreigners' suffering. You're an American. You need to suffer in some shithole outside the USA. Return with the story. That's what people want to read. Your suffering assuages the national guilt."

"What national guilt?"

"For having so much money that even a publication like *Hell* can prosper."

Chapter 12

When thirty thousand dollars and two lives are on the table, it's easy to remember what the players said. On the plane back to Cincinnati, I wrote everything down. Teaching only one course, I had plenty of time to read a lot about Algeria and Lalla Kahina's translated writings. The ones smuggled out since the death sentence was pronounced were partly autobiographical. My grad students would have killed—or died—for this material. Lalla grew up in a village on the Mediterranean coast east of Algiers. Her family was middle class, but she needed and got a scholarship to attend the university in Algiers. There she became interested in the plight of women, particularly poor and divorced women under the recently passed Family Code, which appeased Islamists by defining women as minors, requiring widows or divorcees to marry their former husband's brother (if he wanted), legalizing polygamy, and severely limiting what a woman could inherit. The organization Lalla founded—Association for the Victory of Women's Rights—was tolerated until she graduated, got a job teaching history in an Algiers high school, started agitating for political change, and became a minor celebrity when she embarrassed a government minister in a television debate. She was fired from her job. After demonstrations against this action, the government outlawed her group. Then came the fatwa and a bomb outside Lalla's home that killed two of her associates and wounded her in the leg.

These facts about her life emerge from her writings, but they are essays on historical and political subjects, not the narcissistic narratives my American students were composing. There is nothing creative about Lalla's prose, just a recitation of what she has done, the consequences, and what she has observed. Maybe her essays would be called Cognitive Non-Fiction, offering knowledge and understanding. Instead of constructing a water slide, Lalla uses her personal experiences to exemplify the plight of Algerian women. Wearing the veil and passing through streets from one safe house to another, Lalla is like every Algerian woman who fears being attacked—and possibly murdered—in public for the impiety of an uncovered face. Unable to work, supported by her male relatives, confined to shuttered rooms, Lalla the fugitive represents millions of other suppressed women. Lalla never knows if her travel—her walk or ride through Algiers—will lead to a safe house, to prison, or to her death, a terminal tour. No wonder she is willing to risk a flight to the safety of Paris or Detroit or wherever she would end up.

Lalla Kahina's piecemeal autobiography made me embarrassed by my aversion to traveling with the terminal, by my autobiography, even by my attempt to save Alice's life. What had I been risking with that tour? A few weeks' pay and Ann's wrath, but I wasn't risking my life, not the way Lalla was by staying in or trying to leave Algeria. I knew I shouldn't let guilt influence my thinking. But as I thought about the practical details, the image of Lalla putting on a veil and passing from one safe house to another kept interfering with my coach-like calculations, the game plan's necessities.

1) The ticket has to look plausible. Mr. and Mrs. Keever spend three nights in Paris (at Franklin's expense), go to Algiers to escape the March cold of France,

return for two or three nights to see museums they missed when first passing through.

2) The people have to look plausible. Mr. and Mrs. Keever should be wearing stereotypical tourist clothing. If one fake wife isn't the same size as the other, the Keevers will have to bring tourist clothing for Lalla. There has to be enough American luggage for each of the wives to carry out.

3) The American Mrs. Keever's early return has to be easy and smooth. Maybe she's sick. A fight with her husband? A screw up by the travel agent on the ticket? Or maybe she's just one of those heroic lesbians traveling on her own.

4) How to switch one Mrs. Keever for the other resisted me. This was not a bait and switch operation. I might have to depend on Lalla's people there to figure out a way to make the quick change.

The main problem was thinking of someone to collaborate with me in this elaborate ruse. Algeria wasn't like telling Ann about basketball and letting her work my facts into her fiction. I couldn't just make up a companion to fit Henderson's plot. A terminal patient would be perfect. Lauren would probably want to do it for the material, but I couldn't very well go on a vacation with one of my students. June wouldn't go to Algeria to force Richard's hand. Rakhshanda wasn't the right color. Eden was too young. I couldn't ask Kara. But when I realized there was no one I could ask, I considered telling her about the trip to see if she would volunteer.

Then Sara and Bucky dropped in one evening. I didn't know if this was new familial casualness or if they wanted to catch me off-guard. I turned down the volume on a Pistons-Heat game but couldn't activate the camera. No shenanigans or jokes by the young couple. In fact, standing in the middle of the living room they seemed rather grim. Even before Sara said anything I wondered if her mother told her I was fucking Jason or vice versa. By the looks of Bucky, who kept glancing at the game on TV, Sara was running this show. She didn't ask what there was to eat, not even if I'd turn off the TV. I could see this was going to be a quick strike.

"It's decided," she said, "we're going to look for an apartment during spring break, and Bucky's parents will come out the last weekend of the break for a civil ceremony. That way, you won't have to make a dorm payment for the second half of the semester."

She added, "I hope you'll want to come."

"That's hard and unfair," I told her. "Of course, I'll come to your wedding. I love you, and I trust I'll come to love Bucky."

Given what I'd told Ann, maybe this wasn't the right thing to say. I realized too late, though, so took a look at Bucky. He was checking to see if both his boots were tied and were not tied to each other.

I continued on, "My questioning of your decision wasn't personal. I'd have questioned any two eighteen-year-olds. I know you're not just any two eighteen-year-olds, but even so I wanted to challenge your thinking, make sure this is what you both wanted. But now, as you say, it's decided, I'll do whatever I can to help you."

"Thanks, Dad," Sara said from the middle of the room.

"Thank you, Mr. Keever," Bucky said, but neither made a move to come over to the sofa to give me an appreciative hug or handshake. I had to get up and go to them. Both of them were stiff in my hugs, and I was convinced that Ann had told them my lie. Who would listen to the views on marriage of a man who was two-timing his girlfriend with one of his male students? But I had no way to ask Sara, and I decided it didn't make a difference, not right now.

"I'm afraid I don't have any champagne," I said, "but there's some red wine and some beer in the fridge. Will you sit down and have a toast? I'll even turn off the game. I can tape it and watch it later."

This last was meant as a joke, but Sara and Bucky weren't laughing.

"Not tonight, Dad," Sara said, "we've got to get back to the dorm to study. We just wanted to tell you what we've decided."

"Well, this is certainly better than an email, but I feel there's something that isn't being said here."

Given that opening, Sara spoke up: "If you really want to know, Dad, we feel you tried to frighten Bucky last time. We don't want to hang around and be scared again."

"I'm sorry," I said, "I write about some hell every three months. I suppose it's on my mind more than it should be. When I found out Bucky's parents are Catholics, I thought it was a consideration. But I am sorry. And if you sit down, I won't talk about divorce statistics, I promise."

Another attempt at levity that failed. Sara and Bucky seemed to be embarrassed by my efforts to restore some normalcy. Sara said she'd come for dinner soon, and Bucky thanked me for being honest with them, and they backed out the door.

I'll be damned, I thought, not even practicing Catholics are afraid of hell. It had become a synecdoche or metonymy. Not even Algeria was really hell, a place of fiery, eternal incarceration.

The following night I told Kara about Sara's visit, and then I told her everything about the proposed trip to

Algeria: the enthusiasm at *Hell*, Henderson's plot. I held back nothing including the fee I was asking for.

Her first question was, "Could I take my cameras?"

"You'd consider going?"

"What about the cameras?"

"It would be one camera. Not the Hasselblad. A tourist's camera. Point and shoot. You couldn't look like a journalist. You may not even be able to leave the hotel grounds."

"Those lawyers up in Michigan would pay all our expenses in Paris and Algiers and pay me $300 a day to boot?"

"I think so. I'd offer you part of the fee, but I refuse to sweeten this risky deal."

"What could go wrong, Michael?"

"For you, nothing that I can think of, and I've been running this in my head for quite a while. For me...I don't know. If Lalla Kahina is identified at the airport...that I'd rather not think about too much."

"But you're willing to take the risk?"

"I need that money. I'll never have the chance again to make that chunk of money."

"And?"

"'And?'"

"And what else?"

"I don't know. I guess if someone asks you something like this, something that could save that person's life, well, it's hard to turn down. But I don't mean to pressure you. The best I can promise you is the chance to see Paris."

"What about Frisky? Could he come along?"

"Frisky would need to be detained in a kennel of your choice."

"I'd be traveling on my own passport, right? Because, unlike Sara, I'm not sure I want to get married just yet."

"Glad to hear that. Because if I'm the person you're considering, I'm not divorced just yet. But we would have to pretend to be married in Algiers. I expect the people at the hotel see passports of women who haven't taken their husband's name. But if you go, you should get a gold band to wear."

"This could be our honeymoon. I hope they have single beds."

"This could be, but we wouldn't want to call attention to ourselves."

"Would I walk around with a scarf over my face?"

"You may be joking, but that's not a bad idea. I've seen Western women do that in Egypt. They want to be sensitive to local practices."

"Would I be able to shop for a rug?"

"Another good idea. Yes, you should bring back the bounty of beautiful Algeria."

"This sounds like fun, Michael."

"And you're beginning to sound like Jody and the other undergrads. This isn't going to be fun until you and Lalla and I get to Paris. I don't want you to think that."

"Oh coach Keever, such a hardass. I suppose you'll tell me to run a few suicides as punishment."

"Let's not talk about the suicides right now."

"Okay, but I want to go."

"Tell me again in two days."

I didn't want to recruit Kara, but I also didn't want to talk her out of accompanying me so I didn't ask her why she "really" wanted to go. Fun and photos couldn't be her only reasons for this kind of tour. I wondered if Kara wanted to prove something to me. Or to someone else, perhaps the mother Kara hadn't visited in the hospital.

Two days later, I got an email from Kara: "I know what happened when you took old Mr. Rorque to Lourdes. This is my written acknowledgement that you have explained the risks of going to Algeria. I waive any right to hold you legally responsible for whatever might happen there. I do want to go. Please feel free to forward this email to *Hell* and the lawyers in Michigan. When you do, ask them if they'll advance the per diem so we can eat in a manner appropriate to two people engaged in a lifesaving mission."

Mission. Alice's was the remission mission. This trip would be the tuition remission mission. I'd tell Sara about it at the wedding reception. I'd show off Kara's and my tans, and tell Sara the truth, finally: that I went to hell so she could go to QCC.

I called Henderson to see what he'd heard from Franklin.

"His client is grumbling about the fee."

"That's too bad," I said, "because we need three nights in Paris on each side of the main trip. So it doesn't look like we're just passing through Algeria, you know what I mean?"

"You said 'we.'"

"That's right. I have a volunteer."

"How much did you lie to her about the risks?"

"I'm playing this one straight up, James. She knows everything, and made some good suggestions about keeping up pretenses."

"There's stuff you didn't think of?"

"You know how women are, James. The clothing and shopping angle. By the way, we need to know how tall Lalla Kahina is, how big she is. We also need to talk about the wife switch."

"Okay, what about the timing?"

"The volunteer teaches at Queen City, so it's spring break or nothing."

"I'll call Franklin and get back to you."

"When you decide, I need something in writing James."

"Franklin will balk at that."

"From Henderson and Henderson then. 'You will pay me thirty thousand dollars to deliver an important document to Algeria.' It can be simple but something my lawyer down here will approve."

"You've become legalistic, Key."

"Two-on-one, that I'm used to. But there are three of you lawyers up there, and Ann's down here, so I need some paper. Our late agent would insist. You remember how it was in Athens. Contracts always fucked up, players cheated out of their money."

In a week, the deal was done. I got all the expenses and fee I asked for. Henderson and Henderson bought our tickets and advanced us the per diem. *Hell* was excited. Dirk Ryan mentioned again the life insurance policy to let me know I'd finally come through for them. It was time to narrow the focus, fourth-quarter time, when the point earns his keep by controlling the action. "Money" is the players' term for last-quarter guys like me, either shooters or passers. I met with my autobiographers but remember nothing of what was said. I didn't communicate with Sara or Ann. I no longer worried who Sceptic was. Kara and I quizzed and tested each other almost every night, looking for advantages, searching for hidden dangers. We set up a contingency plan: if anything went wrong for me at the airport, Kara would tell our rescue story to whomever she thought best. Assuming she would talk to Lalla in Paris, Kara read her essays. "We have to do this, Michael," she said. "You have to get her out of there." I finished writing what you've been reading, getting onto my hard drive what was on my tapes, in my notes, in my head. Just in case, I thought, Sara and Ann want to know the truth. I gave Kara a key to my apartment and told her about the *Passing Through* file. If I didn't come back, she'd know the facts too. Non-fiction. I liked that idea. With the open ending of *Passing On*, I'd concealed a truth in an attempt to pass on hope. This time, I don't expect publication. I'm just putting down the truth for the people I have loved and do love.

Part IV

Chapter 13

March in Paris was not much different from March in Cincinnati. It rained most of the time, and we had to drink and eat inside or huddled next to gas heaters in the outdoor cafés. Kara had never experienced jet lag, so we spent lots of hours in the hotel, preparation for the more luxurious confinement of the Sheraton Club des Pins Resort and Towers in Algiers. We did buy large golf umbrellas and walk some avenues, but the light was bad for photography. We ate in the Greek tavernas of the Latin Quarter so I could show off my Greek and introduce Kara to next summer's food. But no matter where we put our bodies our minds were on Lalla, what she would think of Parisian girls wearing miniskirts beneath long coats, the images of nude bodies in cosmetic ads displayed in pharmacy windows, a couple kissing in a back booth of an Isle St. Louis café. How would she feel about just walking hand in hand with a person not your spouse, being afraid only of getting splashed by a bus or being poked in the eye by another umbrella? Pretending to be Lalla and a companion became a game for Kara and me, perhaps a way to cover our anxieties about entering and leaving Algeria.

***

"The last time I was in Paris I went to a lot of swimming pools. There's one just two blocks away."
"What days do women go?"

"It's not like the baths. Women and men swim in the same pool at the same hours. They even take showers together."

"They are free?"

"The people are, but you must pay to get into the pools."

***

"Wow, look at all those newspapers."

"You can't get those French papers in Algiers?"

"Not even some of the Arabic ones on this kiosk."

"Would you like to buy some?"

"I would, but I have no money until I can find a job."

***

"Did you see them?"

"Yes, I'd read that many Muslim women wear the veil or scarf here, especially in Algerian neighborhoods. It's a way to prevent trouble for yourself. Otherwise, the old men will put their hands on you, and the young boys will call you whore. I would rather live in a convent. At least those women chose their lives and clothes. And don't have to have contact with men."

"Would you rather I not hold your hand?"

***

"Salut."

"I don't believe I should be drinking champagne so soon after leaving home."

"Drink up. Maybe you'll change your mind about contact with men."

"Did I tell you about the trick a fundamentalist teacher in our school played? He asked the students to bring in corks for a scientific experiment, something about flotation. When a few of the kids did show up with corks, he scolded them for living in a household that drank alcohol. No one else would have corks."

"Drink up. It's our last night in Paris."

"But we'll be back."

"With tans. Salut to the sun."

***

There was plenty of sun on the famous Bay of Algiers and the white city surrounding it as our plane approached Boudemeine airport east of the city. After we went through passport control, I spotted a man holding up a sign that said "Sheraton Club des Pins."

Kara and I walked over to him. His blazer and sign had a little Sheraton logo on them, but I knew about Internet "phishers." The guy could be a phisher of women and men.

"Who am I?" I asked to throw him off.

"I also think that," he said.

"Okay, who are you?"

"The man that drives you?"

"And we are?"

He reached in his pocket and pulled out a sheet of paper.

"Mr. and Mrs. Keever," he read.

"Will you take us to the Kasbah before we go to the hotel?"

"Michael," Kara said.

"You make laugh, Mr. Keever," the driver said and forced a little laugh.

"Just being careful," I told him—and Kara.

The hotel looked like two white cruise ships that had not passed in the night: one had hit the other broadside at midship, and they were now welded together. They were sitting a hundred yards from the beach and were surrounded by trees, flowers, and a ten-foot wall. The grounds reminded me of Spring Grove cemetery. The two guards at the gate knew our driver and didn't ask who we were. They weren't wearing pistols, but we did have to weave around truck-bomb barricades to reach the gate and I noticed a submachine gun standing in the guardhouse. I trusted there were two.

No dying client had ever paid me to stay in such a hotel, which just proved that rescue missions were more lucrative than terminal tours. The Sheraton had its own private beach (with fences and guards at each end), outdoor and indoor pools, an exercise and game room, a spa, four restaurants with different cuisines, everything but a roller coaster and water slide for my students. Our eighth-floor room had a view of the sea and Algiers to the west.

"Welcome to the world of professional travel writers," I told Kara while she took some photos from our balcony. "Free, all free. All you have to do is write a thousand words with superlatives in every sentence. You wouldn't even have to lie about this place."

"Forget *Hell* and *Prodigies*. Let's start *Sybarites*. Why do we have only three nights here?"

"Two nights for you."

"I could have left after you."

"When you're riding to the airport with someone who doesn't have the Sheraton logo on his jacket, you may feel differently."

Kara's pleasure was not to be diminished.

"I know why the mullahs want to get in and hack us to pieces," she said. "This is their idea of heaven. Paradise on earth. An oasis with plenty of water. And we get it without dying."

"Life as the afterlife. I like it."

"And no waiting," Kara said.

"I wonder what Lalla will think about the hotel."

"And about spending the night with a man she's just met," Kara said, returning from the balcony and flopping on the king-sized bed.

"Not so different from Algerians' arranged marriages. 'What did you say your name was?' What a honeymoon. The husband's relatives are standing around outside, waiting to make sure the bride is a virgin. You'd have to smuggle a live chicken into the room to bloody the sheets if you had dillydallied with one of your village homeboys."

We dillied and dallied for two days and two nights. We spent hours by the pool, despite its associations with Alice. We went to the beach and took our lunch under an umbrella. Though there were few other guests, we projected the illusion of honeymooners, a private zone which others, whether guests or hotel employees, were discouraged from entering or even observing too closely. In our safe hotel, we tried to imagine Lalla's series of safe houses. What if the toilet overflowed? Who would make the call? What if you had a toothache or sliced your hand peeling vegetables? Would you be afraid to talk on the phone? Could you get a pizza delivered in Algiers? What if the person bringing you food was run over in the street or arrested? Could your lover come and visit on Saturday nights? Were there Saturday nights in a Muslim country? If you suffered from seasonal affective disorder, as I did, how would you get any sun? Were safe houses really houses or basement apartments? What if your father or mother died? Or your sister got married? Or you wanted to raise your voice, scream out against your contracted life?

Since I was the one who would be walking through passport control with Lalla, I fixated on how she passed through the streets from safe house to safe house. She'd have to have a male companion. Would he be her "father," "brother," or "husband?" Would they pretend to be sauntering, looking in shop windows in broad daylight when others were in the streets? Would they move slowly in the late afternoon heat, when others would be sleeping? Would they prefer the night or a car and risk being stopped by a random police roadblock? How much would they dare to carry? The advantage Lalla had in Algiers was the veil or scarf. In the streets, it was her curse and her deception. At the airport, she would have to hide behind her bleached blond hair, sunglasses, lipstick, tourist clothes, and me.

After a morning at the beach and too much lunch on the second day, we went to our room for a nap. Before falling asleep in the heavily curtained room, I thought Lalla must do a lot of this. PT. Passing time, not playing time. When I woke up, Kara wasn't beside me. She wasn't in the bathroom. I assumed she was down in the lobby poking around in the jewelry or crafts shop. I turned on CNN and watched for a while. When I got up, I found a note on the floor: "I'm asking the concierge to arrange a quick visit to the Martyrs' Memorial for some photos. Be right back."

I hustled down to the lobby to talk with the concierge. After explaining that this was a completely safe trip with an utterly dependable driver, he laughed and said, "Your wife was wearing a scarf on her head and around her face. In her trousers, she looked like an Egyptian. When she and the driver left, she was sitting in the back like a proper lady."

"Why did you let her go without her husband?" I asked.

"But, sir," he said, "do not American women go where they want without husbands?"

He had a point. I hoped the people at the airport felt the same way when Kara got there. But leaving the hotel was a dumb and risky thing to do, which is just what I told Kara when she showed up about fifteen minutes after my talk with the concierge: "dumb and risky."

"I wasn't pretending to be married to my driver when we got to the memorial. Besides, it was so damned hot there not a person was stirring. Now I understand why the terrorists attack at night."

"Why didn't you wake me up?"

"Because I knew you'd never go if I asked. I decided I'd rather have this argument after rather than before the fact."

"So you knew there'd be an argument one day before 'you know what,' and you still went?"

"'You know what' is your operation, Michael. I wanted to have something to show for this trip besides the per diem and my sunburn."

"But going off by yourself was selfish. You could have been disappeared."

"And then you'd have no one to switch with Lalla?"

"I didn't mean that. I was thinking about you."

"So was I. You weren't thinking about me when you went to Greece by yourself."

The best I could respond to this was, "Greeks don't cut the throats of foreigners."

"Besides," Kara said, "I was also thinking of you. How are you going to prove to *Hell* you've been to Algiers if all you have are photos of the Sheraton?"

"I can get photos off the net."

"Maybe, but these will have my name on them. I also got some shots of people in the streets from the car. They may not be the greatest quality, but they'll have an authentic blur to them. You know, as if I was afraid to stop and shoot."

"You should have stopped at the hotel gate and passed up this little tour."

"You've already said that, Michael. If you're this stressed about a ride that has already happened and turned out fine, how are you going to pull off leaving with Lalla?"

There was a long answer to that question. It involved about fifteen years of competitive basketball. The point guard has the ball in his hands, he makes the decisions in the last few minutes. I was always nervous when my other players were choosing between pass, shoot, or dribble. The short answer was, "Because I'll be in control."

"If you say so," Kara said, but without much enthusiasm. I didn't know if she believed me or was lying to me to keep up my confidence.

After Kara cooled down in the shower and after the guard called "Low Key" came down from his fear, Kara showed me the digital photos she'd taken. The images of the Memorial—three intertwining concrete palm fronds as tall as the Eiffel Tower—were good but boilerplate tourist shots. The photos of people were, as Kara promised, vivid proof that we'd been in Algiers. Either Algerians were afraid out on the sidewalks or the moving car made them look as anxious as I was waiting in the lobby for Kara.

Maybe it was good that we had the spat about Kara's leaving the hotel because our last night's dinner was more relaxed than I expected. Although we were one of two couples in a large dining room and had plenty of privacy, we didn't speak at all about Lalla or the next day. Instead, we talked about QCC, about what we thought we'd be doing next year, about our families—how they'd be shaking their heads at Kara's photos of the hotel and grounds. After a couple of glasses of wine, the subject of Patrick came up, and on this last night together, I started feeling guilty again about the trip to Greece I hadn't taken. If something went wrong at the airport, I wanted Kara to know the truth from me, not from the computer file back in Cincinnati. Or maybe I was just trying to assert some control and purify myself for the test at passport control.

"There's something I want to confess," I told Kara.

"Me too," she said.

"You too?"

"Yes, but you go first."

"I've been wanting to tell you…I never went to Lavrion."

"That's not much of a surprise," Kara said, surprising me. "I always felt there was something fishy about that trip. The details in your piece were a little fuzzy. So where did you go, Cancun with one of your students?"

I told Kara about the trip to Vermont; I explained my embarrassment about journalistic ethics, my lack of money. I apologized and asked her pardon.

"You didn't trust me to understand, did you?" she asked.

I didn't answer and she filled the gap: "That's okay, Michael, because I didn't trust you. That's why I wrote you those anonymous emails."

"Jesus fucking Christ, you're Sceptic. Do you have any idea how those emails scared me? The wacky things I did because of them?"

"I'm really sorry, Michael. I didn't understand how much they affected you until that night you told me about your going along with Sara getting married."

"You could have admitted it then."

"I wanted to, but I was afraid. Just like you were afraid to tell me about not going to Lavrion. You know, if you'd told me the truth about that trip, I'd never have found out the truth about Alice."

I just shook my head. Kara was the one person I hadn't suspected. On the court, I'd made a career out of blind passes. Kara was my blind spot. Of course she was. Like athletes, we'd sweated together, played off and on with each other's bodies.

"I still don't understand why you went to all that work," I said.

I'd told my students, "Travel to learn about other people and other places." In the last few hours I was learning more about Kara than I wanted to know. Learning, too, that I was not in control, not the way I wanted to be.

"The emails started out as play," Kara said, "as a game with you. But your answers—or evasions—piqued my old reporter's curiosity, so I kept pressing."

"All the way to Lebanon?"

"Once I got going, I wanted to know the truth. I was interested in you, but I was also upset with you for not taking me to Greece."

"Upset enough to expose the fiction of Alice's recovery."

"No, Michael. That's between you and your readers. I just wanted to see if you would tell the truth to me."

"Why not just ask me?"

"I was waiting for you to choose."

Somehow this sounded like Ann, and made me angrier.

"And you also wanted to make sure you went along on the next trip, right?"

Kara smiled. "Maybe so when I wrote the emails. But I didn't exactly blackmail you to come here, did I?"

"No, but you did get yourself some photos for your portfolio."

"And you got some photos for your piece. But I can see you're not in a pardoning mood. I just want you to know before you leave with Lalla that I'm sorry if those emails brought you here."

So that's the missing motive for Kara's tour. Guilt—what I thought never moved her.

As a long-time fuck-up, I wasn't used to receiving apologies. This one eased the truth out of me. "No," I told Kara, "Sceptic didn't bring me here. Lying did. Because I lied about being Greek-American, Ann lied in *Passing Off*. Because of that book, I lied in *Passing On*. Because Richard hired me with false expectations, I ended up lying to you. I don't remember what Dante did to liars, but they should have long chains attached to them, the linkages a single lie can create."

If I've been passing through, I thought, I've been dragging the chain with me. Carrying the ball and dragging the chain.

I put my head in my hands and looked down at my unfinished couscous.

"And now," I said, "we're both lying to the hotel and authorities."

The hovering waiter, our personal waiter in the almost empty dining room, thought we were through eating and started to remove our plates. We let him.

Kara had her chance to say "you should have" or "you could have," but instead she said, "Let's not be too quick to honor the truth, not until the three of us are sitting around one of those gas heaters in Paris."

The waiter was standing at a respectful distance, pretending to be pleased with his job.

Kara said, "We need to be like our man there. Wait. Later we can decide who should be pardoned for what."

I thanked her, and we went up to our room. This was no honeymoon. Kara watched CNN, and I sat on the balcony with its view of the sea and Algiers. I thought of the balcony in Athens where Alice and I waited through the night, waited until we could find a doctor to pronounce her death sentence. Lalla was waiting in one of her safe houses. I couldn't imagine what might be in her mind now. I didn't try to imagine what was in Kara's mind. And I refused to imagine all the things that could pass through my mind. Imagining was a form of lying. Keep it simple, Keever.

Chapter 14

In the morning Kara and I didn't look back. We were in the present, rehearsing the next few hours. We'd settle our differences in Paris and Cincinnati. I went down to the concierge to start in motion the switch that Lalla's people had set up. I told him my wife was ill, and we wouldn't be able to leave the hotel and shop for a rug as planned. But I had the number of a store that an Algerian friend in the U.S. had given us, and the owner and his wife were going to bring a few small rugs for my wife to look at in the room.

"These merchants won't have any trouble getting into the compound, will they?"

"Of course not, Mr. Keever. If you have the name of the man, I will call the guard at the gate. And when the merchant gets here, I will call you."

"Great. I believe Mr. Liabes will have his wife along to help him carry the rugs."

The concierge rolled his eyes, as he'd probably been taught to do for Western guests who might find offensive Algerian males' treatment of women.

"No problem, Mr. Keever. Would you like me to call for our house doctor?"

"No," I said, and now it was my turn to roll my eyes. I rubbed my stomach and said, "Just tourist problems."

I went back upstairs and called Mr. Liabes's number. The entry was set. Now Kara and I had to wait for our call from the concierge.

Two minutes after the concierge phoned, one of the bellboys, of which there seemed hundreds, knocked at the door. Mr. Liabes was next to him, and Lalla was standing behind her "husband." He was carrying a couple of rugs under his arm. Lalla had a bunch of rolled rugs in a cotton bag on her back. Mr. Liabes was about fifty, portly, a successful rug merchant with smooth hands, not one of those suspicious-looking lean young men that Sheraton had converted into bellboys. He was wearing a gray suit and open-collared yellow shirt. He was selling rugs, after all, not bonds. Lalla was in a loose-fitting blue robe and had a scarf covering her hair and the bottom half of her face. I couldn't see her eyes because she kept her head bowed in the presence of the bellboy. I welcomed Mr. Liabes and tipped the bellboy. But he didn't leave. "I wait here," he said and nodded at his distrusted fellow citizens.

Inside the room, as agreed beforehand, Mr. Liabes gave me his rug pitch, describing each one of the carpets, while Lalla and Kara did their quick change. They silently shook hands and Lalla took off her robe and scarf. Underneath she was wearing rolled-up jeans and a black tee shirt. The blond hair was a decent match. The rug patter went on as Kara put on the robe, and Lalla showed her how to correctly wrap the scarf. We all acted as if the room was bugged, not because there was any chance of that or even because the bellboy was standing out in the hall but, I think, because no one wanted to interfere with the illusion. Kara picked one of the largest rugs; Mr. Liabes complimented her on her choice. He and I pretended to haggle over the price while Lalla rolled up Kara's clothes, camera, and cosmetic kit in the space left by the rug. She had her passport and ticket in a fanny pack. Kara put on Lalla's one-size-fits-all sandals. Mr. Liabes had a carry-on in his car. In two hours Kara should be on the flight to Paris.

"Thank you very much, Mr. Keever," Mr. Liabes said in a big moneymaking voice. He beckoned to Kara. Then he motioned me closer to hear what he whispered to her: "Outside I will curse you in Arabic. Keep your face down." Kara nodded, and I put the bag of rugs on her back. I kissed her goodbye on the forehead, the only bare skin I could find. She bent over to disguise the two inches of height she had on Lalla. I opened the door and tipped the bellboy for waiting. Then I stood and watched while he led Mr. Liabes and the bowed and shuffling Kara to the elevator. Halfway there, Mr. Liabes turned and barked at his carrier, which made her even more downcast. I hoped Kara could keep the robe, along with the rug and her photos, for making this trip possible.

I hung the "Do Not Disturb" sign on the door and double-locked. No maid could get in and recognize the woman devoted to the lives of maids. Lalla was looking around the bathroom, the double sink, the glass-encased shower, the toilet and bidet, the spread of cosmetics and soaps, everything but the little paper cover on the toilet. I walked to the door and said, "Welcome to America."

Lalla turned and smiled. Maybe it was the flattering light of luxury hotels, but she looked younger than twenty-five and prettier than her photograph. Her nose was French, not Mediterranean like Kara's. Her eyes were darker, her skin just as light, and the contrast made Lalla look exotic, her national origin mysterious. Wearing sunglasses and tourist clothes, she was close enough to Kara to get through the lobby.

"You possess a toilet like this one, and you came to remove me?"

"No," I told her, "this bathroom is about half the size of my apartment."

I extended my hand and said, "I'm Michael Keever. You must be Kara Schmidt."

Lalla shook my hand and said, "Tomorrow I will be, but in this moment I am Lalla Kahina."

She spoke formally, like Rakhshanda but with a French accent, and Lalla's usages were sometimes a little off. But since English was, I found out, her fourth language—after Algerian Arabic, classical Arabic, and French—and since just about all we did for sixteen of our twenty-four hours together was talk, I've not exactly transcribed here Lalla's sometimes curious locutions. And couldn't if I wanted to because I had left in the States anything that might identify me as a journalist, such as a tape recorder and laptop. I didn't even bring a notebook or pad of paper.

Lalla was soft-spoken; I didn't have to remind her to keep her voice down. Only ships at sea could see our balcony, so she was free to check out the view after inspecting all the furniture, including the king-size bed. I pointed to the rather short sofa and said, "I'll sleep over there."

"Yes, please," she said, "I am a lesbian."

Aaiight. Sure. Just my luck: married to a lesbian. I should have tried to get closer to Lauren to prepare for this one-night stand. Or maybe, like June, Lalla was pretending—to get safely through the night with a strange man.

"Ah," I got out.

"And you are a homosexual, correct?"

"Ah," I managed again, glad this wasn't a job or exit interview.

"Ah, no," I finally said, careful not to express any surprise or disapproval. But I was mystified. I didn't have a moustache. The reputation of Queen City College couldn't have penetrated to Algeria.

"Your gaydar must be off in the hotel," I said.

"What is this 'gaydar'?"

"Like radar. What gay people use to identify other gays."

Then, as if the question was about the weather here in sunny Algeria, I said, "So, why did you believe I was gay?"

"I believed only a homosexual would take the chance you are taking for a lesbian."

I thought about Richard's fear of being mistaken for a sissy. In Algeria or in Lalla's mind, gays are courageous.

"To be completely honest, I didn't suspect you were gay," I said.

The pleasures of international touring: come six thousand miles to Algeria, meet someone for five minutes, and discuss her sexual orientation.

"You don't mention being a lesbian in the essays I've read," I added.

"That was impossible for an Algerian woman. It is bad enough that I am a secular democrat and a feminist and a supporter of Berbers. To confess to homosexuality in a text would require more courage than I have. 'There are no homosexuals in Muslim countries.' You must know this falsity."

"I do now. If there are no homosexuals in Algeria, I guess that shows I'm a breeder."

I'd forgotten again that Lalla's English was not colloquial, so I had to explain "breeder." She thought the word was humorous because it reminded her of Arabic terms for women. This gave me an opening to talk about Sara, being married, being almost divorced, coming here with Kara, my girlfriend and two-night "wife." Lalla then told me about the practice of "temporary marriage" that some Algerian Islamists had imported from Iran. Young women are forced to "marry" for a few hours or days to satisfy the desires of men. If the girls refuse, they are, according to Lalla, raped, then mutilated or killed. Anyone who refused because she was a lesbian would be killed immediately. I commented on the severe penalty for "sexual orientation."

"I hate this phrase in English," Lalla said. "It is also in French. 'Orientation' means turning toward. Literally, facing the orient. But I do not stand in myself and turn around and around, choosing which way I will orient myself. My sexuality is something natural and necessary to me. It is not a choice. Yes, I can choose to act upon it or cover it up, but this is not 'orientation.'"

I nodded, at first simply to go along and then sincerely because I realized how Lalla and I were alike. I'd never thought much about my sexual identity because it was "normal," the default position. But I'd thought a lot about being an athlete, that tropism—it never seemed like a choice—that I'd been following as long as I can remember, long before I was interested in girls. Like Lalla, I could be deprived—by my metal and plastic hip replacement—of living as an athlete, but I had been unable to replace that identity. Husband, father, tour guide, teacher—none of those functions reached as deep down into my bones and sinews and synapses as athlete. The athlete passes through tight spaces and passes timed tests. I had not been able to get beyond that. Maybe I was even in Algeria because of my failure to change, either quickly or slowly.

My identification of Lalla as an athlete was, I admit, a self-centered way to understand her and to more fully sympathize with her plight. The athlete represents freedom from ordinary physical bonds. Lalla should not be in prison, whether figurative or literal.

Maybe the identification was an illusion, a way to keep up my heterosexual courage for the next day. Whatever the source of the identification, afterwards I felt more at ease with this stranger—and now athletic "teammate" if not temporary "wife." I asked Lalla why Muslims were so adamant about denying homosexuality.

"The imams want to control all sexuality," she said. "So they pretend homosexuals do not exist. If they can get away with this lie, they can dictate how women live. They adopt a Family Code that deprives women of basic rights to live alone or bring up their children alone if they are widowed or divorced. A woman like me who chose to live by herself is a scandal and threat."

She paused and asked, "Did you have your penis cut at birth?"

Discussing sexual orientation was one thing. This was an entirely different kind of question. I'd already mentioned Sara, so Lalla knew I wasn't a eunuch.

"Do you mean 'Was I circumcised?'"

"Is that the English word?"

"Yes," I said, but seeing her embarrassment I added, "I was too young to remember."

Lalla smiled and said, "Men here remember because they are circumcised at five or six. It is an initiation into virility, a trauma I believe. If you have gone through that suffering, you will do just about anything to maintain the power of your new identity and group."

"Or become a monk."

"Ha, no monks for Muslims. Even the holiest men have a wife or two and many children as proof of patriarchal power."

Somehow this talk of circumcision or the word "power" made me think of the shower. I asked Lalla if she wanted to use it. I could order some room-service lunch, and she'd be out of sight of the bellboy. She agreed and went into the bathroom. I heard the water turn on, and then a call for help. I went to the door and knocked. "Come in," Lalla said, "quickly." She was standing with a wet towel wrapped about her, and the shower—a high-tech semicircular compartment with "massage" jets all around—was shooting water all over the room. "I can't turn it off," Lalla said.

"Slide the door closed," I told her. She didn't understand. "The glass door. Push it toward the wall." The jets were massaging her and everything else in the bathroom. Finally she saw how the glass door worked. When it was closed, I went in and turned off the shower. Lalla was crying.

"If I can't bathe by myself, how will I ever live away from Algeria?" she asked.

"Only luxury hotels have showers this complicated," I told her. "I couldn't figure out how to turn the massage function on. So you're ahead of me."

"I want my own simple bath," she said.

"That can be arranged." I figured out the plug mechanism and started drawing water.

"But now all the towels are wet," she said.

"I'll get more."

Lalla had her bath and got dry and seemed to enjoy the lunch under its fake-silver domes, but the shower dampened the rest of the day. She didn't see being sprayed as comic. Instead, the water-shooting jets seemed to represent the world outside Algeria. She feared that Europe or America was no more tolerant of lesbians than Algeria, that she would not be able to find a job, that she would have no friends. I told her I was sure that she could depend on feminist groups for continued assistance, and that she should easily get a job as a translator of Arabic or as a teacher of French. But just as she couldn't turn off the shower jets, I couldn't at first stem her fears.

"Perhaps I should stay here," she said. "I know the people who care for me."

I needed to stop Lalla from going any further along this line of thought.

"I know the kind of people who will care for you if you come to the United States," I told her. "I teach in a college where many faculty members and students are gay. My supervisor is a lesbian. My best student is a lesbian."

Lalla didn't look impressed or moved by our common jobs, so I became more creative: "The head of my department is a homosexual. We even have a departmental basketball team made up almost completely of gays."

"Really?" she said, and I was encouraged.

"Not only that," I told her, "my daughter and her roommate are gay. They live together openly in a dorm room at the college, and no one ever bothers them. In America, being gay is like a style. You might have problems if you were in some small Southern town, but if you work in a school or in a city you will be free to live how you want."

"But you are not gay," she said, substituting my term for her earlier "homosexual." "So why did you come here for me?"

"I know your life is in danger. I once tried to save the life of a woman about your age, but I failed. So I agreed to come here."

She asked about Alice, and I told her about Terminal Tours, the business itself and the problems it caused me with my family.

"So I am like one of your old clients?"

"No, because you have years to live after you have escaped."

Lalla shook her head and corrected my English for the second time: "Not 'escaped.' No, I don't think so. 'Exiled myself' are perhaps the true words."

Passing Through

She started to cry again. I said, "When people pronounce a death sentence on you, almost kill you with a bomb, and wait to hack you to pieces, 'escape' is the right word."

I wanted to escape any further discussion that might lead Lalla to doubt the wisdom of her choice. She was beginning to sound like Sara: stubborn, insistent, troublesome. Because leaving seemed to me Lalla's only choice, I figured her anxieties about life outside Algeria expressed a more immediate fear—passing through passport control. I told her that maybe "escape" was not well chosen after all. We are going to walk through the airport. No running, no car chases, no gun play. Ours is an academic story, I say, not a movie. We're both teachers, not students. We present our confident faces and written documents. Perhaps I say a few authoritative words. Away we go. We're not like pupils who are examined, asked questions, tested. And like teachers in America, we get to travel during our vacations. Paris in March. Croissants. The Louvre. Under this shower of assurances and pleasures, Lalla brightened. I asked her if she had watched satellite TV. "Just once," she said, so I turned on the TV and found CNN and a French station for her. She sat on the bed and clicked around the channels like a veteran traveler.

"Wait," Kara had said the evening before. Waiting for the time to pass was slow going. Lalla asked about things on TV, I asked her about her family, she wanted to know how I felt about having a lesbian daughter.

"I probably won't have any grandchildren," I said, "but then again I'll never have to pay for a wedding." Or tuition, I thought to myself.

Lalla understood I was joking. "Yes," she said, "you will be able to keep all of your sheep and goats." She told me more about the Family Code and asked about my parents. I didn't want to get into explaining my mother's suicide, another life I'd failed to save, so I told Lalla my parents were living in Florida and switched to Patrick, whom I transformed into an openly gay policeman in that liberal, though very cold, state of Vermont.

I'd confessed the truth to Kara, and she'd confessed to me, and I knew I probably shouldn't be inventing all these gay lives for Lalla, but she spooked me with her remark about staying in Algeria. And it was easier to keep the conversation going about gay matters, which she found most congenial and reassuring. Queer, I thought, that I should be pretending to have so much experience with gays when I knew almost nothing before starting at QCC. Then I realized that, except for Kara, the two people at the college who had responded most positively to me—June and Lauren—were lesbians or pretending to be. As the afternoon and evening dragged on, I discoursed on gay marriage in Massachusetts, other legal protections afforded gays, and various support groups. I didn't know how much I knew; the pressure was like a game or competition, bringing out secret resources. Lalla was so impressed by my knowledge that she asked, "Do you write about these subjects?"

"Not really," I said. If she knew I was a writer, she might think I was here for material.

"When you're out of Algeria," I told her, "you'll be able to write freely about these subjects. Autobiographies are very popular, especially if you have secrets to reveal."

"Perhaps I will be forced to write my life if I can't find a job. But I am very *jeune*, so maybe I will need to tell stories."

Like Lauren, I thought.

"So," I asked, "is being gay a story you've told me?"

Passing Through

At first, Lalla didn't understand or pretended to not understand. Then she laughed and said, "Now I am certain you are not gay."

"Why do you say that?"

"Because heterosexuals always suspect homosexuals are pretending, are keeping a secret from you 'breeders.' Do you think I have secrets? Because you secretly came here for me, I will tell you one that I cannot put in my autobiography."

In case Lalla never has the chance to write her life, I'm giving her narrative its own title and typeface here:

Passing Up

I have known since high school that I was attracted to women, but of course I could do nothing about it even if girls, though more taboo, were more accessible than boys, who were carefully chaperoned. Perhaps I needed to break rules step by step because in my second year at the university I somehow fell in love with a boy, a rich boy who had rooms of his own. He was very gentle, not like the boys I knew at home. Anyway, I soon got pregnant. I did not want to marry. I did not want to have an abortion. I couldn't go back to my parents' home, but a cousin in another city agreed to let me come and live with her. She had studied in France, and she and her husband were more liberal than anyone I knew. They were also childless, so we created a secret plot. No one knew I was living there, so my cousin kept me hidden and pretended to be pregnant. For six months, I did not leave the apartment. I was, how do you say, in the closet. When the midwife delivered my child at home, my cousin bribed her to report the child as my cousin's. The child's father never knew; he thought I left the university because of my shame for having sex with him.

I returned to the university in the fall, continued my studies, and began my rebellion against the government's Family Code, which would have imprisoned me for my offenses. I used to visit my cousin and see my little "second cousin" several times a year, but since the assassination attempt I have not seen my son. It would be too dangerous for me to leave Algiers, and too dangerous for him to visit me here. It is even dangerous to speak on the phone or to send letters to him, and besides I do not want him to ever suspect that I am anything more than a distant relative or that my cousin is not his mother.

After two years in hiding, I decided it will be best for my son if I disappear. I suppose I will find ways abroad of learning about him, but it will be best for him if he knows nothing of me. So I am leaving him and my country. About Algeria and its Family Code, I will be able to write, but not about my family—my son—not for many years. Even more than my sexual orientation, he must remain a secret.

After Lalla told me about her son, neither of us felt like talking anymore. Lalla lay on the bed and stared at the ceiling. I sat on the balcony and tried to keep her story a secret from my present consciousness. I retreated to the preparation I learned from basketball, repeatedly visualizing how the next day would go, what the shooter calls positive imaging. It's the way to bury your mind, focus your imagination, discipline your emotions, and remind your body—the shot leaves your hand, follows its fated arc, and always passes through the center of the rim, never touching metal. Repeat. The shot leaves your hand....

We present our tickets, we receive our boarding passes, we present our passports, we walk through to the gate. Repeat.

Chapter 15

The couch was uncomfortable but probably better than sharing the bed with Lalla. I could hear her thrashing around as if she were in a literal tight spot and fighting to get free. Around seven, when I got up to pee, Lalla wasn't in the bed or the bathroom. Oh no, I thought, an escape, and then saw Lalla on the balcony. When I went out there, she was bent over, holding on to the railing. I thought she was crying again, but when I touched her back she turned a scowling face to me.

"I'm not leaving," she said.

It was early in the morning and late in the mission to be sensitive and nurturing, but maybe my post-Sceptic dealings with QCC students prevented me from saying "You're fucking well leaving." Or maybe it was all those years collaborating with and competing against my own teammates. In the game's last two minutes, I called the shots. First the passes, then the shots.

"It's going to be easy, Lalla. Don't be afraid. You're going to be an American bimbo, and nobody will question you."

"I'm not afraid of the airport. I'm afraid to leave my home."

"Is it your son? Maybe he can join you abroad."

"No, no, you don't understand. This is my home. I've never been outside Algeria. I came out here and smelled the sea and the pines. Even in my little prisons I can smell the sea, the bread from the bakeries. I can hear all of my languages outside the shutters. Through cracks in the shutters I can see the Mediterranean light."

"Light" was the trigger, the word that suffused Ann's descriptions of the Greek islands in *Passing Off*.

"I felt the same way about my home in Vermont," I told Lalla. "Then I moved to Greece. I didn't want to, but my wife had to go for her work. I thought I would hate it, but I found I could reorient myself. I found another home, one I loved more than my original place. I thought I couldn't live without the sound of snow crunching underfoot, the smell of cows in my family's barn, everything from my childhood. But in Greece I loved the shushing sea, the dry heat, wild oregano in the mountains. I know you can't escape your body, your sexuality, but I'm telling you that you can leave your home. You must leave to get rid of the fear and the shame Algeria has imposed on you."

Finally, I thought, a use for Ann's book, her praise of the rural Greece she loved and I didn't.

But Lalla was not convinced by my autobiographical romance of re-placement.

"You are constantly traveling," she said, "it is easy for you to feel at home in a new place. I've never been away from Algeria. I'm sorry, but I can't leave. I'm very sorry you came here, but I just can't go. I will call Mr. Liabes, and he can come and take me home."

More and more Lalla was sounding like Ann, a home-girl even if home was a series of safe houses.

"Let me think about this for a minute," I said and went back into the room and hid the phone. I'll freely confess that the thirty thousand was first on my mind. Second was my own safety. Could Lalla return to her safe houses without exposing me? Third was Lalla. Naïve and vulnerable, she was more like my daughter or Eden than my temporary wife or my soon-to-be former wife. I was here so Sara could do what she chose, but she wasn't risking her life by marrying Bucky. I couldn't let Lalla choose. She was afraid and not thinking clearly. *In loco parentis*. I'd let my students believe they were prodigies, but I knew more than Lalla. I knew she could find a new home somewhere, maybe even in Greece if she needed Mediterranean light. Yes, I'd been exaggerating her gay life. I'd been lying to her. But the truth was that outside Algeria Lalla could live freely, if not always happily. Like me after Terminal Tours, Lalla could have a new life. There was a chance that by "removing" Lalla from her home I was condemning her to my old life of wandering, of passing through. We would also be risking her life for a minute at passport control. But she was already condemned in Algeria and was risking her life every minute she stayed here. Her life and possibly her son's.

I returned to the balcony and made my arguments why Lalla should leave. She wouldn't discuss them. Like me refusing to do any more Terminal Tours, Lalla said, "No, no flight." I repeated my arguments. She repeated her refusals and her apologies. But I wasn't pardoning her. She asked me to show her how to use the hotel telephone system. It was my turn to refuse.

"No telephone," I told her. "If you won't go with me, I'll use the telephone and call the police. You have a choice. You go to the airport with me or you go to prison."

"You wouldn't expose me!"

Sceptic passed through my mind.

"Yes I would, Lalla. I'm an American. A former athlete. Players have a killer instinct and hate to lose. I'll be paid fifty thousand dollars if I deliver you to Paris. Without you, I'll lose the fee and will have to pay all my travel expenses."

"Bastard," she said and started to cry again.

Fear and anger were working for me, just like they used to on the court. At crunch time, the point guard must control his emotions, use others'. That was the advantage of being temperamentally low Key. Full of adrenaline, Lalla couldn't see through my bluff or think through to the next question: how would I explain to the police that a fugitive was in my hotel room?

Lalla was crying and speaking Arabic to herself. I took her arm and got her off the balcony. I didn't want anyone hearing my wife speaking in tongues, and Lalla lying dead beneath my balcony would definitely put me in prison. I thought of Mr. Rorque, dead in Lourdes. Lalla was even more dangerous to me. I told her if she didn't stop speaking Arabic I'd put a gag in her mouth or a pillow over her face. She couldn't scream for help. As she became more afraid of me than of leaving, she began to calm down.

"This is a kidnap," she said.

"A disappearance."

More crying and snuffling but no more Arabic.

"You are just another man controlling me," she said.

"A man risking his life to save yours," I said.

"Always the man chooses for the woman."

"You're really just a girl, Lalla. You've been living your short life under a veil of ignorance. You're an expert on Algeria, but you know less about the world than my daughter."

"Another father-man telling me about myself."

"A traveling man. Look, Lalla, if you don't like what you find out there in the world, you can come back. Use the same passport and return to your safe houses. I'll even give you money for the return flight."

"Return," Lalla said, as if that hadn't occurred to her, just as it hadn't occurred to me earlier. The word "return" might have saved me the threat, for Lalla stopped crying and said, "I could return?"

"Sure, why not?"

"How do I know you're not lying?"

"Think about it. My wife and I were welcomed here. Algeria wants tourists. You now have an American passport. No one will be looking for you coming into the airport."

"Yes, you are right, I think."

I wasn't apologizing or taking back the threat. I didn't want Lalla changing her mind at the last minute. I wanted her to fear me, fear the police, and show neither.

After room service breakfast, I told her to take a shower to build her confidence. And then I watched as she put her game face on, the thick lipstick and eyeliner that made her an American. I didn't want a Sara or an Eden to emerge from under the makeup. I needed a Lauren or, better yet, a slim Brenda. So I gave Lalla a little Henderson brother-man tough-talking.

"No more tears now," I told her, "that makeup runs down your face and both our asses will end up in jail. Time to play big."

"Okay," she said.

"Are you sure?"

"Yes, I am ready to leave."

I kept the "Do Not Disturb" sign on the door and went down to the front desk to check out. "My wife is still ill," I told the concierge, "and in quite a bit of distress. So please call me when the driver is at the door. Oh yes, could we get a different driver? The man who brought us was very slow. I want to rush my wife to the car and to the airport. She cannot be away from the toilet very long."

"Yes, sir," he said, probably wondering why I would share the state of my wife's bowels with him. Just another Western eccentricity. But I didn't want anyone in the lobby demonstrating Algerian hospitality, possibly insisting on kissing the newlyweds goodbye. In the car, if we had the same driver, Lalla could lie down in the back seat, get out of mirror range. He might wonder at Kara's quick change, her loss of ten years. If he did, I hoped he'd chalk up the transformation to the wonderful Sheraton spa.

The driver was new, so once we raced through the lobby, Lalla put on her airport face, a self-assured, possibly even slightly condescending American who worries more about her blond hair than observing silly native customs such as scarves. In fact, Lalla was so haughty that she didn't even speak to her husband all the way to the airport. She just looked out the window, silently saying goodbye to the home she loved despite what her countrymen had done to her.

There was no line at the ticket counter. Lalla kept her sunglasses on while the ticket agent glanced at our passports and issued our boarding passes. As we'd agreed, we moved immediately—but slowly, so slowly—to passport control. Once through there, we felt, we could relax. There was no sense in staying in the waiting area and fidgeting.

Only four or five Algerians were waiting to present their passports and boarding passes. None of them said, "Aren't you Lalla Kahina?" I stood in front of her, guarding her. When the young policeman in the booth motioned me forward, I moved aside to let my wife go first. Stepping toward the booth, she removed her sunglasses and looked down into her handbag. No passport! Ooops. She turned and motioned me toward her, as we'd planned. We were obviously together, husband and wife, and of course the man was carrying the woman's passport, even if we were both Americans. I pulled out the two United States of America passports and handed Lalla hers. She handed it to the policeman, he looked quickly at the picture, glanced at Lalla's blond hair and lipstick, found the entry stamp that one of Henderson's acquaintances had forged, and stamped her pass out. She stepped through the narrow passage between booths.

I handed the policeman my passport. The picture was almost ten years old but the same buzz cut, same blank expression. He glanced at the photo, glanced at me, and started turning pages to find my entry stamp. All the pages of my passport were full of stamps from my years as a European player and my year in Terminal Tours. Agents like this policeman had begun overlaying and criss crossing their stamps. He couldn't find my Algerian entry. He turned pages back and forth, and then finally found it. But instead of giving me my pass out, he kept my passport and motioned me around to the back of his booth.

Lalla was waiting a few steps behind the booth. "You go on ahead to the gate," I said in a confident voice. "I'll catch up with you in a few minutes. There's no room in my passport for an exit stamp."

She gave me a questioning look, and I gave her a grim, insistent nod. Go on ahead, get out of sight, keep your head down, don't ask any questions.

In a couple of long minutes, another policeman came to where I was standing. *"Parlez-vous français?"* he asked.

"Non," I said.

He opened the back door of the booth and took my passport from the young policeman. My new opponent turned all the pages of my passport. He then motioned me to come with him. We walked to a door with no sign on it and entered. Inside were two men sitting behind desks. They looked like they could have been brothers. Though not in uniform, they were identically dressed: blue shirts with the sleeves rolled up, ties pulled down from their throats. The policeman nudged me toward the one on the right. He was talking on the phone. He pointed to the chair in front of his desk. The policeman stood behind me. There was nothing on the desk except the phone and a computer. There was nothing on the walls of this cubicle. I wondered how the two "brothers" worked in such a place all day.

When my brother got off the phone, the policeman handed him my passport. Again the page-by-page inspection.

"What is your profession, Monsieur Keever?"

He pronounced my name Keev-air. Air Keever. Not right now.

"I'm a college professor," I said.

"Does your position require so much travel," he asked and held up my passport.

"I used to be a professional basketball player in Europe."

He did a subtle double take that showed he didn't believe me: American, white guy, only six-three. I knew I could prove who I was, why I had the stamps, but I didn't know why I was being delayed.

"What is your academic specialty?"

"Communications."

He seemed puzzled. *"La littérature?"* he asked.

"No, writing."

"Do you write also, Monsieur Keev-air?"

So there it was. A person with this many stamps must be a drug courier or a journalist.

I was guilty of passing through too many places. About writing I was afraid to lie.

"I published a book a few months ago."

He didn't ask the title or the subject. Instead, he looked carefully at my passport and typed—I realized in a few seconds—my name into Google. He turned the monitor so we could both see the screen. There was my book in the first three entries. Then Ann's book.

"You are modest, Monsieur Keev-air. Two books."

"Well," I started and thought better of correcting him.

Then he clicked on Google's second page, and the three articles in *Hell* came up.

"An author and a journalist. It is necessary for a journalist to have a special visa to visit Algeria. You have a tourist visa."

"My wife and I came here for the sun. I never left the hotel grounds. You can search my bag. No computer, not even any paper."

He smiled, pointed to his head with his right hand, and said, "Journalists are like policemen. They must have excellent memories. You will need to answer more questions, I'm afraid."

"My flight leaves in thirty minutes."

He smiled again and said, "Someone else will ask you some things. But he is in the city, so you will not leave for Paris today. The man behind you will take you to your wife. She may leave today or stay in Algiers as our guest while we ask you these questions."

He spoke to the policeman in Arabic, and we walked to the gate where Lalla was waiting to board. I hoped Lalla wouldn't lose her nerve when she saw me approaching with a policeman. To keep her calm, I put on my best tourist or satisfied travel-writer smile. When we got to where she was sitting, I put my body between her and the policeman. He didn't step away to give us privacy. I didn't believe he spoke English, but I couldn't be sure. I hoped Lalla remembered her coaching—say as little as possible with her French accent.

"They believe I've come as a journalist," I told Lalla—and the policeman, if he understood English. "They want to ask me some more questions, so I'll be in beautiful Algeria for another day."

Lalla didn't jump out of her chair and hug me, as if she feared she wouldn't see me for months or years. She played along with my casual attitude and forced a curious expression on her face though she must have been trembling inside, not knowing why the policeman was standing there, possibly wondering if I was turning her in to save my own ass.

"You go on to Paris," I said, "and I'll meet you at the hotel tomorrow. You could stay if you wanted," I said for the sake of the policeman, "but I think you should go. You still haven't seen the Louvre, and we'll be leaving for home soon."

Lalla looked sad and stood up. She kissed me straight on the mouth and then hugged me. She placed her mouth to my ear away from the policeman and whispered "thank you" and "courage," the last with the French accent I wanted no one to hear.

I eased her away and said, "It's just one night alone in bed. You'll be fine."

"Okay," she said, and it sounded American to me.

I wanted that policeman out of there and Lalla on the plane, so I gave her a gentle push toward the gate. She pulled out a handkerchief and pretended to be crying as she approached the ticket agent, the last trap she had to pass through. After the agent took her ticket, Lalla turned and gave me a quick wave. Get in the fucking plane, I wanted to shout, but I guess the wave was necessary for the deception.

The policeman might think she was a dumb blond, someone who could muster only an "Okay" in these circumstances, but the show was, I felt, the best we could do. As long as a flight attendant didn't recognize Lalla, she was through.

I was not.

The policeman walked me back to the brothers' office. He spoke to my brother in Arabic for what seemed to be a long time, possibly reporting his interpretation of our parting as well as the facts. Then my brother said, "You will wait outside with this policeman. Soon two men will come to take you to the city. What is the name of your hotel?"

"The Sheraton," I said. "Will I be returning to the hotel?"

My brother laughed loud and long. Then he had to translate my stupid question for his brother and the policeman, who also got a good laugh from Keev-air's dumb question. I even started laughing at myself, which seemed to diminish the fun the other three men were having. In fact, my brother seemed to resent my laughing.

"This is a *'situation grave,'* Monsieur Keev-air, *'tres serieux,'*" my brother said, shifting into some French to express the gravity. "You will be taken to a prison in the city for *l'interrogation.*"

Even with his French accent, I understood "interrogation."

"Non-sanitaire" flashed through my mind. But instead of being denied entrance, I was being denied exit.

My keeper took me outside. I kept looking in the direction of the gate. As long as another policeman didn't show up with Lalla in hand, I felt my trouble could be minor. Though we'd not discussed my being detained alone, I trusted Lalla would know not to kiss French soil when she landed. If she didn't breeze through French passport control with her fake American passport, she would quietly explain the situation and ask for political asylum. So I hoped.

After about twenty minutes, two men not in uniform came to take me and my guilty passport off the hands of my keeper. They led me out of the airport and put me in the back of an unmarked car, a little Renault. They spoke to each other in Arabic but not to me as we drove through the city to the prison. Plenty of photo opportunities here. But no Kara, no camera. I was happy about both.

The prison had no identifying sign, not that I could read. From the outside, it could have been a three-story rug factory. Nobody was gesturing out through barred windows. But there were plenty of cops standing around the entrance. We were waved through into a courtyard, and I was led into a first-floor room where my escorts handed over my carry-on and I was asked for my wallet and watch. Then I was patted down and led to a room like the one the brothers occupied, though smaller and without the computer. There was a desk, a phone, two chairs, and nothing on the white walls. I sat down and waited. This is civilized, I thought. No cell, just a room that reminded me a little of my office, a room for a conference or interview. I waited for the person doing *l' interrogation*. I don't know how long I waited. The room had no windows, I had no watch. For about two hours, though it could have been more or less, I rehearsed what I would say. Yes, I have written travel essays but am not here on assignment. Yes, I have written two books but am not here gathering material for the next stage of my autobiography. The problem was not lying but lying in persuasive detail about what I wasn't doing. I remembered from some college course the sentence, "You can't prove a negative." My cover story was seamless and plausible, but how to persuade my interrogator of the negative?

I didn't need much time to arrive at this question, just a fraction of the time I was in the room. I went through my best arguments over and over. Finally, my body decided I couldn't wait any longer for the interrogator. I knocked on the door. No response. I didn't dare open it. I knocked louder. I turned the knob; it felt like it would open. I knocked louder. I still didn't dare open the door. I hammered on the door, and a uniformed policeman opened it.

"Toilet?" I said.

He nodded and took my arm. Already my captivity had me considering unusual contingencies. Should I just pee or, since I didn't know if my hammering on the door would work next time, should I try to move my bowels, even though my body didn't feel the need? Trust the body, I always used to tell myself in pressure situations. But in this case I wondered if the rule held true.

The policeman led me back to my room. Again I waited for what seemed to be several hours. Lalla should be through the airport in Paris by now. Unless she was being tortured in a room down the hall, being forced to tell where she got an American passport, how she got onto a plane with a meager disguise that even a flight attendant could see through. Even if she didn't talk, the police could quiz the guy in the booth, and he'd remember the two "Americans," one of them kind of tall, maybe not basketball tall but taller than most Algerians. Even with all the time I had I couldn't think of a story that would explain my standing in line and being familiar with a fugitive. I hadn't met Lalla at the hotel and gone to the airport after a one-night stand—because the police could ask at the hotel. Besides, I'd already identified her as my wife. And there were the damning documents, the passports with the Keever name and address in both. Ann was right: dumb. How could I forget the documentation, the facts?

I tried to think through basketball, what I knew best. Coaches call timeouts at the ends of close games to "ice" foul shooters on the other team. Maybe the interrogator was sipping coffee down the hall, enjoying watching me fidget. I looked around the room. No little cameras I could see.

Coaches also practice deception, teach self-deception. Even if you're behind by seven with twelve seconds left, they all say, "We're in a tight spot but we can win this one, it's a long shot but we're going to win it." I never had the chance to tell that lie to the "The Unnamable," but I'd heard it plenty of times and recognized the usefulness of a crazed confidence.

I tried to maintain that self-deception after I was led away from the interrogation room to a cell. A meal was pushed through a hole in the door. Not bad: couscous and meat of some kind. I had my cot and toilet to myself. The cell was a cell, a lock-up rather than a locker. But it was clean even if the walls were covered with graffiti, some of it in English and French and maybe Spanish or Italian. Nobody had written "spent twenty years in this room" or anything like it. The cell was isolated, so I decided it was a holding cell, maybe even designed for temporary detainees, visitors who were just passing through. I tried not to think about Kara in Paris or Sara in Cincinnati. I might leave Algeria tomorrow, and we would be back as scheduled. Less successfully, I tried not to think about Lalla. I didn't worry too much about the visa issue because I didn't think of myself as a real journalist, maybe because I still hadn't been to a place to write about it, but I was a real accomplice or accessory to Lalla's flight.

In *Passing Off*, Ann invented ways for me to use my point guard skills to wriggle out of tight off-court situations. Sitting in my cell, I couldn't even begin to imagine some means of escape. My video-trained x-ray vision couldn't penetrate mortar. My practiced ability to slip through defenders and change direction was up against steel bars. I couldn't trust my body or my athlete's intuition. No neurological creativity would evade this door. A tough Key wasn't opening this lock. Keeping it simple and positive imaging were useless. Self-deception didn't help. Not thinking would not get me through this.

I hadn't played ball since my hip replacement, but it was in this cell that I finally and truly changed, shifted, switched. I became a former athlete, a non-athlete. I gave up basketball and began thinking like a professor of Creative Non-Fiction.

Chapter 16

The next morning a guard takes me to the room where I waited the first day or a room that looks just like it. After perhaps an hour, a young man, no more than twenty-five, wearing a beige suit and tie comes into the room and sits behind the desk. He has dark brown hair cut short, but his complexion is almost as light as mine or Lalla's. Except for the suit, he looks a little like Gary Gallagher, the same suspicious eyes, similar wire-frame glasses. No tattoo or piercing though. He opens up a folder that contains my passport and what seem to be downloads from the Internet.

"Mr. Keever," he says, "my name is Samir Hadj, and I have been directed to ask you some questions."

His English has none of the French or Arabic inflections I'd heard at the hotel or airport. In fact, Samir Hadj sounds like he just stepped off a plane from London. Maybe he had. Maybe that's why I waited all day yesterday to hear these questions. His English fluency is a good sign for me. I can try to sound like Richard or, better yet, June.

"I'd very much like to answer them," I say, projecting a professor's helpfulness rather than a detainee's fear or an interviewee's nervousness.

"I've not read your books, but I've read reviews of them on the Internet. I've also read your journalism for *Hell*. I was especially interested in the most recent essay where you commented on the Human Rights violations that drove people in countries bordering the Mediterranean to enter Greece. Do you think Algeria is such a country?"

Hearing this first question, I'm relieved. Yes, it is about people fleeing countries like Algeria but makes no mention of Lalla. I feel I'm not going to be imprisoned for assisting a fugitive.

"I'm sorry to admit this," I say, "but my knowledge of Algeria is rather spotty. I came because my wife wanted to. She loves North African food and read a novel about sunny Algiers. I was busy with my teaching and my new book, so I just let her make the arrangements."

"Were you aware that journalists must have special visas to visit Algeria?"

"My wife is in the travel business. She prepared the visa application. I had no idea I needed a different visa, not until I was stopped at the airport."

"Do you know that journalists visiting the United States, even journalists from England, must now have special visas?"

"No, I didn't. I'm afraid I've been rather obsessed with my autobiography and not keeping up with current events. Since I wasn't planning to write about Algeria, the visa issue never occurred to me. We were tourists. You can ask at the hotel. The Sheraton. I never left the grounds. We mostly soaked up your wonderful sun by the pool. I didn't interview anyone. My wife took a few snapshots to show my daughter. Writing something was the last thing on my mind. In fact, I wanted a vacation from writing and thinking about writing, my own and my students'."

"And yet you came to Algeria, a controversial country, and not Tunisia or Morocco, our equally sunny neighbors."

My pose as an ivory-tower, female-dominated, and lazy-ass sun-soaking professor is not going well, but Samir Hadj's introduction of what I had not done gives me an idea.

"You have my passport there. If you look very carefully, you will see that there are no entry or exit stamps for France just before I wrote the piece on the catacombs or for Greece before I wrote the piece on Lavrion. I don't necessarily visit the countries I write about."

"So you make up material about these countries?"

For some reason, I think of Patrick, my interrogation of him in Vermont.

"I'm not saying that. I'm only saying that just because I'm visiting Algeria doesn't mean I'm going to write about it."

"That's not very good logic for a professor, Mr. Keever. If you were not planning to write about Algeria, you will now, isn't that right?"

That's when I realize I'll be leaving Algeria, though I don't know when. Being a journalist from the United States is both my offense and my protection. The interrogator can't make me disappear like Algerian dissidents, not with my wife able to testify that I've been detained. If I'm the "professor," Samir Hadj is like a department chair at QCC: he wants to be tough, uphold the country's laws, give me a scare, but eventually he'll let me pass through. What I need to do is shorten my "colleague's" concept of "eventually." I don't know how long Lalla will or can keep her escape secret, and I don't want to explain any coincidences.

"I write essays only for *Hell*," I say. "I don't believe they'd be interested in my three glorious days at the Sheraton."

"But might be pleased if you were placed in a dirty cell with three other criminals who, because of their Islamic beliefs, hated Americans?"

"I guess that could be hellish."

"For a professor, even being forced to respond to questions might seem like hell."

"Not as long as I can answer them."

"Yes, of course. So here is an assertion: we suspect that you entered the country under false pretenses."

Maybe the pressure is getting to me or I'm listening too closely, but I boggle at the phrase "false pretenses."

"I don't understand," I say, "wouldn't a false pretense be true, like multiplying two negative numbers and getting a positive?"

Samir Hadj is likewise boggled by my question. He thinks about it for a few seconds and says, "False pretenses is just a phrase."

"But it's what you suspect me of. And it's plural. How many pretenses are you accusing me of?"

"We're not engaging in academic word games here," he says. "'False pretenses' may be redundant, but the facts are clear: you are a journalist and you have broken Algerian law."

For some reason, "Algerian" sounds like "American," some of the same vowels and consonants. I know what people in other countries think of Americans. Greeks call us "Americanakia," little Americans, children.

"I simply had no idea," I say.

"Ignorance…" he starts and then stops for me to complete the thought. Lalla may have gotten out because she was a dumb blond, but not me. A professor might be effete and absent-minded, but is still expected to be logical and informed.

"I know," I say. "Can I contact my embassy?"

"We have notified your embassy. Under Algerian law, you do not have the right to speak with your embassy at this stage of investigation. If there is a trial, of course, you will be allowed to arrange legal representation."

Maybe it's because Samir is so young or because of the way he uses formal language or because I'm deceiving myself, but I just don't believe him about a trial. He's bluffing, lying, putting me through some shit. I have something in mind, a way to change his mind and my situation, but I need to prepare him for my story. And I need time to prepare it. I lied too quickly to Ann about being bisexual, and that fiction boomeranged.

"I understand," I say, "that it would have been prudent to have a journalist visa. I understand why you're suspicious and sceptical. I can't prove I wasn't planning to write something. All I can do now is ask you to investigate what I've told you about the hotel. And to do further Internet research on me."

"And what will I find?"

"If you read Queen City College's web site and if you go to www.terminaltours.com, you'll begin to understand why I came to Algeria without a journalist visa."

Back in my cell, I ask for paper and pen but am refused. Mine will be an oral composition, like telling Ann material she could put into *Passing Off*, like those first in-class narrations by my autobiographers. The bases have to be factual, Richard's stuff. Then I need vivid details and persuasive momentum if my story is going to be a creative solution. My improvisational lies to Lalla were easy to tell but didn't work. I won't be able to move Samir by threatening him. For some reason, I think of my last conversation with Lauren.

I quickly outline what I'll say, but it's two days before I'm summoned to the interrogation room. During those hours my jailers didn't allow me out of my cell for exercise. I had plenty of time in my cramped space to revise, extend, and reflect back on my story. It incorporated recent events. But I was not, as I thought when I began this book, through with the dying and the dead. They came back into my story, and I realized the past is not dead. We may be passing through time or time may be passing through us, but memories come bouncing back to us. The right word for prior experience is "passed," not "past," because what is passed—like a ball or a gift or even a story—can be passed back. Now that I couldn't pass through my cell door, I realized how much I'd adhered to the places and people I'd known or how much they'd adhered to me. Ann said that I was slippery, that nothing stuck to me. She was wrong. Some of those adhesions I could use for my story. Some were random, adhering only by association to those I could use. But even those extra details seemed to demonstrate that I could think outside the box, the rectangle, the court that had organized most of my responses to the world. On the court, it's what you do that counts. Trying to evade an Algerian court, I realized it's what I say that will be key. I used to videotape as an aid to action. Now I needed my audiotapes. Tape. How every player prepares. Watch the videotape, tape the ankles. Tape, the sticky stuff, adhesive.

In *Passing On*, I'd concealed the fact of Alice's death. In my Algerian box, I saw ways to liberate my life from fact, to create a fiction that would sound like non-fiction. Even if my story didn't liberate me from the cell, imagining it freed me from my belief that I had been just passing through. Passing through, yes, but not "just" or "only" or "merely" or any of those other modifiers that diminished who I was, what this skinny "I" remembered and could transform, could change and articulate.

Then again, I also thought, it may be necessary to be self-deluded to create an illusion for a captor.

Then again, I further thought, it may be healthy that I'm thinking and saying to myself "then again." Before I came to this imposed full stop, three walls and bars, I was thinking then and then and then, on and on and on. It was the athlete's desire—keep it bouncing. "Then again" was looping backward or upward or downward or even forward to have another look, to see through the "and" and "and" and "and." "Then again" was even reason to write a sequel or a trilogy.

My story for Samir would not incorporate everything I remembered and learned while thinking it through. The story was designed for his easy listening and simple retelling. I wanted Samir and his superiors to ride my water slide. I'd use my academic knowledge but give up my professorial pose. I'd speak directly, like a former player, like a coach. From their first recruiting visit to the game's last minute, coaches always lied.

When finally summoned to the interrogation room, I immediately try to control how the dialogue with Samir will go.

"Did you speak to the people at the Sheraton?" I ask right away.

"Yes. They confirmed what you said. Though the names on your passports were different, they thought you might be on your *lune de miel*, your honeymoon."

"Something like that. And the web sites?"

"Yes, I also read your web site and the web site of your college."

"So you read about Alice?"

"The woman who swims in Paris, yes."

"Right."

There is no way Samir can know about Alice in Athens because that installment would have to be emailed to him. Now he's set up.

"I want to confess," I say, trying to sound like I did on Saturday mornings when my father would take Patrick and me into town to whisper our misdeeds to a priest who'd heard too many masturbatory fantasies.

"Ah-ha," Samir says, unable to conceal the interrogator's surprise and pleasure.

"Yes," I say, "the woman with me at the hotel is not my wife."

"You told me she was your wife."

"But you know that she isn't."

Samir just smiles, his first. He thought he'd catch me out with Ann Logan's name on the site and Kara Schmidt at the hotel. But I want to admit these facts right away so they won't emerge later and interfere with my story's momentum.

"I apologize for the deception," a word I like better than "lie." "If you will hear me out, I believe you'll understand. The woman I brought here is dying of a brain tumor. She read about Alice on the web site, and she wanted to do the same thing—go to Paris with the hope that she would be cured. But not just Paris. She wanted to go someplace that she considered dangerous, somewhere that she would be, she said, 'risking her life.' For some reason, she thought this might be the way to beat her death. First she wanted to go to Somalia, but Algeria was closer to Paris. I knew that Algeria was a conservative country, so we registered at the hotel as husband and wife in order not to offend anyone's sensitivities. I also knew that you have problems with Islamic militants here, but I figured if we stayed on the hotel grounds we'd be safe and the client could have the illusion of risking her life. For all I know, she may even have wanted to die in some political event. If that's true, my keeping her around the hotel may have saved what's left of her life. And saved your government the embarrassment of a dead American tourist."

I give Samir a quizzical look to see if he appreciates what I've done for Algeria. He nods, slightly. Bring him to you, fuck him up.

"Anyway, Kara thought that I was an immortality agent, that I had the secret of living forever. Keep moving, keep changing time zones, keep passing through places. Alice did recover her health, but I assumed that was just an accident, not a miracle. But I wasn't sure. And, besides, when someone who is dying asks you for something, it's hard to turn the person down. Do you know what I mean?"

"I can imagine," he says. Yes, imagine along with the teller.

"Well, as you know from the web site I was retired from Terminal Tours, but the woman I brought here insisted that I was to be the one who escorted her. The woman was offering me a great deal of money, a lot of money. If you looked carefully at my college web site, you know I was reduced to teaching only one course this semester."

Yes, Richard, praise the Internet and its dissemination of information to as benighted a place as Algeria.

"I really needed the money. Like civil servants, teachers in the United States are very poorly paid. I have some gambling debts from when I was involved in sports. My teenage daughter is pregnant and has to get married. I don't have to provide a dowry, but she will lose her free tuition at Queen City. It's a terrible thing. Even very young women do whatever they choose in America. They break all the family codes. You understand?"

"Yes," he says.

"My wife wanted to do this tour and make the money, but the client refused. Well, my wife and I are in the middle of a divorce, and she's angry at me for leaving her, but she and her damned lawyer finally agreed to let me take the client if I paid my wife twenty per cent of the fee. I agreed. My wife then arranged the visas and tickets for my spring vacation. Now I wonder if she knew I needed a journalist's visa and sent me here with the tourist visa. It's the kind of thing she might do to punish me for escaping the prison of our marriage. Put me in jail in Algeria."

I shake my head in wonderment at the vengefulness of wives. Samir has no ring on his hand, but he was no doubt brought up to be suspicious of women like my wife and Sara.

"Now there's another secret I want to confess," I tell him.

He is not so pleased to hear "confess" this time. I haven't admitted to emailing a scathing story about Algeria to *Hell*.

"The woman I brought here believed that the way Alice got better was to have sex with me, even though there was nothing in the web account. I didn't know this until we got to Algeria. You have to understand that this is a person with a brain tumor. She's fearful and not thinking very clearly. I mean, this person is so disoriented by her fear she couldn't even figure out how to turn off the shower at the hotel. Not only that, she said she'd always been a lesbian but believed that if she shifted her orientation and had sex with a man, she might save her life by changing it. She said she would double my per diem. When I declined, she then threatened to not pay me if I didn't have sex with her. She even left the hotel compound for an hour to scare me. I didn't want to do it. Think about it: sex with a lifelong lesbian?"

I don't give Samir time to think about this. Hustle him along. Yes hustle—speed and cheat.

"I felt that if we stayed around the hotel and had sex then we would lessen our chances of being chopped up by those Islamic militants that your government is trying to put down, a policy that as an American, by the way, I fully support. Therefore, the appearance of a 'honeymoon' at the Sheraton. Unfortunately, the brain tumor demanded that the client be horny as a goat and that I take her from behind. It was terrible. We had to do it in a dark bathroom that Kara kept calling 'the shelter' when she wasn't making these horrible bleating noises. I'm no sexual athlete, but I was able to keep up my end, so to speak. By the third day the 'goatess' said she hadn't known what she'd been missing as a lesbian, so I suppose my reorienting her to normal sex could be seen as one positive result of this tour, even if she doesn't have long to live."

Not bad, so far—the kind of story a man in an Arab country should believe: a Muslim-fearing American doing deceptive, sinful, disgusting, and eventually sickening things with a sex-crazed woman for money. Complete disclosure, full exposure. But is there anything else, something I haven't rehearsed?

Recovery. How in hell did I overlook that? Recovery is why autobiographies and memoirs sell. The Change. My students haven't gotten that far, but I can shift my life. Recovery and return, coming back from physical, moral, and spiritual degradation. Yes, coming back, not Alice's passing through to a dead end. Coming back: the place where autobiography, travel writing, and sports stories intersect. If not exactly a happy ending, I can give

Samir the recognition—my recognition—that might lead there.

"When I was stopped at the airport, I was afraid but I have to say that I also felt relieved, you know? Somehow I was going to be punished for the sins I'd committed. You see, I'm an Irish Catholic, and we're almost as guilty about sexual offenses as Muslims. If I do penance here, I felt, I won't have to spend eternity in hell. But I didn't want the woman to be detained. After all, she has only a few weeks left to live. Maybe she'll see the error of her perverse ways. So that's why I pardoned her and pushed her toward the gate. Now I find I'm being punished for a technicality I wasn't aware of, not for being an expensive male escort."

I pause, look at the floor like a dumb recruit, and shake my head in disgust.

"Money is a terrible thing," I sum up. "It makes people in America do crazy things, like come to Algeria with the wrong visa."

Or, I think, make up stories about the same subjects.

This is as thick as I can lay it on. Samir isn't laughing at me, not like the "brother" at the airport. But he doesn't ask any follow-up questions. Instead, he says, "What is this Creative Non-Fiction?"

His expression is blank. I can't tell if he has seen through my story and is mocking it or if he is really curious about what I teach. It has to be the opposite of what I've just told him.

"CNF," I say and chuckle. "It's just an advertising term. Students write ordinary events and trivial facts, really boring stuff, in poetic or 'creative' language, lots of metaphor and allusions and literary crap like that."

"I see," he says, "there were no courses like that in Wales where I studied. Of course, we were interested mostly in translation and cross-cultural studies."

"We have cross-cultural studies at Queen City College, too. One of my students is from Pakistan. She is writing a very interesting study of her family past."

"So you have international students there? I heard it was impossible for students from Muslim countries to get visas now."

That's when I realize—late—that we aren't being taped. Samir wouldn't want this personal chat on tape. He won't be able to re-listen to—review—my story, analyze its water-slide quality. I can shift back to professorial language, June talk.

"Visas are possible still if you are acquainted with someone at the college. Are you interested in pursuing your studies in the States?"

"It is very expensive."

The money. Just like me, Samir needs dollars.

"Not if you are granted an assistantship. You'd receive tuition remission and a living stipend. And housing in Cincinnati is quite inexpensive. With an undergraduate degree from Wales and with your English fluency, an assistantship should be just about assured."

I ask Samir if he plays any sports. He "did" soccer in Wales and was a huge "football" fan, so I tell him about the new Creative Sports Writing program at QCC. Maybe it's my using again that word "creative" that brings Samir to his senses.

"Well, this is all very interesting, Mr. Keever. I will report to my superiors and let you know if they decide to bring you to trial."

Recovery, one last shot at moral recovery and forgiveness.

"Please be sure to tell them I came here to save a life if I could. It's kind of a Christian thing, but maybe they'll take a humanitarian view."

Passing Through

Again I have to wait. I'm like the food-server Kara pointed to in the Sheraton restaurant: stay still until my masters say I can move. But no waiter spends months or years at his station. And still I have to wait patiently, allow my story to have its effect before I demand contact with my embassy. I want to avoid, if I can, all the legal complications that could ensue and might somehow introduce Lalla into the situation. I need to be passive, something I've never been good at. Passive not passing, whether off or on or through.

As my story was being disseminated, I had more time to think about why I'd had to tell it, why I was stuck in an Algerian prison. My last sentences to Samir seemed to be true and maybe the key to unlock Keever's life, if not his current cell. Jesus, the nuns used to tell Patrick and me, gave his life to save you from damnation. We never had a chance to save our mother's life; we were in school when she gassed herself. When my father's pickup plunged into the Black River, neither Patrick nor I was around to throw him a lifesaver or dive into the icy waters. Patrick learned CPR and tried to prevent drivers from killing themselves on Vermont roads. I learned the point guard position and became a specialist in last-second shots and game-saving assists. When Ann wanted to abort Sara, I asked her to marry me instead. When everybody around me was dying, I took the long shot of trying to save Alice's life. People I knew were passing through, passing away, but not passing on. I wanted to stop the process.

Understood, all. But waiting for the judgment of faceless men, I still wondered why I risked my new life to save Lalla. Jesus, after all, had the security of being the son of God. But maybe even he felt he had to prove it. Like an athlete. Carry that weight. Walk, don't run, the suicides up to Calvary. Maybe my coming to Algeria was the final unrecognized consequence of thinking most of my life like an athlete. No, not like an athlete. But like a player, the person who proves himself over and over and over in public performance. Always some opponent, a score to be settled. Always some audience, a public to please or alienate. Being a player was not so different from being a teacher. I was both and not quite either. But coming to Algeria proved some things to family, loved ones, friends, and colleagues. Too bad I couldn't prove the story I'd passed off to Samir. If he didn't believe it and pass it on, whatever I had proved about my love to Sara, about my ingenuity to Ann, my moral worthiness to Kara, and my dumb courage to Henderson would have to go on without me.

I waited another two days in my cell. "Show, don't tell" say the CNF handbooks that Richard gave me. But all I have to show for those days is the thinking above. That and some nasty diarrhea, prison food passing through me, the "runs" a mockery of my immobility. If Kara and I could imagine Lalla in her safe houses, you can imagine, if you'd like, the way my solitary minutes and hours passed. But I assume you're more interested in the conclusion of my interrogation.

This time Samir is waiting for me and stands up when I enter the room. He shakes my hand for the first time and motions me to sit down.

"Congratulations, Professor Keever," he says, "my superiors believe that you did not enter Algeria with the purpose of writing about it."

So, I turned a sceptic into a believer, even if I wasn't really a professor.

"Thank you for telling them what really happened."

"Yes," Samir says, "but the fact remains that you are a journalist, so the government will show you our country. We will keep your passport and you will return to the

Sheraton Hotel. For now, you will not be allowed telephone or Internet access."

"It's hard but fair," I tell Samir.

Like an earnest student, he seems pleased by my measured, truthful approval.

"Here is the best part," he says. "I have been assigned to be your interpreter and guide."

"Nice," I say, "and how long will this tour last?"

"That I don't know," Samir says, "but it should be fun."

Overtime

Passing Through

I'd missed my flight from Paris to the U.S. I'd miss Sara's wedding and the beginning of classes. I didn't know how long my overtime stay would be. Algeria was a large country, and I was a captive audience. The government could kill me with kindness, show me the Sahara and Oran and Kabilye, where many Berbers lived and where Lalla's family was originally from. The longer I stayed, the more I was at risk that Lalla would come out and I'd somehow be implicated when the Algerians connected us. Then I'd just be a captive. I would need an official pardon, maybe when I was fifty and had written my prison memoir. Or maybe after my death at the hands of the mullahs Lalla was fleeing.

I should never have shifted point of view in "Halftime." Now you know that I did get out of Algeria.

I stayed in the Sheraton for another week, and each day I got into a different car with Samir and we were escorted by two unmarked police cars with two plainclothesmen in each to various sites around the capital. We always returned before dark. We never ventured into the countryside. I never spoke to people other than officials at dams and factories and athletic facilities. All of the interviews were videotaped so that, I suppose, after I left I couldn't lie about what my interviewees said. I never heard any complaints about the government, but then again Samir was translating. I never saw any atrocities, but I did go through a lot of military checkpoints and was almost always happy to have escorts, though I sometimes wondered if they didn't make us a target. A tall Westerner and freckled Christian, I slumped in the back seat and probably didn't see as much as I could have.

Algeria is not a place to be known by a visiting journalist. You need something more than first-person data, whether travel narrative or autobiography. No creative telling of my arranged trips and escorted visits can reveal what was happening outside my limited purview. I'm sorry to disappoint, but if you really want to know about Algeria you need to read web sites such as Journalists without Frontiers and Human Rights Watch. Or reports by Algerians who, like Lalla, have sent their manuscripts out or have escaped the country. What's the point, then, you may ask the former point guard. Suspicion of "factual" stories, I suppose.

The personal consequences of my extended stay in Algeria I can report with confidence and pleasure, but briefly. There's no reason to send this narrative into double overtime.

I talked with Henderson on the phone when I got to Paris: "You did it, Key! You got her out and got yourself out."

"Thanks for keeping things quiet until I could sneak out."

"Lalla insisted, man. I think she may be ready to cross over."

"To the States?"

"The gender barrier, my man. She's in love with her new husband."

"The power of white sexuality, James."

"What they do to you there?"

I was tempted to tell James about the Algerians' subtle methods of torture to see if he'd up the fee, but I told him the truth. I did ask him to pay my $300 per diem all the days I was in captivity.

"Sound like a double dip to me, Michael. They providing five-star room and board, and you want the per d?"

"How do you want to look when I write this up, James? You want me to say Sahar turned down the job as Mrs. Keever?"

"I'll talk to Franklin."

"Tell him I can make him ugly."

Henderson and Franklin paid the thirty thousand but not the extra per diem.

Once I was back in the United States, I spoke with Lalla on a very good phone connection. Among a multitude of thanks, she laughed at how I'd persuaded the Algerians I was not there for journalism. I saw no reason to tell her that I'd lied to her as well. Lalla and the American feminist organization that paid me wanted to keep her liberation secret. The organization to head off any harassment, Lalla to make the Islamists waste their time searching for her in Algiers. So when I broke the story in *Hell*, I changed Lalla's name and some biographical facts to "veil" her identity, just as I have changed the names of the law firms that hired me. Because the real "Lalla Kahina" remains a secret, I felt I could expose the secrets she'd been keeping. Dirk Ryan loved my account, gave me extra space, went easy on the fact checking, and paid me more than double my usual fee. Although he didn't use Kara's photos, he's no longer talking about Somalia, at least not for now.

Having missed two weeks of classes, I was afraid I'd be fired at QCC. But once Kara told Richard about the circumstances, June met my classes and Richard used my captivity to burnish the department's reputation as a collector and disseminator of real-life, if not in my case real-time, information. After my role in Lalla's release was known, Richard said I'd surely have undergrads in Extreme Travel next year and, needless to say, plenty of grads who'd want to study Engaged Autobiography with a Human Rights hero. June persisted in her pretense of being a lesbian and spoke to me about how heterosexuals and gays could work together. She even talked of starting a group of straight men and gay women called "Dears for Queers." Maybe she really is gay. Perhaps my athlete's x-ray vision was wrong about her and Richard.

My students were happy to have me back. They said June was too tough on their sentence structure and was too literary. They also knew I'd take up plenty of class time with my oral account. Gary asked if I'd been able to tape any of my interrogations, but the others told him that was unrealistic. I told Rakhshanda that details from her autobiography had served me well in a Muslim land. Jason asked if I could have gotten out earlier by pretending to be bisexual, and I wondered why I hadn't thought of adding that to the story I told Samir.

After class Lauren walked down the hall with me.

"How much of all that did you make up, Mr. Keever?" she asked.

"Faction, every bit."

"Damsel in distress?"

"Can a lesbian be a damsel?"

"I really am a lesbian, you know."

"Maybe you should move to a less tolerant country to have something to write about."

"And have you come rescue me?"

"More material for both of us."

"No game, no gain," she said and thumped me on the back like a hoopster. I still don't know if she was telling the truth about her sexual orientation. But hearing my faith bounced back at me, I realized the game is always ultimately for and against the watchers, the hometown fans and the away-game hecklers, those who want to see you lose.

When Ann and Sara found out where I was, they called off the wedding. Neither one went so far as to accuse me of faking detention to stop Sara's marriage. When I got back, Ann gave up her email-only rule and called me:

"That could have been a terminal tour," she said.

"Just an extended one, possibly months or years."

"You can't ever complain again about *Passing Off.*"

"Why's that?"

"Because you're a bioplagiarist. You were dumb and greedy enough to actually do what I only made up."

I could hear a note of affection, possibly even respect, that wouldn't have come through in email.

"You're responsible," I said lightly. "You and your lawyer drove me to it. Now I'll have enough cash to pay mine."

"So now that you really are a hero, we're officially going to split. I waited a long time. It doesn't seem fair. But I have to say that Kara is one tough woman. I was afraid she was going to kidnap me to keep my mouth shut. But now that you're safe, I do want to ask you something."

Ann was not Sceptic. "What is it?"

"Why did you tell me you were gay, Michael?"

"I'll explain everything to you at the wedding."

Sara came to see me, and I told her I was sorry about putting off her wedding.

"It worked out okay," she said. "Bucky's parents decided to keep supporting him, so we now have the apartment and three toasters and some other wedding gifts without getting married."

"Whenever you want, just say the word."

"Maybe next fall. As long as Bucky's parents don't take his money, we're fine as we are."

I felt it had never really been Sara's idea to get married, but didn't reveal my suspicion. We talked some more about Bucky's parents, and then Sara asked why I'd risked my life for Lalla. I told her Lalla was part of it, but I also admitted my financial problems and explained the tuition remission.

"I didn't know that, Dad. You mean you went to Algeria so you could pay my tuition at Quasi College? Why didn't you tell me I'd lose the remission?"

"I wanted you to do what you chose to do."

"That was crazy. You've done some dumb things, but going to Algeria was crazy."

"I figured if I was imprisoned for four years, you wouldn't get married and would have your tuition covered until you graduated."

"I should smack you, Dad."

And she did, a big sloppy kiss on the cheek.

"If you were in prison, who would cook for me? Bucky can't make scrambled eggs."

"Tuesday nights. I'll come to your place or you come here, and I'll teach Bucky everything I know."

"Except for the lying, okay?"

"If you insist."

Yes, patient reader, I have scrambled chronology and saved the "best part," as Samir said, for last. When Kara heard in Paris that I was detained, she immediately called Henderson and told him that he and Franklin had to keep Lalla invisible. Then Kara called Ann and told her what we had done. If the news media called the real wife of Michael Keever, Ann was to be absolute in her "no comment" and should avoid having her picture taken. Kara called Richard, swore him to secrecy, and warned him that I might not be back for the beginning of classes. She then used her journalistic contacts to get connected with the State Department. She explained to the person on the Algerian desk what had happened and suggested that they go slow. Kara didn't know why I was being held, but she asked a friend in the French department to read the Algerian papers online. There was no mention of Lalla, so Kara assumed, rightly, that I was held on some kind of technicality.

Then she sat still and waited, the best thing she could do. I was waiting; she was waiting. Though we didn't know it, we were collaborators in waiting. It was hard for both of us not to force the issue, demand action, but somehow we both knew we had to wait, to be still. To have agitated for a speedy resolution might have somehow uncovered the facts. Kara knew I had to carry through the deception of tourism if I was going to pass through passport control and the Air Algeria gate to Paris.

What Kara and I said to each other on the phone when I reached Paris and what we did with each other when I returned to Cincinnati are private materials not necessary for the public autobiography this has become. But I will say that she asked me to alter her names in this account. I did, even though I told her that all of my problems the last decade stemmed from changing my name to Kyvernos to play in Greece. Once my divorce goes through, I'll ask Kara to quick change her last name to Keever, to make true what we pretended in Algiers. After all, by telling our story and then waiting, Kara did, in a manner of speaking, save my life. If she resists the name change, I'll remind her: "If someone asks you something...."

I also changed Samir Hadj's name, but I'm afraid he'll be identified if *Passing Through* is ever read in Algeria. I hope he's not punished for believing and passing along my story. At the end of *Passing Off*, Ann had me gloat about taking in readers, but now I know that even educated people will ride the slide. Terminal tales, along with rescue reports, are the hardest to be suspicious about, the most difficult to see through. Maybe my story was one Samir wanted to hear. Then again, perhaps he had his own ulterior motives for passing it on. Anyway, Samir, if you are reading this and still considering studying in America, check out the University of Cincinnati web site. Once I had a contract and advance for this book, I showed the manuscript to people in the English Department at U.C. They liked the "false pretenses" and offered me a full-time position as a real Assistant Professor in their Creative Writing program. U.C. is not Michigan or Miami, but now Sara won't have to attend Quack College. And I can promise you, Samir, that if you show up in one of my graduate classes I'll tell you the truth, only the truth.

One last sports metaphor from the ex-athlete and new professor. "One and done" players say when a shot misses and the ball goes to the defensive team. "Two and through," I say. Two of my own autobiographies are enough. True and through, through and true. Maybe I'll become a poet or a novelist, something truly and thoroughly creative.

Passing Through

Acknowledgements and Disclaimers

Although it may be quixotic to append facts to a fiction within a fiction about fact, I want to say that, like Keever, I have changed the name of an Algerian woman, Khalida Messaoudi, whose autobiography, *Unbowed: An Islamic Woman Confronts Islamic Fundamentalism*, I have relied on and modified for the character of Lalla Kahina. I would like to thank Jane Kuntz, a longtime resident of North Africa, for research suggestions on Algeria. Thanks also to those who read and commented on the manuscript: Russel Durst, Gil Gallagher, Heather Hall, Lee Kellogg, and Cynthia Ris.

Although Keever ends up teaching at the University of Cincinnati, where I'm a professor, Queen City College bears no resemblance to the university, my colleagues, and students. Keever also bears no resemblance to Rabbit Angstrom, who was always a shooter. Www.terminaltours.com is an actual web site, but the services advertised there are fictional.

— Tom LeClair

Author

Tom LeClair:

A widely published critic, Tom LeClair was a member of the jury that chose the 2005 National Book Award for fiction. In addition to his novels—*Passing Off, Well-Founded Fear, Passing On,* and *The Liquidators*—LeClair has published two works of literary criticism: *In the Loop* and *The Art of Excess*. He has reviewed books for *The New York Times Book Review, BookForum, The Nation, American Book Review, Atlantic Monthly,* and many other national periodicals. LeClair is currently proprietor of the website www.terminaltours.com and Nathaniel Ropes Professor of English at the University of Cincinnati, where he can be reached at Thomas.LeClair@uc.edu.

Printed in the United States
204463BV00001B/118-132/P